Donated to
Yreka Library by
Lolly Hammond Estate

Blackbird Lake

Center Point
Large Print

Also by Jill Gregory and available from
Center Point Large Print:

Sage Creek
Larkspur Road

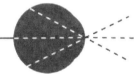

**This Large Print Book carries the
Seal of Approval of N.A.V.H.**

Blackbird Lake

JILL GREGORY

CENTER POINT LARGE PRINT
THORNDIKE, MAINE

This Center Point Large Print edition is published in the year 2014 by arrangement with The Berkley Publishing Group, a member of Penguin Group (USA) Inc.

The text of this Large Print edition is unabridged. In other aspects, this book may vary from the original edition. Printed in the United States of America on permanent paper. Set in 16-point Times New Roman type.

ISBN: 978-1-61173-913-8

Library of Congress Cataloging-in-Publication Data

Gregory, Jill.
Blackbird Lake / Jill Gregory. — Center Point Large Print edition.
    pages cm
ISBN 978-1-61173-913-8 (Library binding : alk. paper)
1. Homecoming—Fiction. 2. Family secrets—Fiction.
    3. Large type books. I. Title.
PS3557.R4343B53 2014
813′.54—dc23

2013030068

To Rachel and Jason.
With love.

Blackbird Lake

Chapter One

LONESOME WAY, MONTANA

Carly McKinnon's day had been cruising along just fine—a perfectly calm, typical, somewhat slow Wednesday in her Spring Street quilt shop.

Until late afternoon when she heard the news that Jake Tanner was back in town.

Suddenly, everything seemed to freeze for a full thirty seconds.

Of course she could still see Gloria Cartright, finished with her afternoon shift at the Lickety Split Ice Cream Parlor, thoughtfully fingering some new calico fabric on the shelves at the far side of the shop. She could still hear the sound of light traffic outside on Spring Street, and she could feel her own breath catch hard in her throat at the mention of Jake's name.

But she couldn't move, couldn't speak, couldn't *think*—not until the first ice-cold shock of the news had settled into her brain.

"Jake Tanner . . . are you *sure,* Laureen?" she finally asked her assistant, struggling to keep her voice calm and her face composed, as if she were talking about the chance of rain tonight or today's ninety-nine-cent caramel brownie special at A Bun in the Oven bakery.

"Jake Tanner?" Gloria shook her head skeptically. "That man hasn't been back more than a handful of times in the past dozen years. Not since he first fell in love with rodeo."

Shoving the bolt of calico back on the shelf, she eyeballed Laureen as if trying to ascertain if the other woman knew what the hell she was talking about.

"Well, I didn't say *I* saw him." Laureen Rowan glanced back and forth between Carly and Gloria, the small paper bag from Benson's Drugstore containing her new red lipstick and a pack of sugarless gum still clutched in her hand. "But Deanna Mueller is positive she did. The second I stepped into Benson's just now she rushed over in a big hurry to give me the scoop. Deanna was at the gas station filling up her minivan when Jake cruised by in his truck. She said there was a big dog leaning over his lap, its head hanging out the window. I never knew Jake to have a dog before, but Deanna insisted they were headed for Sage Ranch. Turned onto Squirrel Road right quick, she said. Deanna swears it was him. She told me, who else could it be, no one is as handsome as that Jake Tanner."

Tell me about it, Carly thought. A flush of heat raced through her body.

"Well, duh. That's for sure." Gloria nodded

knowingly. "That man is smokin'. And he's all over the TV these days, between the rodeo coverage and those beer commercials of his." Her bright little black pepper eyes brimmed with interest. "I know if I was a dozen or so years younger, *I* wouldn't think twice about climbing between the sheets with him."

"Carly?" Laureen moved toward her boss in concern. "Hey. Are you all right?"

It was only then that Carly realized she was biting her lip, her hands were clenched, and her neck felt as tight as a washrag twisted in the clothes dryer.

"Sure. Fine," she said airily, forcing her lips into a smile, casually pushing a thick strawberry blond curl back from her usually dreamy green eyes.

"Well, you don't look fine. You look like you're going to fall down in a dead faint or something." Laureen studied her carefully, her own round, pretty face worried. Forty-four and divorced, she was the proud mother of two mutts and three cats, all adopted from Lonesome Way's overwhelmed shelter.

Laureen didn't know how to say no to a sad pair of feline or canine eyes. She had a heart as big as Montana and Wyoming combined. With chin-length white blond hair and hazel eyes she was still as pretty as she'd been in high school when she was named prom queen, but she'd gained twenty pounds since her divorce—and had convinced herself she was too fat to ever attract the attention of a man again. But still. . . . Tonight she had a date with a rancher from the nearby town of Big Timber.

A blind date that had been set up by her sister-in-law in Butte.

Laureen had been insisting to Carly all week long that this was going to be her very last shot.

No more dates, blind or otherwise. They never panned out, not a single one of 'em. If this guy didn't call her back, Laureen was done.

"Maybe you should sit down. I'll get you a glass of water. There's a bad flu going around Billings. Could be the bug made its way here and you caught it."

"No, I'm . . . okay. It's just . . . I didn't get much sleep last night. Emma kept waking up," Carly lied.

It was only a half lie, though. Her eighteen-month-old daughter had woken up several times after Carly put her to bed, but it had all happened long before Carly went to sleep for the night.

A semi-lie is okay, she assured herself shakily. *Especially in extreme circumstances.* And Jake Tanner coming home to Lonesome Way— definitely an extreme circumstance.

She felt her heart lurch. Memories burned through her, along with a sprinkling of guilt and a pinch of unease. That thick, longish, jet-black hair. All those rock-hard abs. The slow, sexy kisses trailing down her throat. . . .

The man had returned to his hometown only once since she had moved there from Boston nearly two years before—and even then he'd hit town for only a day. Which was one of the reasons she'd felt comfortable settling in Lonesome Way in the first place. Because Jake hardly ever came home. He'd told her as much that one night they'd spent together in Houston.

And that's what everybody always said.

Jake Tanner was a roamer through and through.

But his family was all here. His brothers, Rafe and Travis, along with their wives, Sophie and Mia, and their children.

All of whom were Carly's friends. Some of the nicest and best people she'd ever met. The last time Jake *had* come home—when Mia and Travis's daughter, Zoey, was born a year ago—Carly had heard in advance that he was coming in for a day to meet his new niece and had made sure she and Emma lay low.

Of course when she'd decided to move to Lonesome Way she'd always known Jake might drop into town on rare occasions for a visit, but most of the time she relegated that possibility into the far recesses of her mind as she savored her own sense of peace and delight with small-town life.

"I bet he's here for his niece's birthday party." Gloria's dark head bobbed up and down. "Zoey

13

Tanner turns one this weekend. I have it on good authority that Travis was none too happy when Jake said he wasn't going to be able to make it to her party."

"You're probably right," Laureen said distractedly. She was digging out her new, very red lipstick from the drugstore bag and ripping at the packaging with her nails. "Everyone knows family means everything to the Tanners. Jake must've got wind Travis was pissed and changed his mind."

Panic whipped through Carly. She felt breathless and a little sick to her stomach. She and Emma were invited to Zoey's party.

If Jake was there, they wouldn't be able to go.

But that was the least of her problems. . . .

She needed to get home. To hold her daughter. To think.

But it was only four thirty and she didn't normally close Carly's Quilts until five. Gloria looked like she wasn't going anywhere, not while this juicy topic of conversation was on the table. And Laureen—Laureen seemed to have forgotten all the urgency of her big date tonight as she drew a mirror out of her purse and began applying her new lipstick with the careful precision of a surgeon performing a lobotomy.

Time to remind her about that date, Carly decided desperately.

"I know you want to get ready for tonight,

14

maybe get a manicure, wind down, or whatever, so maybe we'll just close up early," she began with what she hoped was a breezy smile. Moving briskly across the shop, she began folding bolts of gingham and calico left on the long table beside the shelves and gathering up pattern books the few customers of the day had been browsing through. "I want to go home and check on Emma, too—what with her getting up so much last night. Just to make sure *she's* not coming down with some-thing."

True enough. Emma *had* been restless last night. She probably sensed her daddy was headed to town, Carly thought wildly, knowing the thought was totally irrational. Nervousness flowed through her like a chill autumn wind sweeping down from the Crazy Mountains.

Stop it. Pull yourself together. She gulped a couple of breaths and dug deep, searching for the hard-won serenity and sense of peace she'd worked so hard to achieve over the years.

Her own childhood hadn't exactly been a picnic—more like an odyssey of lonely confusion, uncertainty, and fear. But now, at thirty, all of that was behind her. She'd built a life here for her-self and her daughter—a life that was solid and steady and filled with the warmth of this tight-knit community. Nothing was going to change that.

She reminded herself that Jake didn't know about Emma. He had no clue that he even *had* a daughter. Much less that she and Carly were living in Lonesome Way.

He probably doesn't even remember *me,* she thought, drawing a breath.

Jake Tanner had women falling all over him in every town from here to Alaska. But he was the last man to ever want any ties, any family of his own, any kind of commitment—except to the rodeo life.

He'd made all that very clear the one and only night they'd made love.

What am I talking about? We didn't make love. We had sex. Intense, incredible, rock-the-world and light-up-the-night-with-fireworks sex.

It was the lone one-night stand of Carly's entire life. She'd acted completely out of character. But then, she'd already downed two glasses of wine at the bar of that hotel in Houston and was sipping a third, trying to expunge her lying, psycho ex-boyfriend from her head, when she spotted him.

Jake Tanner. In all his hot cowboy ruggedness. He'd seemed like the ideal candidate to eject Kevin Boyd from her brain for good.

So when Jake glanced over from across the lobby, cocked an eyebrow, and grinned that sexy cowboy grin, she'd made the first impulsive move of her life.

She'd downed the third glass of wine and gone for it.

The next ten hours had been momentous in

every way. But then, of course, there had been nothing. Zip. No phone call from him a day or two later, no *maybe I'll see you again sometime.* Just nothing. Slam, bam, and . . .

Of course, she'd known that was exactly how it would be. She'd counted on it, even. He'd made it clear over dinner in the hotel restaurant that he wasn't the kind of man who was into long-term relationships or commitments or anything remotely hinting at permanence.

And we both wanted it that way, she reminded herself, trying to thrust Jake Tanner and his sexy smile, lean, powerful body, and impossibly hunky muscles from her mind.

That one night they'd spent together in his cushy Houston hotel suite had been, for her, all about rebound sex, pure and simple. They'd made crazed, incredible love all night long. And every bit of it had helped her to forget just a little more about her scumbag ex.

She'd discovered only four months earlier that Kevin Boyd had lied to her. Not just once or twice, but the entire time they were together. It turned out Mr. Fancy Schmancy genius architect wasn't divorced after all. And he wasn't a good, upstanding guy, searching for a serious, stable relationship as he'd claimed.

Just the opposite. He was married. With children! Three children, to be exact, one of them a two-month-old *infant.*

Carly had gone numb with shock when she discovered the truth. Kevin was a player. A liar. An elegantly good-looking blond jerk with a high IQ and a talent for hiding his wedding ring.

It had taken her long enough, but she'd finally started to grow suspicious and followed him one day when he left her apartment.

She actually caught him with his family, after he'd told her he was headed to the airport and an out-of-town consultation with a new client.

Watching in horror, her knees had sagged as Kevin hugged twin little boys who looked to be about eight or nine, scooped a pink-clad baby girl into his arms, and embraced a woman in a stunning Chanel suit. She'd grabbed onto a brick storefront for support as she watched them all bundle into an elevator in an exclusive doorman building that was *not* the place she'd thought was his home.

It was definitely not the apartment where she'd spent countless nights in his king-sized bed, where dozens of designer suits, pairs of slacks, shirts and polos hung in the walk-in closet. An apartment always stocked with gourmet food and wine and an extensive collection of antique clocks and timepieces, where expensive works of art hung on all the walls.

And in that last huge fight with Kevin at *her* apartment in Boston she'd glimpsed a side of him she'd never seen before.

The angry, snarling, bordering-on-violent side.

Mr. Genius Architect didn't even think what he'd done was wrong! Even when she'd forced him to admit to his lies, to admit he'd told his wife he was traveling on business all those days or nights he spent with Carly, he'd shouted at her, and then snatched up the crystal ballerina sculpture her college friend Sydney had given her for her birthday. Even as Carly screamed, "Don't!" he hurled it at the brick wall behind the fireplace, shattering the exquisite dancer into a thousand shards.

He'd screamed that everything he'd done had been for *them*—so *they* could be together without the financial messiness of a divorce.

In shock, Carly had stared at the man she'd thought she knew. Listened to him try to gloss over his lies—all the things he'd said and done to make her believe that he was working tons of overtime at the office or conducting out-of-town meetings with clients.

When all along he'd been home with his wife and kids.

It was devastating to discover what an idiot she'd been. A naïve, gullible fool who'd swallowed hook, line, and sinker all his crap about the stresses of being an overworked, in-demand architect. She'd believed him when he claimed he couldn't have dinner with her regularly or attend her friends' parties—or even leave town for a romantic weekend getaway—because of a killer schedule and his boss being a demanding pain in the ass. She'd nearly thrown up when she learned there was a *Mrs.* Boyd—and a young family to boot.

At first Carly had been sickened, but that had quickly turned to fury. Fury not just with Kevin but with herself. She'd concluded that either she was as dumb as a brick or she'd inherited her mother's knack for picking losers. That making stupid romantic choices must run in her family, like allergies or cancer or freckles in other families.

Bad romantic karma was *in her genes.*

And she'd figured out one other thing—she wouldn't have a chance of finding peace again until she found a way to exorcise that entire fiasco with Kevin from her head.

So when she'd flown to Houston on business several months later and run smack-dab into Jake—tough, drop-dead sexy, rodeo champion Jake—whom she'd met briefly years before when they were both kids—she'd suddenly lost every single one of her brain cells and had done something stupid, something crazy, something she'd never done before in her life.

One-night stands were *so* not her thing.

Caution. Good sense. *Those* were her things.

But that night . . . that one amazing night . . .

There *should* have been no consequences, she'd

thought faintly several weeks later when she stared at the results of her home pregnancy test.

True, she'd gone off her birth control pills after the fiasco with Kevin, swearing she'd never get seriously involved with another man again—but she and Jake had used condoms that night.

And yet . . .

A baby had been growing inside her. Emma.

Now a vivacious little blue-eyed charmer, eighteen months old—Emma was bright, active, and more precious to Carly than all the stars in the sky.

From the instant she first saw her daughter, Carly had never, ever thought of Emma as anything but the most treasured gift in the world.

So pull it together, she ordered herself again as she caught Gloria staring at her, while Laureen scooped up coffee cups from around the homey quilt shop with its walls of buttery warm yellow and its floors of burnished wood. *If you don't, the moment you get home, Madison might see something is wrong. And Emma could sense it.*

Emma's daytime babysitter, Madison Hodge, was a smart, down-to-earth twenty-year-old who adored Emma just as much as Emma loved her. Carly didn't know how she'd ever get by without Madison. A former pageant princess, this girl worked harder than anyone Carly knew. When she wasn't babysitting Emma four days a week, she was working toward her online degree in childhood education and playing keyboard in a local country band at night.

"Closing up early works great for me," Laureen was drawling. "I can use the extra time. Maybe I can fit in a really intense workout and lose twenty-five pounds before eight o'clock. Ya think?"

She headed toward the sink in the back of the shop, the cups hooked on her fingers. "This isn't going to turn into anything, you know," she called over her shoulder. "After tonight, I'm never going to hear from this guy again. He's probably expecting a skinny girl. A size two. Or four. You watch, when he sees me, he'll run fleeing into the night."

"Stop." Carly managed to drag her thoughts from her own worries. "Don't talk that way. You're beautiful, Laureen. You're stunning. And smart. And amazing."

"You're my friend. You have to say that."

"Well, *I* think you could stand to lose a few pounds," Gloria chimed in, sauntering toward the shop door. A grandmother of three teenagers, she was small and as skinny as a scrap of tree bark, and her bright orange sweater, the color of a ripe pumpkin, hung loosely on her wiry frame. "But some men think more pounds is just more to love. So you need to think positive. And hope this date of yours likes red lipstick, because that one you bought is awfully red. I'm just sayin'."

In typical Gloria fashion, she yanked open the door and was gone.

For a moment there was dead silence. Laureen and Carly stared at each other.

"Can you believe her?" Laureen finally gasped.

"Don't you dare pay any attention to a word she says," Carly ordered.

"Tell me the truth. Do *you* think the lipstick's too red?" Laureen's hazel eyes locked on Carly. The lipstick she'd carefully applied was full-on, red-carpet red, a lush, richly voluptuous color that looked bright and prettily vivid with her fair hair and creamy complexion.

"No way. It's perfect. Gloria's just being Gloria. Go home. Primp. I mean it, Laureen. Drink a glass of wine, and have fun tonight. I'll expect a full report tomorrow."

"No way. *You* go home." Setting the cups down with a clatter on the countertop at the rear of the shop, Laureen hustled up to the front where Carly was putting away the toys scattered around the small children's play area.

"I'll close up." Her red mouth was firmly set. "*You* check on Emma—that's a whole lot more important. My date isn't until eight, so go. Go see your daughter."

Straightening, Carly took another deep breath. "You sure? You don't mind?"

Laureen grabbed the stuffed Big Bird from her. "Get outta here, boss."

Carly didn't have to think twice. Grabbing her purse from beneath the front counter, she managed a quick, grateful grin. "That does it. You're officially employee of the month."

"Last I heard, I was the only employee, this month or any other."

"That makes you the best. Every month." It was all she could do not to sprint to the door. "This guy better treat you right tonight or he'll answer to me," she called over her shoulder.

"Yeah, what are you going to do? Stitch him to death?" Laureen gave a small huff of laughter before the door of Carly's Quilts clicked shut behind its owner.

Then Carly was bolting across Spring Street toward her Jeep, her tan wedges tapping the pavement. A cool September wind nipped down from the mountains, tousling her thick, curly mane of strawberry blond hair, making her shiver in her sea green cotton sweater and jeans.

I'm not *going to have a panic attack, I'm* not, she told herself, taking deep breaths, repeating the mantra over and over, trying to turn her mind from every disastrous thought.

It was hard to get in enough air, though, and she felt a little light-headed. But she hadn't had an attack in years, hadn't even had one when she found out about Kevin being married, or when she discovered she was pregnant. She certainly wasn't going to have one now. . . . She couldn't *let* herself have one now, not after all this time. . . .

She had nearly reached her Jeep when she heard Martha Davies's voice call out from behind her.

"Yoo-hoo. Carly! Where's the fire?"

Can't get away with a thing in this town. Carly's stomach clenched. Turning, she managed a smile for her foster mother Annie's cousin, the eighty-something owner of the Cuttin' Loose beauty salon, waiting as Martha bore down upon her, beaming. A long purple knit skirt swished around the older woman's legs and a turquoise crocheted sweater covered her tall, spare frame. Not a smidgen of gray showed in her chin-length hair. It was freshly dyed a light blondish auburn and gleamed with reddish highlights in the autumn sunshine.

Martha was famous in Lonesome Way for changing her hair color the same way some women changed shoes. But her heart was as steady as a rock. She was Emma's godmother and, now that Annie was gone, the closest person to family Carly had left in the world.

If not for all the times she'd accompanied Annie on visits to see Martha in Lonesome Way over the years, Carly might never have discovered the town that had become her home.

"I was just on my way to find you," Martha went on briskly before Carly could respond. "Closing up a little early, honey, aren't you?"

"I wanted to squeeze in some extra time with

Emma." Leaning forward, Carly gave the older woman a quick kiss on the cheek. She hoped Martha couldn't sense the tension flowing through her. Martha might be in her eighties, but she still ran her business with a firm hand and was as sharp as a toothpick. "It was a slow day; you know how it goes."

"Oh, honey, you bet I do." Martha's dangling jet earrings swung as she shook her head in annoyance. "Wouldn't you know, Georgia Timmons canceled her tint at the last minute and now I have twenty minutes to kill before my next client comes in for a manicure and cut. What am I supposed to do, twiddle my thumbs?"

She stopped grimacing suddenly and stared at Carly with sharply narrowing eyes. "You know, you look sort of tense, honey. Everything all right? Emma isn't sick, is she?"

"Emma's great. She blew me about fifty kisses when I left this morning. I'm just tired." Carly hated lying but she could hardly tell Martha that Emma's daddy had breezed into town. Even Martha didn't know that Jake Tanner was Emma's father. No one knew. And Carly intended to keep it that way.

"Can I give you a call later?" She edged toward the Jeep. "Madison needs to study for an exam, plus she has a gig tonight. I want to let her leave as early as possible—"

"That's exactly what I want to talk to you

about—Madison! Can I switch days with her and watch Emma tomorrow instead of Friday? I'll be shorthanded Friday and have a full day of appointments booked, including two perms and three manicures. But I don't want to miss out on any time with my little miss."

Ever since Emma turned one, Martha had insisted on having Emma spend the day with her at least once a week and then sleep over that night at her apartment. She'd even bought a crib that fit into a corner of her small living room and had sewn a gorgeous quilt for her goddaughter. Emma always squealed in excitement at the sight of "MaWa"—and not just because each time she slept over at MaWa's apartment there was a new toy or doll waiting for her.

"No problem—or we could skip this week if it would be easier for you—"

"Not a chance." Martha waved her hand, an amethyst and jet bracelet jangling cheerfully on her wrist. "I look forward every week to having my time with her. And—I bought her a little something new. I can't wait to give it to her."

"You don't have to buy her things all the time, Martha." A mixture of emotions rose in Carly, an overwhelming combination of guilt, love, and tenderness for this woman who had taken her and her daughter so deeply into her heart and woven their lives into hers. "Emma loves you for you, not because you give her—"

"Shoot, don't you think I know that, honey? I *like* buying things for her. Gives me a kick to see her face light up. Never had a little grand-daughter of my own. And it's my business if I want to spoil her, isn't it? I think Annie would want me to do just that. Remember, it's *your* unpleasant job to say no to her now and then—not mine." Chuckling, she turned back toward the Cuttin' Loose. "You go ahead now. But don't forget to tell Madison," she instructed over her shoulder.

"I won't."

For a moment Carly watched the older woman saunter back toward her shop. There was a lump in her throat as she studied the tall, retreating figure. Martha had always been so kind to her, so kind to Emma.

Just as this town had been. . . .

Drawing yet another long breath that was supposed to be calming, she climbed into her Jeep, snapped her seat belt, and roared out of her parking space a lot faster than she'd intended.

She couldn't believe any of this. That Jake Tanner was here, that this was really happening. But the sick feeling in the pit of her stomach brought reality vividly home.

Only an hour before, the biggest problem in her life had been the charity dating auction coming up next week. Ava Louise Todd, Sophie Tanner's tiny, silver-haired grandmother, had roped her into being part of it. The dating auction was the first installment of the town's big Thanksgiving fund-raiser to build a new animal shelter. Carly had volunteered months earlier to donate gift certificates, fabric, and quilting lessons as her contribution—and to sew a square for a community quilt.

But that hadn't been enough for Ava.

Oh, no.

That petite little old lady might be as sweet and beautiful as the cinnamon buns sold by the dozens at A Bun in the Oven, but she also had a spine of industrial-strength steel.

It was not in Ava Louise Todd's nature to ever take no for an answer.

"All we're asking you to do is go on one tiny little date," she'd pleaded with a gleam in her eyes. "And you need only spend a couple of hours with whichever man casts the winning bid. Where's the harm in that, dear?"

Carly had tried to explain that she had zero interest in dating, that she was done with men— *done* with a capital *D*—and that the thought of parading across a makeshift stage at the Double Cross Bar and Grill before a roomful of shouting, stamping, whistling cowboys was as enticing to her as a night out on the Crazy Mountains, stark naked, in the midst of a February blizzard.

But Ava had merely chuckled and waved a hand at all of her objections.

"Now, don't be silly, it's going to be fun. You know Tansy Noble who works over at the post office, don't you? Well, *she's* up for our charity dating auction, and she's been through three divorces, poor thing. And your own babysitter, Madison Hodge, volunteered, too, and that young woman is about as eager to parade across that stage as a gazelle would be to step into a lion's den, especially after everything her mama put her through with all those beauty pageants she signed the girl up for—why, she got poor Madison started when she was only six! So if those two can brave it, something tells me you can, too. Especially for such a worthy cause. Only think about those poor needy animals!"

So Carly had. She'd thought about the animals, the strays, hungry, neglected, or abused—all of them needing a new shelter. Her heart went out to them. She'd been pretty much a stray herself, growing up in the homes of reluctant relatives who'd shuttled her off somewhere else whenever they got tired of having another mouth to feed.

A toss-away child, she remembered a case-worker saying once, in an undervoice. But Carly had overheard.

She knew all too well how it felt to be unwanted.

To have no place that was home.

And so, in the end, she'd caved. She'd agreed to put herself up for auction. It was a big icy plunge for someone who had dreaded standing before her third grade class to give a book report.

But now, at this moment, driving home toward Blue Bell Drive, knowing that Jake Tanner was here in Lonesome Way, the charity dating auction suddenly shrank to an insignificant blip on her emotional radar. No bigger than an ant at a picnic. A moth on the moon. Nothing compared to the fact that her daughter's father was here in his hometown and it was almost inevitable that he'd run into them.

He can't find out about Emma, she told herself, her chest tightening with fear.

It would change everything. If his family learned the truth, they wouldn't understand why she hadn't told him—or them—that Emma was part of their family.

She'd only wanted her daughter to be close to them . . . to know them, and for them to know her, even if they didn't know who she really was. . . .

She'd almost told Jake she was pregnant way back then. She'd debated with herself for weeks and finally had tracked him down at a rodeo in Prescott, Arizona, fully intending to tell him.

But when she'd spotted him, he was surrounded by a bevy of beautiful young women, all clamoring for his autograph. He'd had his arm around one dainty, laughing brunette as he signed. And she'd suddenly changed her mind. Backing away, she'd melted deliberately into the throng of people attending the rodeo before Jake ever spotted her.

She had no regrets about that, she told herself now. None.

Because it would have been a disaster. They'd only spent that one night together but it was as clear as a glass of spring water that Jake Tanner hadn't the least desire to be a father. Or a husband. Or a boyfriend. He was a cowboy, a roamer.

A tumbleweed.

Jake didn't even want a permanent *address,* much less a family!

Carly had strong feelings about men who left the women in their lives. Who didn't do well with commitment. Her own father had abandoned her and her mother when Carly was only three. She barely remembered him—his face was merely a square-jawed shadow in the darkest recesses of her memory. She couldn't recall his voice, his smell. She hadn't seen or heard from him since the day he left. There had never been a phone call or a letter.

Even after her mother died, her father hadn't come back for her. She'd waited, telling herself every night before she fell asleep that he'd know somehow that she needed him, that he'd call or come. That he'd take care of her, hold her hand, tell her he was sorry for ever leaving her. He'd sweep her away from her aunt's noisy jumbled house, or her cousin's crowded trailer, and find a new place for them to live, a place where it would be quiet and happy and safe, with just the two of them.

She waited and waited.

But Les McKinnon never came back to rescue her.

So Carly knew all the way down to her innermost soul that she could only depend on herself. And that it would be far better for Emma to have *no* father in her life than a reluctant, resentful, or unreliable one. One who might take off at any time, disappear for weeks, a month, a year—or forever.

Just as hers had.

Jake was a bull-riding, rodeo-following, freaking famous cowboy, after all, with the world at his feet. And no inclination to settle down. He was as tough and independent as he was handsome. He was a risk taker, who liked to live life on the edge, with no roots, no attachments. A cowboy through and through, with zero desire ever to be tied to one woman or one place, even Lonesome Way.

He'd told her so himself that night over dinner—and in the hotel room in Houston. Laid it all out for her, nicely, lightly, but clearly before he allowed her to tug him toward that sumptuously made-up king-sized bed.

Oh, she'd known what she was getting into before she'd tumbled onto those one-thousand-thread-count sheets with the hottest man she'd ever met.

And she'd also known when she'd backed away from telling him she was pregnant that she *didn't* want a reluctant, unhappy, rodeo-following father anywhere near her baby's life.

Let Jake do his thing, you do yours. Or you'll all be miserable, she'd told herself when she was six weeks along, alone and throwing up at least twice a day.

She didn't need him in any way, shape, or form. She would take care of her baby just fine all by herself. Thanks to Annie, her foster mother, the first person in Carly's life to recognize her math aptitude and intelligence, she'd earned an MBA and had been working for several years as a senior financial consultant for Marjorie Moore's Home and Hearth—one of the largest home goods and lifestyle companies in the country.

She had the financial means to raise a child alone.

And more than enough love for two parents.

So much love.

But still, her stomach churned as she left the town behind and hung a right on Coyote Road, heading toward her own small neighborhood. By the time she finally turned onto Blue Bell Drive she was barely keeping panic at bay. She needed desperately to hold Emma. To think this through before she ran into Jake or even Lissie or Sophie or Mia, his sister and sisters-in-law, who, along with Karla McDonald and Laureen, were her closest friends in Lonesome Way.

As she drove past Karla and Denny's house, two doors down from hers, she saw their son, seven-year-old Austin, shooting baskets in the backyard—and through an open window caught a glimpse of almost four-year-old Ashley toddling around in dress-up clothes in the living room.

At least everything was normal over there. Blissfully normal. The way it should be. Carly suddenly yearned for normal. For yesterday.

For Jake not to be here.

There was a knot in her stomach as she turned into her own tree-lined driveway where her rambling Victorian house sat amid the row of other rambling Victorian houses. Parking at the top of the driveway, she sat for a moment with her fingers still gripping the steering wheel, staring at her beautiful wraparound porch, at her apple tree, at her neat little flower garden tidied up for fall.

Through the window, she saw Madison in sweatpants and a tee and heard the girl playing her guitar and singing "Old McDonald Had a Farm" for Emma, who stood swaying and clapping, her stuffed dog, Bug, at her feet.

It was all Carly could do not to burst into tears. She felt like everything she had, everything she loved and cherished, was at risk.

Sitting in the Jeep, her throat thickened with

unshed tears. She needed to hold Emma in her arms, to hear her soft baby laughter. She needed to feed her daughter supper and read to her. To rock her to sleep tonight as the Montana sky slid from peacock blue to deep, cool purple. While a million stars popped out and the peaceful quiet of home enfolded the two of them like a thick, safe cocoon.

She could only have dreamed of a life like this one when she was a young girl, trying to make herself invisible in corners while the relatives she lived with after her mother's death argued and screamed, while TVs blared, her roughneck cousin Phil's feet pounded up and down hallways, and doors slammed all through the night.

She couldn't lose this. *Lonesome Way*. She couldn't lose any of it.

Stepping down from her Jeep to the sound of a lone bird chirping in her apple tree, Carly prayed for nothing to change as she swallowed the lump in her throat and hurried up the steps of her home.

Chapter Two

The big dog lifted his head and peered mournfully at Jake as he parked his truck in the Sage Ranch driveway.

It was a look that said, *Is this where you push me out and leave?*

"Yep, I'm leaving you, pardner, but in good hands," Jake said gently. "No fear. Look, you've got friends here."

He grinned as his brother Rafe's two dogs, big galloping Starbucks and the tiny, desperate-to-keep-up Tidbit, raced from the corral behind the ranch house, both of them barking their heads off.

"See, plenty of company," Jake assured the mutt. He stroked a big hand along the animal's matted fur, scratched behind the drooping, golden brown ears. "You like horses, fella? Rafe and Sophie have plenty of those, too. Not to mention a couple of kids. You'll love it here, I promise."

He spotted Rafe heading over from the barn. There was a look of pleased astonishment on his face, and Jake's grin widened. His brother hadn't known he was coming but he looked plenty glad to see him. Springing out of the truck, he clasped his arms around his brother's shoulders in a bear hug. Seeing as he hadn't been home in a year, he'd been bracing himself for his family to be good and mad at him.

"What are you doing here?" Rafe demanded, thumping him on the back. "I thought you were competing at that rodeo in Devil's Lake this weekend—and then doing the Bighorn Bull Rodeo over in Wyoming. And wasn't there something about filming some new commercial outside Salt Lake City?"

"That was the plan, bro, but the shoot got rescheduled for a few weeks from now, and I canceled on the rodeo in Devil's Lake. Travis called me and—hell, didn't he tell you?"

"No. But let me guess." Rafe tipped his Stetson back on his head. "He reamed you a good one for not planning to come home for Zoey's birthday party."

"Bingo." Jake couldn't hide a smile as his broad shoulders lifted in a shrug. Birthdays, weddings, anniversaries—all happy occasions were huge with the Tanners, and Jake loved being with his family as much as the rest of them did. But his schedule had become even tighter than usual this past year. Ever since he'd signed on five months before as the spokesperson for a charity that was raising awareness about bullying, and had also agreed to an endorsement deal for a new shaving cream in a national advertising campaign, his life had been one revolving hotel room door after another.

He hadn't had a chance to get home. Until now.

"How long are you staying? And who's this pitiful guy?" Rafe looked over at the dog in the front seat.

Jake glanced at the dog, too. The poor thing *was* pitiful. A big, sad-looking mutt. Probably part yellow Lab, part golden retriever, with something undetermined mixed in. Not a puppy, not a senior citizen. He was thin and weak looking—probably hadn't been eating much lately—not until Jake scooped him up from the side of the highway and fed him his own take-out burger and a couple of French fries.

"Don't have a name for him yet. He's been checked out by a vet in Billings—doesn't have fleas, worms, or a chip. So I thought I'd leave his name up to you, seeing as he's a present."

Opening the door, Jake watched the dog clamber out, landing on the driveway with a clunky thud. "I figured the kids might want to come up with a handle for him."

He watched as Starbucks and Tidbit rushed up, and all three mutts began sniffing and wagging their tails, checking each other out.

"Well, we've always got room for one more," Rafe said as they headed toward the ranch house. "But it looks like he'd rather stick by you, bro."

It was true. After about thirty seconds of

39

sniffing, the dog was ignoring Starbucks and Tidbit and trotting right at Jake's heels, as close as he could get. The other two were scampering after him like he was the Pied Piper.

Jake laughed. "He'll forget about me once we get some more food and water in him and he gets to playing with your two."

The aroma of fresh-baked cinnamon buns greeted him the moment he stepped in the door of the ranch. Inhaling the sweet scent, he managed to avoid stepping on the three dogs clambering around him as he followed Rafe to the kitchen.

"Man, it smells good in here. Sophie and the kids home?"

"Sophie and Aiden are over at Travis's place. Sophie volunteered to help Mia decorate the house for the party. Ivy's on a date."

"A date? Ivy?" Jake stared at him. Hard to believe his little niece was old enough to go on a date. She was only fifteen. He remembered when she was born, a tiny helpless and beautiful little bundle who grabbed onto his thumb and didn't let go. He didn't like the sound of her going on a date. Probably because he remembered the kind of stuff *he'd* done on dates when he was fifteen.

"You think that's a good idea, letting her go on a date so young? If you remember when we were that age—"

"Hey, I remember." Rafe sighed as he poured water and then kibble into a couple of spare bowls for Jake's stray and set them on the floor near Starbucks's and Tidbit's food dishes. "But this isn't like that. It's a study date. At the library. Sophie said it was okay. And you know, I trust Ivy. According to Sophie, I guess I have to."

"Sure, trust her." Jake nodded. "Trust her all you want. But don't trust any fifteen-year-old boy."

"I can't—not if they're anything like you were," his brother retorted as he took down a couple of dark blue mugs and poured freshly brewed coffee into them.

"Look who's talking," Jake shot back as Rafe handed him a steaming mug. He strode to the counter, snagged one of his sister-in-law's famous cinnamon buns from a white bakery box, then glanced fondly around the kitchen as he took a seat in the same chair he used to sit in as a kid, and stretched his long legs out beneath the table.

The hungry dog he'd found finished the entire bowlful of food, took a long, lapping drink, then came to lie beside Jake's boots. In fact, his chin was resting on top of Jake's left boot, he noticed idly. Couldn't go a step without the dog knowing all about it.

The Sage Ranch kitchen still looked pretty much as he remembered from when he was growing up. New granite countertops, backsplash, and windows, but the same layout, the same cherry-wood table where he'd sat with his parents, Rafe, Travis, and Lissie every day for meals.

41

Man, this room, this house had been noisy back then. Noisy in a good way . . . the best possible way, with everyone talking, arguing, laughing at once.

Good times. A close family. Homework and chores, roughhousing and rules. Hot cocoa and Scrabble tournaments and lots of shouting and racing up and down the stairs whenever he and his brothers or sister forgot their homework or their books before school.

He remembered his mother, and that no matter how annoyed she was after someone spilled milk across the floor, or if Jake and one of his brothers wouldn't stop hitting each other while she wasn't looking, she still always kissed each of her children before they headed off to the bus. And how his father would reach under the table and hold his wife's hand as all around them circled the chattering voices of their children.

But not everyone came from a home like that. Which reminded him of the other reason he was here.

His best high school friend, Cord Farraday. Cord had followed the call of the rodeo, too, and had been killed in a bull-riding accident just over two months before. Jake had taken it hard, but Cord's twenty-two-year-old brother Brady had taken it even harder.

Brady had always been a good kid, solid as they come. He was low-key, hardworking, reliable. But now, from what Jake had heard and seen for himself, he was veering toward trouble.

Setting his coffee cup down on the table, Jake's midnight blue eyes lasered in on his brother.

"The truth is, I didn't come to town only for Zoey's party. Or because Travis might take it into his fool head to *try* to kick my butt." The flash of a good-natured smile faded as he began to speak again. "Ever since Cord's funeral, I've been worried about Brady. I've tried to get in touch with him, but no luck. You seen him lately?"

"You mean before or after he got out of jail?"

"Jail?" Jake's heart dropped. So it was as bad as that. "What did he do?"

"You mean, what *didn't* he do? Take your pick." Sighing, Rafe leaned his shoulders back in the chair. "Drunk and disorderly. Fighting. Assaulting an officer. You name it."

"Brady hit Sheriff Hodge?"

"Not Hodge. Hodge's deputy, Zeke Mueller. Which is just about as bad."

Jake groaned.

"Luckily for Brady," his brother continued, "he didn't hurt Zeke too bad, but whoa, Jake. That kid's pretty messed up. Did you know he quit his construction job with Sam and Denny McDonald a month after Cord died? Just up and walked out one day while they were in the middle of this big remodeling project. He really left them in the lurch. Far as I know, no one's seen much of him since."

A frown tightened Jake's face. Brady Farraday was a dozen years younger than Jake and Cord. He'd always been a dependable kid, the star defenseman of his high school football team, a whiz with tools and fix-up projects. When he was eighteen, he'd saved a little boy's life. A family had gone camping in the Crazy Mountains, and one of the three young sons had wandered off.

A seven-year-old boy, Alex Dursky.

It was only October but an early snowstorm was blowing in. An alert had gone out as well as a request for volunteers to help search. Brady heard about the missing boy and joined the hunt. He'd combed the foothills, then started on some of the back trails in higher areas. Dark was falling, the temperature had dropped, and snow was whirling, but Brady didn't quit.

And he found Alex. The boy was discovered, cold and scared and crying, on a remote ledge. Brady had wrapped him in his own jacket and carried him in his arms through the darkness, down to safety.

He'd been written up in the *Lonesome Way Daily*, hailed as a hero—and the story had even been picked up in the national media and featured on the nightly news.

It was one of the rare bright spots in the hardscrabble life of the Farradays. A bright spot that quickly faded when Cord and Brady's parents died in a car crash a scant two years later.

Les Farraday had always denied he had a drinking problem. Insisting he was as sober as a rock, he drove drunk one night coming home from a neighbor couple's anniversary party at the Lucky Punch Saloon—refusing to let his wife take the wheel instead. Holly Farraday had scrambled into the car with him anyway. Les missed the turn on Mule Road leading to their house and tried at the last minute to make a sharp U-turn, but he'd spun the wheel too fast, too hard. The car plowed straight into a tree. Ned and Holly both died instantly.

But even then—even with Cord on the road, hardly ever home—Brady had hung in there, keeping up the house alone, working steadily, plugging away at life.

Until Cord died, too.

"I called Brady half a dozen times after he roared off from Cord's funeral like a bat out of hell, but I only reached him once," Jake said quietly. "He sounded lower than an earthworm and two sheets to the wind. Not to mention angry. Real angry." His brows drew together as he remembered the boy's bitter tone. A tone so unlike him.

Brady had refused to listen to a word Jake had to say.

"He used every cussword you or I ever heard—and then some. Then he cut off the call. I figured I better check on him, see if there's anything I can do to haul his ass back on track." Jake sighed, remembering the pain he'd heard that day beneath Brady's words.

"A while ago Cord asked me to promise I'd keep an eye on his brother if anything ever happened to him. Ever since their folks died, they've only had each other. Brady's a great kid, but he's had a tough life. He and Cord both."

"You think Cord had a feeling something bad was going to happen to him?" Rafe looked surprised.

"No way. Nothing like that. It's just that Cord couldn't catch a break. I know for a fact he was barely scraping by. He put up a good front—kept telling me he knew things were going to get better, that he was due to win some major purses soon, but it never seemed to happen. He started diving into the bottle, just like his old man. And he found out Brady had taken a notion into his head to sell the house and try his own hand at rodeo, but Cord didn't want him going that route. He didn't want Brady facing the same hard times he'd found on the circuit. Besides, their grandparents had built that house, every inch of it, and he hated the idea of selling it, just letting it go to someone outside the family."

Jake fell quiet for a moment, remembering his friend in happier days. Grade school. High school. Playing touch football or video games, fishing in Sage Creek during the summer. The two of them driving with the radio blaring to the Bear Claw bar in Livingston, armed with fake IDs when they were only seventeen, looking to buy a couple of beers and to pick up girls. Actually, they were looking not for girls but for women. Older, more experienced women. And, Jake recalled, they'd been pretty damned successful at finding them.

A few years later, home on a short break from the rodeo circuit, Jake had also found something else at the Bear Claw. Someone else.

Melanie . . .

The muscles in his neck clenched as her small cameo face floated into his mind, and he instinctively shifted his thoughts away. Away from her . . . away from what had happened that night . . .

He focused them back toward Cord and Brady.

His long-time friendship with Cord had endured long after they first took up rodeo. They'd started out at the same time—two cocky young cowboys with mad roping and riding skills who dreamed of making it big.

Unfortunately, Cord hadn't ever found even close to the same kind of success Jake had. Plagued by injuries, he'd worked like a mule just to scrape by. As time went on, he watched his earnings decrease even more.

Though the two of them branched off onto starkly different paths, they'd kept in touch and caught up whenever they happened to be in the same town or even the same state. But over the last ten months, the losses and the injuries and the stress had taken an increasing toll on Cord. He'd turned to drinking in a big way, steeping his troubles in a pint of whiskey whenever he was scrabbling for enough prize money to keep going.

Jake had lent him cash several times to help him get by, had paid his hospital bills, had tried to talk sense into him. He'd recommended AA, tried to convince him to cut out the liquor, take a break from rodeo until he'd fully healed.

But Cord insisted he knew what he was doing, that he could handle it and was going to win some big-time prize money soon.

Instead, two months later he'd been thrown from a bull at seven seconds. He hit the dirt hard and got stomped on before either the clowns or anyone in the stands could do more than blink. Cord's chest had been crushed. He'd died before he even reached the hospital.

It was a horrific accident but not a completely surprising one.

Jake knew just how dangerous the rodeo could be, and bull riding posed the most danger of all.

Those eight seconds you needed to stay on that bull didn't seem like a long time unless you were the one riding that two-thousand-pound beast. Then those eight seconds ticked by as slow as frozen syrup while those monsters heaved and bucked. Jake was used to it—he had the rhythm of the ride in his veins, pulsing through his blood.

He'd had his close calls, plenty of them—all the times he'd needed to roll aside real fast, but the rodeo clowns had always dashed in front of him, arms waving, distracting the bull before it could reach him once he was bucked off.

Cord hadn't been as lucky that night. The clowns had raced in—but the enraged bull had cut toward Cord even faster. And Cord had been too stunned by the impact of the fall to roll or leap out of its path. . . .

Jake still found it hard to believe he was gone. Everyone who'd ever met Cord Farraday took to the guy. Total strangers bought him drinks within minutes of the most casual conversation.

Even his ex-wife still loved him, though they'd been divorced for more than a year. Tiffy Farraday couldn't take the stress of the rodeo life, of not having money to pay the bills, of not seeing Cord for weeks, sometimes even a month at a time. She'd given him an ultimatum and he'd chosen rodeo over her.

Still, when he died, she handled all the funeral arrangements and buried him in a plot near her home in Mesa. She'd cried in Jake's arms at the funeral and there was a world of regret, anger, and lost dreams in her red-rimmed eyes.

Brady had been there, too, but the boy hadn't seemed to really grasp what was going on. When Jake threw an arm around his shoulders and tried to offer his condolences, the kid had pulled away. He'd seemed still half in shock. Brady had remained mute during the entire service, his eyes almost glazed—then, the moment Cord was lowered into the ground, he'd roared off on his motorcycle without a word to anyone.

Jake had been trying to get in touch with him and make sure he was all right ever since.

"If there's anything I can do to lend a hand, let me know," Rafe told him quietly. "If Brady decides he wants to have a go at ranch work, I know the Double J is shorthanded. I can talk to Jerry Johnson, put in a good word for him."

"Thanks, bro, I'll tell him." Jake didn't mention the idea that had been circling in his head for a while now. It had first come to him a year ago, just a vague notion. With his schedule, he hadn't had time to really develop it. But every once in a while, it returned and began taking hold in his mind.

Now, while he was here in town, with Brady needing a job and all, maybe it was time to set things in motion.

"Any idea if Brady's still living out at the house?"

"Seems like the logical place, but I can't say for sure. Not too many people have spotted him since he got out of jail."

"Well, I'll be heading over there later to find out. Soon as I check out my cabin, see if it's habitable for tonight." Jake got to his feet, mindful of the lightly snoring mutt whose golden head still rested on his boot. He eased his foot away but even as he did, the thin dog clambered up, staring at him with deep, worried brown eyes.

"Come back and have supper with us," Rafe suggested as they headed to the kitchen door. "Sophie will bite my head off if you don't. And you can always bunk here if your cabin needs work before you can spend the night. When are you heading over to Travis's place?"

"Right after I scope out the cabin, clean up a little. Been driving for ten hours and don't want to hug little Miss Zoey wearing my travel dust." Striding out the door, just as a horse whickered from the corral, Jake noted wryly that the dog was still right there on his heels.

"Hey, buddy, you're staying put," he said firmly, as Starbucks and Tidbit trailed eagerly after their skinny new pal. "You've got yourself some friends now. Ivy and Aiden will want to get to know you, and if I know my brother, even young Aiden knows how to be gentle with animals. Trust me, you don't want to hook up with me. I never stay in one place too long and it's no life for a dog."

Rafe had stopped for a moment to speak to his foreman, but he caught up with Jake as his brother opened the door of his truck.

"So how long *are* you sticking around

Lonesome Way this time?" Rafe asked drily.

"Not too long, bro. I'm taking off for the Bighorn Bull Rodeo in Wyoming two days after I sing 'Happy Birthday' to Zoey."

Though it was tempting, he decided against telling Rafe yet about the plan he intended to set into motion. It had been rattling around in his brain for a while, but things had really begun clicking into place when he got involved in the antibullying crusade. Then he learned about Brady quitting his job and suddenly—now that he was back in Lonesome Way—there was a picture in his head of how this all might come together.

It was the right time. And the right place. He'd get it started, and after he took off, he could get updates from the road. With the right builder in charge—and Jake knew just who that builder ought to be—all he'd have to do was give his okays via phone or email and foot the bill.

"Wait until you see Zoey." Rafe's words interrupted his thoughts. "She's a hoot. She might be the spitting image of Mia—only tiny—including all that blond hair, but trust me, she's got a will of iron, just like Travis. That's one fearless, plucky little girl, and you won't believe how she idolizes Grady."

Grady was Travis's adopted stepson from his first marriage. A brilliant kid, all of thirteen, and last year he'd won first prize in the countywide science fair.

"I've seen her picture. Looks like an angel. But if she's anything like Travis, heaven help him and Mia," Jake said with a grin.

The smile stayed on his lips as he thought about his niece. Mia had been emailing him photos since the day Zoey was born. He had them all saved on his phone, along with pics of Grady, and the ones Sophie had sent of Aiden and Ivy. *Ivy*. His teenaged niece was morphing way too fast into a knockout young woman. It scared the hell out of him. And his sister emailed him pictures practically twice a day of her beautiful four-year-old, Molly, who'd snagged his heart the moment he set eyes on her—which happened to be the day after Sophie and Rafe got married, when Lissie barely made it to the hospital in time for the delivery.

He was crazy about all of his nieces and nephews. Which was probably why every time he talked to Lissie, she kept pestering him, telling him he'd make a great dad and since he was now thirty-four he needed to seriously think about settling down. First she wanted him to snag himself a wife, then get started on a passel of kids. Lissie insisted he didn't know what he was missing.

But Jake saw things differently. Marriage, kids, a normal life, that wasn't for him. His life suited him; it was exactly the way it should be. He had freedom with all that riding and competing, every week a different crowd, a different town. And best of all, no one depended on him. He'd failed once at the most important commitment he'd ever made. He'd decided after Melanie died that he wasn't going to make any more promises to anyone—especially a woman—that he might not be able to keep.

So he planned to go right on winning championships until he was too old to saddle a horse. He relished being in a position to raise awareness and funds for the charities and causes he supported.

Rafe and Travis kept razzing him, telling him he'd feel differently if he met the right woman. They didn't have a clue why he intended to ride right away even if he did meet her. They didn't get it. He wasn't cut out for long-term relationships or marriage or promises that needed to be kept. He'd known the truth about himself since he was twenty or so, when he was young and stupid and just starting out in professional rodeo. Melanie Sutton had danced into his life one night bright as a candle, incandescent.

And he'd failed her.

After that, Jake knew that family life and the kind of love Rafe had with Sophie, and Travis had with Mia, wasn't in the cards for him. Not ever. Maybe if he'd stayed with Melanie that night, things could have been different. . . .

But he hadn't stayed. And Melanie . . .

Jake had met a lot of smart, cool, sexy women

in subsequent years, and he'd liked them all—enjoyed them all. All shapes, all sizes, blond, redhead, brunette.

But if he hadn't been there for Melanie, how could he promise to be there for anyone else?

"Let me know what time to show up for supper—" he began abruptly, deliberately cutting off the painful memories, but suddenly, with a burst of energy, the mutt tried to spring up onto the front seat of the truck, then almost didn't make it and would have slid backward, except Jake grabbed him swiftly before he hit the ground. He lifted him up into the driver's seat.

"Who invited you, fella?" His tone was gruff. But somehow he didn't have the heart to set the scrawny creature down on the driveway again.

"I think you've got yourself a dog there, bro. Whether you want one or not."

"Naw. He just knows me better than he knows you. He'll be happy to hang with you guys once he meets the kids. Tell Ivy and Aiden they should start brainstorming names for him."

But glancing over his shoulder, he caught an amused—and skeptical—grin spreading across his brother's face.

Jake shook his head and turned back to the mutt crouched behind the wheel of his truck. "You want to drive this thing, pardner, or you going to move over?"

As if he understood, the dog lumbered over to

the passenger seat and sat staring out the window as if he hadn't a care in the world and was studying the sweeping view of the lavender mountains in the distance.

Behind Jake, Rafe laughed.

"You think this is funny?" But Jake was fighting a smile, too.

"You've been adopted, bro. Hold on while I grab your new dog a few days' worth of pet food." His brother was already striding back toward the ranch house. "Just to tide him over until you bring him back."

Jake swore he could hear Rafe chuckling just before the screen door slammed.

Twenty minutes later, Jake turned off of Squirrel Road and onto Wild Mule Pass. He drove another two miles through lonely, beautifully wild country until he reached the bumpy gravel path leading to his cabin.

His grandfather had willed him nearly seven hundred acres of lush rolling grassland practically within spitting distance of mountains and lakes ripe with wildlife and fish. This gorgeous spot was only a ten-mile hike from Blackbird Lake and surrounded by jagged mountains, magnificent sky, and wildflower meadows that seemed to roll on forever into the hazy distance.

In addition to his own renovated cabin, there were three older, smaller cabins scattered across the property. He sometimes rented them out to fishermen, hikers, or tourists. But he'd never rented out his grandparents' original cabin on Blackbird Lake.

Five years ago, Jake had hired the father and son construction team of Sam and Denny McDonald to transform his personal fifteen-hundred-square-foot cabin into a two-story, six-thousand-square-foot house. That was right after he nabbed his biggest championship purse ever and won a fat commercial endorsement contract for a premium beer. Now, after investing the bulk of that money, Jake had big plans for those other three cabins.

"Don't get lost, buddy," he told the mutt softly as he unlocked the massive solid oak front door and the dog brushed past him into the hall, his feet pattering across wide dusty hardwood floors.

The living room and dining room furniture had been draped in drop cloths while he was gone and the place had a big, lonesome feel to it, thanks to the lofty ceilings and wide open, flowing floor plan.

Way too big for one cowboy. Even one with a dog.

But he didn't expect to be spending too much time here this week anyway. He had too much catching up to do with his family, not to mention tracking Brady down and hauling the kid back in line.

So after showering in the upstairs master bath, changing into clean jeans and a blue and gray flannel shirt, he fed Bronco—only a temporary name for the dog, he told himself, just until his niece and nephew came up with something better—then made sure all the lights and plumbing worked everywhere before taking off again. He pointed his truck north toward rolling foothills and the Farraday place.

Sure, Bronco was curled on the passenger seat of his truck like he'd been there all his life, but that didn't mean Jake was planning to keep the mutt.

It just didn't seem right to leave him alone in that big house—not right away. From the looks of it, this dog hadn't had anyone looking after him in quite a while, if ever, and he had to have some abandonment issues. Which was why Sage Ranch, with Sophie and Rafe and the kids around most of the time, was the place for him to light. Someone was always around; he'd have Tidbit and Starbucks to play with and never a lonely moment.

Hell, speaking of lonely . . .

Jake frowned as he turned onto the rambling drive leading to the Farraday home. It could have been a setting for a sad, spooky painting about desolation.

The clearing where the small frame house squatted was quiet. Too damned quiet. There was no sign that Brady was anywhere around. No sign of his Harley or any other vehicle. No windows seemed open, there wasn't a light on, and not a sound came from the remote clearing surrounded by a lone treehouse and a scattering of cotton-wood trees and pines.

Only silence. Except for the faintest rustling of leaves.

The sun slid lower in the September sky and a lone hawk wheeled lazily as Jake stared at the Farraday place. The small frame house, shed, and garage seemed to stand watch over the clearing like three tired old gray soldiers.

Jake remembered the flowers Cord's mom used to meticulously plant all around the ranch house. Roses, he thought, and some kind of big yellow flowers, bright and happy looking. All spring and summer, Mrs. Farraday was out there working on her garden.

He took the old porch steps two at a time, knocked on the door he remembered from his teenaged years. He rang the doorbell, but heard no sound from within. He wondered if the bell was broken. There was a missing floorboard on the porch. Not a good sign, considering Brady was a wizard with tools and carpentry and had built that treehouse for himself and his friends when he was only twelve years old.

"Brady! Open up!" His fist hammered the door.

More silence.

Checking the shed and peering through the windows of the garage, he determined that both were deserted. He called Brady's name one more time. And heard nothing.

"Guess, I'll have to catch you later. Don't think for a minute this is over," he muttered under his breath as he started up the engine and swung the truck around, back up the drive. A new option popped into his head.

He knew just where he was headed after his visit with Travis and Mia and the kids, and his supper at Sage Ranch.

He'd call ahead to Denny McDonald and get the ball rolling on his new project. Considering the scope of it and the good it would do, he was pretty sure he could persuade Denny to rehire Brady, give him another shot. Then he'd reel the kid in when he caught up to him.

Jake had no intention of taking no for an answer. Whether he liked it or not, Cord's brother was going to quit throwing his life away and do some good in Lonesome Way.

Just as he swung out of the drive and back onto the road, a beat-up old Silverado passed him from the other direction and turned in toward the Farraday place. Jake had only a quick glimpse, but he thought he recognized the little brunette beauty behind the wheel.

Madison Hodge. She had to be about Brady's age. She was Sheriff Teddy Hodge's granddaughter—

and Lonesome Way's resident pageant queen.

Everyone in town knew Madison. She'd collected a slew of titles before she quit the pageant circuit. The glimpse he'd caught of that girl in the truck was nowhere even close to resembling the glamorously made-up, rhinestone-adorned princess whose photos he'd seen in the local newspapers Lissie used to send him. Tonight the girl's famous sweep of thick, straight, dark brown hair was pulled back into a messy pony-tail and he hadn't spotted even a lick of makeup on her face.

Why was she headed to the Farraday place? Were she and Brady friends?

Or maybe something more. . . .

He suddenly wished she *would* find Brady at home. A female could be an excellent influence on a man. On any man other than himself, that is.

He loved women, loved the way they looked and smelled and felt and tasted, and he respected the way they thought and reasoned on almost every subject—except on that settling-down thing. Some women just didn't get that it wasn't for everyone, and Jake avoided women like that. He didn't want anyone getting hurt. Ever since Melanie, he liked to keep his attachments simple, short term and no strings attached.

But if Madison Hodge was interested in helping Brady get back on track, he was all for it. *If she's not up for it, though,* Jake reflected as he listened to Garth on the radio and the gentle snores of Bronco on the seat beside him, *I'll just have to sit the kid down myself sooner rather than later —and I damn well will.*

Chapter Three

Madison punched the doorbell. Still broken, just as it had been when she stopped by three days ago.

Brady, come on. Have you even been home since then?

She rapped on the door until her knuckles reddened. Called Brady's name.

Damn it, where could he be?

Only a deep, cool silence enveloped the clearing as the first crystal stars popped out in an amethyst sky.

Worry bit through her. She hadn't spotted him in town even once since he got out of jail for decking her grandfather's deputy. As far as she knew, no one else had seen him, either.

She'd slipped a note under his door after she learned what had happened to Cord. She'd come by again when she heard about Brady quitting his job with McDonald Construction. But there was no way of knowing if he'd even been back to find her note.

Not that he'd care.

She was probably the *last* person he'd expect to hear from. They hadn't exactly been friends for years now, not since the seventh grade. They hadn't even spoken to each other since that day he'd gotten so mad at her years ago.

But before then—when they were kids—Brady had been her *best* friend. He was the one who'd always told her she had to stand up to her mom if she didn't want to go the pageant route. He'd actually told her mom himself, when Madison hadn't had the courage to do it. He'd spoken up for her—not, she thought ruefully, that Mabelle Jane Cullen had listened.

Pushing the memories of those days from her mind, Madison vaulted back up into her Silverado and roared out onto the road. Driving toward Lonesome Way and her small apartment on the edge of town, she knew she had other matters to worry about—like making it on time tonight to the last rehearsal with Eddie and the guys before the gig in Big Timber, and having to get up on that dumb stage at the Double Cross Bar and Grill within a matter of weeks and sashay across it during the charity dating event. In front of practically the entire town! Then stand there while men bid on her for a date, like a cow at auction or a painting or a piece of furniture on sale at eBay.

She loathed being the center of attention,

detested being center stage. And she had all along, all through those awful pageant years.

Now, playing keyboard with her country band, the Wild Critters, in the shadows of a dimly lit bar—that was different. She *loved* it. It was music, for one thing, and music was in her blood. For another thing, no one was paying attention to her. She wore her jeans and a T-shirt every night, and no makeup, and was tucked comfortably away from the lights, with Delia and Eddie front and center, belting out the music, while Steve showed off his riffs on the drums.

The charity auction was a totally different thing. An *ugh* thing.

But since she volunteered every other weekend at the Lonesome Way animal shelter, she knew as well as everyone in town how badly the new facility was needed.

That didn't make her any more eager to climb onto that stage, but it did put things in perspective. And, she reminded herself, it was a minuscule problem when she compared it to what Brady was going through, losing both his parents, and then his brother and his job.

He needs help, she thought. He needs to know someone cares.

But that someone shouldn't be her. Just because they'd been friends when they were kids didn't mean he wanted her butting into his life. Or *nonlife, as the case may be.*

I'm so done. Madison drew a determined breath as she passed a raccoon scuttling along the side of the road. *Brady will just have to figure this out for himself.*

For years now, he hadn't given her more than a passing nod when they'd seen each other. And not even *that* when she bumped right into him as she was coming out of Benson's Drugstore. He'd just kept on going like she was a ghost or something.

So what makes you think he wants you getting into his business now?

Nothing. *And starting now,* she told herself, setting her jaw as the Chevy rattled back toward town over the darkening country road, *that's exactly what I'm going to do.*

Chapter Four

Carly changed Emma into her pink bunny pajamas, laughing as her pint-sized dynamo squirmed with buoyant energy in her arms.

"Coookiiiie!" her daughter exclaimed.

"You already had a cookie." Carly did up the last of the buttons and lifted the pink-cheeked toddler into her arms. "How about some yummy grapes?"

"Gwapes." Emma's round little face lit up. She was a child easily pleased. Her wispy reddish blond hair flew across dark-lashed deep blue eyes as she tried to squirm out of Carly's arms, hoping to make a run from the nursery to the kitchen.

"Gwapes!" she shouted gleefully to no one in particular.

Carly swept her daughter close and inhaled the scent of her. A calming scent. Baby shampoo and Dreft. Emma's head immediately plopped onto her shoulder and the little girl wrapped her arms tight around Carly's neck.

That was Emma for you. A rock-'n'-rolling toddler one minute and a cuddle ball the next. Carly's heart swelled with an overpowering love that made her breath catch in her throat.

"I love you, pumpkin, you know that, don't you?" Carly whispered, stroking her fingers through that fine, soft hair. "How much do you think I love you?"

"Dis mush!"

Emma's head shot up and she held her arms out wide and Carly had to laugh as she murmured, "You've got that right, baby."

Emotions swamped her as she set Emma down. Emma took off like a shot, racing with a wobbly gait toward the stairs and the kitchen, Carly right on her heels.

She washed four red grapes and cut them in

fourths, then set them on Emma's little Playskool table in the corner and watched as her daughter plopped on the floor and ate the grape sections one by one.

Somehow, Carly had managed to get through her first moments home this afternoon without falling apart in front of her daughter and Madison. She'd done well enough that Madison hadn't seemed to notice anything amiss when she'd filled Carly in on Emma's day, what stories she'd read to her, what games they'd played, what Emma had eaten for lunch. Carly had taken it all in, her mind racing all the while, and she'd needed to suppress a sigh of relief when Madison finally shrugged into her worn suede jacket, told her that it would be no problem switching days with Martha, then gave Emma one final hug before grabbing her guitar and heading out the door toward home.

But Carly was a wreck the entire time and she still was as she readied her daughter for bed. She hadn't felt this awful clenching tightness in her chest for years now—or that sense of horrible uncertainty over what troubles tomorrow might bring. Ever since the day Social Services had whisked her away from the noisy and indifferent jumble of her relatives' homes, her life had gradually become blessedly steady and calm. All of the turmoil, confusion, and loneliness of those six years after her mother's death had begun to fade away the day Annie Benton became her foster mother.

Now, carrying Emma through the airy hall of the old Victorian back to the nursery, Carly couldn't help glancing at Annie's favorite quilt. It was folded over the blue-and-cream-striped sofa in the living room. Merely the sight of the simple log cabin quilt with its vivid squares of periwinkle, rose, lavender, and yellow calmed her. That quilt and the fairy tale quilt hanging in the nursery, as well as the exquisite Dear Jane sampler Annie had sewn long ago, and which held a place of honor folded at the foot of Carly's own bed, always evoked a flood of wonderful memories. Memories of Annie.

Every time she saw or touched one of Annie's quilts, comforting memories of her slight, soft-spoken foster mother circled gently through her head.

Annie, that first day, so calmly opening her door and her heart to a lost, lonesome child.

Annie, with her fluffy, graying hair, her thin, bony face, and serene brown eyes, quietly leading Carly into a spotless sunlit kitchen where Mrs. Smiggles the cat perched on a windowsill.

Annie had served Carly a glass of freshly made lemonade and a chicken salad sandwich that first day, while she told her all about finding Mrs. Smiggles in a trash can. The poor thing had been mewling her scared little heart out. Annie had scooped her out of there and taken her home, and they'd been together ever since. Annie had also told Carly that first day, that first hour, that *she* was home now, too, and she would soon see—everything was going to be all right.

And it had been.

Of course, Carly hadn't believed anything would be all right again, not at first. Ever since her mother's death, Carly's life had spiraled into an endless cycle of loud people and frequent moves, of confusion and, most of all, loneliness. Cousins, great-aunts, and a half sister of her mother's had all taken her in reluctantly for short periods of time, passing her around between them like last week's leftovers. Letting her live with them in crowded apartments or cramped trailer homes filled with their own children or grandchildren and piles of laundry. She'd found herself surrounded by yelling voices and noisy squabbles —until some-one else came along who could better afford another mouth to feed for the next few months or years.

By the time she was ten, Carly couldn't remember the last time she'd felt like she belonged somewhere. Anywhere.

Nor could she remember a place she wanted to be.

But once she was in Annie's home, set back on a shady street in an old, shabby, but safe neighborhood, all that had begun to change.

Life with Annie had been comforting, stable,

filled with quiet talks, homemade cinnamon cakes, and a tranquil sense of belonging. Annie was a quiet woman, a homebody with no children of her own. She taught Carly how to quilt and how to bake everything from lemon squares to carrot cake with cream cheese frosting. She took her to the library every week, and Carly brought home stacks and stacks of books, mostly fiction—mysteries and ghost stories and gothic tales of castles and orphans.

And several times, including the first summer Carly lived with her, she'd taken her on a trip. To Montana—to Lonesome Way. There they'd visited Annie's first cousin, Martha Davies, owner of the Cuttin' Loose hair salon.

After all the rough, run-down city neighborhoods she had lived in, the cozy, close-knit little town of Lonesome Way had seemed like a magical fairy-tale place to Carly.

It still did.

But especially back then, the tiny Montana town nestled in the shadow of the Crazy Mountains struck Carly as picture-perfect, with its astonishing canopy of pure blue sky, its rugged open spaces, and its endless vistas of sage-scented hills and pastures.

Then there were all of its charming Main Street shops, the park, the flower-bordered streets, and the friendly people stopping to chat with each other in the town square.

The spring morning she'd spotted a doe and two fawns picking their dainty way into Martha's garden, staring at her as she sat on the back porch steps, and then nibbling calmly at some shrubs before Martha rushed out to shoo them away, she'd been completely enchanted.

She'd never felt as peaceful, as far removed from her turbulent childhood as she did when she and Annie visited Martha in Lonesome Way.

Of course, there had been that one altercation, Carly thought, as she reached the nursery with Emma in her arms. The fight she'd witnessed on Main Street the first time she'd ever laid eyes on Jake Tanner.

Carly had just turned eleven that summer. Perched on a bench outside of the Cuttin' Loose, she'd been daydreaming while inside Martha snipped away at Annie's wet gray hair. Suddenly a fight had sprung up between a few boys standing outside of Roy's Diner.

Well, not a fight exactly. It was more like three tough-looking young teenagers picking on a fourth boy, one who was shorter, with narrow shoulders. He looked to be about a year or two younger than the others—or else he was just small and skinny for his age. They began shoving him back and forth between them, laughing all the while. The boy yelped as the tallest of the three smacked him suddenly in the face. He tried to break free, to run, but they closed in, surrounding him.

Desperately, he swung a fist at the closest of the bullies, but the blow missed its mark and suddenly he was shoved hard by one of the bullies and careened sideways. He tumbled facedown clear off the sidewalk and into the street.

Carly remembered gasping in alarm. The bullies reminded her of her cousin Phil, who'd always been smacking someone in the neighborhood around. Phil had never hit her, but he'd shoved her hard more than once and he'd gotten a kick out of locking her in Aunt Gertrude's closet for hours at a time. Panic had overwhelmed her whenever he stuffed her into that closet. The darkness, the hanging clothes, the smell of mothballs left her feeling like she couldn't breathe.

And no matter how much she cried and pleaded and screamed, he wouldn't let her out, not until Aunt Gertrude came home from her job at the Quik-Mart.

Thinking about Phil, her breath had hitched in her throat and she felt for one dizzying moment like she couldn't get enough air. But the boys were taking turns kicking the fallen kid in the street, taunting him, and before she even realized what she was doing, she forgot about Phil. The breathless feeling evaporated as she sprang up and shouted, "Stop that!"

Suddenly, out of nowhere, a handsome, husky boy she hadn't spotted before was there in the midst of the fight, launching himself like a cannonball into the fray.

She guessed he was about fourteen or fifteen. He was nearly as tall as the biggest of the bullies, and he was broad shouldered and fierce—so amazingly fierce—with thick jet-black hair that tumbled over his brow. Grabbing the tallest of the bullies, he punched him hard in the stomach, then swung lithely toward the one who'd knocked the smaller boy into the street.

Carly heard the hard thunk of his fist connecting with the second bully's jaw and she had to clench her teeth to keep from cheering.

Suddenly, in a furious blur of sound and movement she heard yelling and cursing, and all three of the bullies swooped toward the dark-haired boy at once—even as the kid he'd been trying to protect scrambled to his feet and ran, leaving his protector to face the others alone.

"Stop it. *Stop!*" Carly didn't remember taking a step but somehow she was in front of Roy's Diner, watching at close range as the husky boy fought off all three.

She saw him get hit hard in the jaw, but he never wavered. He just hit back harder, again and again, punch after punch, cold, concentrated determination on his face, seemingly oblivious of the trickle of blood running from his lip as he dodged some blows and absorbed others and fought ruthlessly back.

"Three against one—that's not fair!" she shouted only a few feet away from them, right before she heard footsteps pounding behind her and spun around in alarm.

But the two young men running toward the fray were older, and they dodged neatly around her.

"You need to step way back now, honey," one of them told her calmly.

And then they each grabbed one of the bullies and dragged him into a headlock. The dark-haired boy punched the third bully one final time, then confronted his would-be rescuers.

"Let 'em go, Rafe! Travis, I mean it! I can take them all!"

And that was the first time she ever heard Jake Tanner's voice.

She'd never seen anyone braver or tougher. Anyone as quick with his fists, or as steady on his feet, or as eager to knock down a bully. And even at that age, he was more compelling and handsome than any male had a right to be.

By that time, several grown-ups had streamed out of Roy's Diner to break things up and Annie and Martha were among those rushing outside to see what all the commotion was about. The moment Jake's brothers let the aggressors go, the three thugs broke for it, pounding away up the street.

After Carly explained exactly what had transpired, Martha promptly introduced them both to the Tanner boys—Rafe, Travis, and Jake.

Little did she know then that the next time she'd see Jake Tanner up close he'd be a towering six foot, two inches of lean, hard-muscled cowboy.

A cowboy offering to buy her dinner at a Houston hotel.

He was all grown up by then—a tall, mouth-wateringly handsome man—with an easy walk and a glint in his dark blue eyes hot enough to melt every ice cube in the hotel bar.

It was that glint that caught her, as much as that incredibly muscular body. That and the need to blot Kevin and all the anger she felt toward him out of her mind had spurred her to go for it. To have mind-numbing, incredible, forget-everything-else-in-the-world sex with Jake Tanner. Just for one night.

She'd figured if Jake couldn't sweep away some of the pain Kevin had caused, no one could.

Now, as Emma stirred in Carly's arms and mumbled something unintelligible, Carly realized how far she'd come. Emma was her world. And Kevin was nothing but a sour-tasting memory.

Even the email she'd received the week before from her college roommate Sydney—an email with a link to a *Boston Herald* article about Kevin's latest legal troubles—didn't make her feel anything but relief that she'd found out the truth and broken things off when she did.

Now she gazed down at her beautiful little daughter.

"Time for bed, baby," she whispered. Emma's eyelashes had already fluttered closed.

Rising from the rocker, Carly settled Emma in her crib, then swept up a stuffed elephant and a doll from the floor. She tucked them into the toy bin near the changing table, dimmed the lights, and returned to the kitchen.

She set water to boil for tea before settling with her laptop at the kitchen table to shoot a quick email back to Syd.

They exchanged emails almost every week, usually about normal stuff, like what new words Emma was saying, or Syd's life as she continued to try to pick up the pieces since her husband's death in Afghanistan two years earlier.

Horrible. What was Kevin thinking? she typed. *He's messed up beyond belief. I so dodged a bullet getting out when I did. How are you and Evan celebrating your three-month anniversary of dating?*

After she hit send, she deleted the email link to the *Herald* article detailing how Kevin had been charged with felony child endangerment for taking his two older kids out of school under false pretenses and trying to drive them to his parents' home in upstate New York. Carly had read each word with wide eyes.

Even worse, he'd been pulled over by the

police for erratic driving with the kids in the car and had tested for a blood alcohol level of .09 and been charged with an aggravated DUI.

That was when he took a swing at one of the cops.

Kevin's wife—now his ex-wife—apparently had full custody of the kids and had not given him permission to take the children *anywhere,* much less out of school or out of state. Though out on bail, Kevin was in big trouble with the law. His ex and her new husband were pressing charges.

Sitting back, she shook her head. *I sure know how to pick 'em.*

A few years ago, reading anything about Kevin Boyd would have set her teeth on edge and had her pacing, unable to sleep, and furious.

Now she felt zip—except sympathy for his ex and her kids, and a fervent gratitude that she'd found out the truth and escaped when she had.

But as she lifted the whistling teapot from the stove and poured hot water over the peppermint tea in one of Annie's delicate flowered cups, a small knot tightened in her stomach. Kevin no longer mattered any more than a pebble scattering under the tire of her Jeep.

But she still had a problem.

And it was a biggie.

What were the odds she'd be able to success-fully dodge Jake Tanner during his visit to Lone-some Way? Next to impossible, if she didn't cancel out on attending Zoey's birthday party.

And if she and Emma didn't pretty much steer clear of town until he was gone . . .

She took a few slow sips of tea, trying to relax, to remember what calm felt like, when suddenly her cell phone rang.

To her surprise the caller ID showed Karla McDonald's name.

"Carly, I'm so sorry. I hate to ask on such short notice, but I need a favor. A big one. If you can't help me, I understand, but—"

Karla's voice broke. She sounded close to tears.

"What's wrong, honey? What can I do?" Scared that something had happened to Denny or one of the kids, Carly's fingers tightened around the phone.

"It's Denny—and his dad . . . they've been in an accident. They were at a meeting, bidding on a construction job in Livingston, and were on their way home. A car ran a red light and hit them. . . ."

Her voice cracked, and Carly heard a muffled sob.

"Oh, no. Tell me what you need. Are they all right? Where are they?"

"Denny's okay—at least, he says he is. But he's shaken up. His dad, though—they think he has a concussion. He's at Long Valley Hospital in Livingston. I need to go there and be with him. I want to make sure they're both all right. But the kids are asleep—"

"I'm coming right over," Carly interrupted. "Let me just grab Emma and I'll stay as long as you need me. Give me two minutes."

"Thank you! I can't thank you enough."

"No need to thank me. I'll be right there, honey. Hang on."

After yanking on a fleece jacket, she tossed what she needed into the diaper bag, then ran to the nursery and eased Emma ever so gently from her crib. She wrapped her daughter in a soft knit throw and headed for the door.

A moment later she had crossed two sets of lawns and was standing on the McDonald porch. Karla's face glowed almost as pale as her hair in the hall light after she swung open the front door.

"Oh, thank goodness. Thank you for coming. I hope I won't be home too late. I just don't know . . . I don't know if Denny will be able to leave with me or not, but I have to see if he's really okay. And to be with him for his dad—"

"Go. It's all right. Everything here is under control," Carly said soothingly, stepping inside. "Call when you can and let me know how Denny and his dad are doing. Okay?"

Karla nodded, her thin fair hair swinging forward with the movement. Her eyes were anxious as she hugged Carly and planted a light kiss on the sleeping Emma's cheek. Only a few years before, Karla had come to Lonesome Way as a single mother, too. She'd first worked as a waitress at the Double Cross Bar and Grill, and then had been hired by Sophie at A Bun in the Oven. Denny McDonald had met her for the first time when he and his father were renovating the former Roy's Diner, where Sophie was opening her new bakery.

Denny had been forty-five at the time, shy, never married. But all that had changed after he laid eyes on Karla and her then three-year-old son, Austin.

"You're the best friend ever, you know that, don't you?" Karla murmured gratefully; then, after one more quick, frazzled smile, she was gone, racing toward her car.

Carly glanced around the neat house with its olive sofa and butterscotch throw pillows, the wide green and tan cushioned armchairs, and a wicker toy chest just like Emma's pushed against one of the living room walls. She crossed to the sofa and settled Emma on the cushions, then stripped off her own jacket and proceeded to make a safe little bed for Emma.

Dragging the upholstered cinnamon-colored ottoman over from the deep armchair, she pushed it flush with the sofa and plopped a thick sofa cushion on top of it, so that if Emma rolled over she'd roll into the cushions and the ottoman, not onto the floor. Arranging the throw across Emma's shoulders, she listened to the sound of her daughter's soft breathing, then settled down herself at the other end of the sofa.

Outwardly she was calm, but her brain was spinning. She wondered how badly Sam McDonald was hurt, and if Denny and Karla would need to stay with him at the hospital all night. She could try to sleep sitting up on the sofa eventually, but she didn't really want to take her eyes off Emma since she wasn't in a crib. Of course later, if she got sleepy, she could always make a cozy bed for Emma on the floor, with cushions and blankets. . . .

She wished she'd brought a book. Something to take her mind off the accident and Denny and Sam. And to take her mind off Jake Tanner being in town. She didn't want to think about that. About having to call Mia and tell her she and Emma wouldn't be able to make it to Zoey's birthday party.

What excuse could she give? What could she possibly say? And was she really going to stay home for the rest of the week, hiding in her house, rather than risk running into Jake somewhere in town?

Carly straightened her spine. *You're not a coward,* she told herself. *You're a strong, smart woman.* Not that terrified little girl who'd hidden all the time, dodging Phil and his roughhousing friends, crawling under the bed when Uncle Nolan got drunk after lunch and started throwing furniture at the walls, and television sets down the stairs.

When she heard a soft tap on the front door, she started, then checked her watch. It was almost nine o'clock—who on earth would be stopping by at this hour?

Still . . . this was Lonesome Way. Maybe someone—another neighbor—had heard about the accident and wanted to check on Karla. . . .

Surging to her feet, she glanced over, reassured herself that Emma was still sleeping soundly. Even when the second knock came, a little louder than the first, the little girl didn't stir.

I hope Austin and Ashley stay asleep, too. Her steps quickened as she strode to the door. She guessed it would be Willa Martin on the porch. The rather crotchety older lady lived two doors down from Karla and Denny in the opposite direction. Willa talked loud and listened harder, always wanting to be the first one to know everything that went on in the neighborhood— she'd probably seen that Denny's truck wasn't in the driveway when Karla took off, and had wondered who was home with the kids.

She opened the door, expecting to see Willa's inquisitive, wrinkly face—and froze.

It wasn't Willa Martin standing on Karla's front porch.

Oh, not by a long shot. It was Jake Tanner, the rodeo champion baby daddy himself.

Chapter Five

For one crazy moment Carly wished desperately she'd drifted into sleep on the sofa and this was just some unnerving dream jolting through her brain. It wasn't really happening. No, she was sleeping . . . waiting for Karla and Denny to come home with Sam. . . .

Then she felt the chill of the night air on her skin, saw the sliver of cool moon glinting in a pure black sky burning with stars. She heard the faint hoot of an owl in the distance and sensed the almost tangible warmth and strength of the man standing two feet in front of her on Karla and Denny's front porch.

This was no dream.

This was her nightmare.

She was five foot seven but she had to look up —way up—to meet Jake Tanner's eyes. Eyes such a vivid shade of midnight blue a woman could easily get lost in them.

She felt her stomach tighten as surprise and hearty male appreciation flashed instantly back at her from their gleaming depths.

He looked every bit as amazing as she remembered from that one incomparable night, yet even in that first instant, she saw subtle differences. He actually looked even handsomer than the cocky, red-hot cowboy she remembered —if that was possible. A little older, but in a good way, even more rugged, and somehow even tougher than he'd looked that night in Houston.

He wasn't a man other men would want to tangle with. But he was a man women would always notice instantly. Tall and rough and muscular, a faint scar on his tanned left cheek. Dark, sexy as hell three-day stubble on his jaw.

But it was his eyes that held her spellbound just as they had that night she'd spent with him in Houston. They were an unflinching cobalt blue, locked on her now like lasers. She remembered the way they'd warmed when he'd slowly kissed her and slid her out of her clothes in that hotel room, and the way he'd grinned as she'd torn through the buttons on his shirt, nearly ripping it from his chest. . . .

She remembered all that, along with the laughter and need and heat that had raced through them both and left them spent in each other's arms by dawn. But she couldn't seem to remember how to talk.

She just gaped at him.

"I'm looking for Denny McDonald. Or Karla. They around?" His voice was deep, polite, but puzzled. "I have an appointment with Den—"

Suddenly his gaze changed, sharpened. Then a smile broke across his face.

"Hey, I *know* you." As his eyes warmed, a small treacherous spark bloomed inside her.

"Houston, right? A few years back . . . you're—Carly. Carly . . . uh . . . something." A slow, adorably sheepish grin touched his lips, a grin that was at once warm and pleased and held a hint of apology.

The whole effect would make any woman's knees melt, she reflected in dismay, even as he shrugged broad shoulders encased in a flannel shirt. "I don't remember your last name, I'm sorry to admit, but I *do* remember you. And that night."

Oh, yeah, well, you're not the only one, Carly thought. *That was me, all right.* The good-girl Carly who never leaped before she looked—until that one night. . . .

A single thought flew through her mind. She had to stop gaping at him and get rid of him. Fast. She had to close this door. Emma was sleeping only a dozen feet away . . . oh, God . . .

"Look," she said in her chilliest tone, hoping it would cool him off fast. She was feeling hot enough for both of them. "It's Carly McKinnon, and I remember you, too, but I can't talk right now. You'll have to come back to see the McDonalds. I'm babysitting their kids. There was an emergency—an accident—"

"What kind of accident?" The grin faded,

replaced by a look of concern. "Are Karla and Denny all right?"

"Denny's dad may have a concussion. Sorry, that's all I know and I really need to go check on the kids. You'll have to come back tomorrow."

When I'm not here.

She began to close the door before he could say another word, but at that precise moment, a dog began howling loudly enough to wake an entire graveyard—long, piercing, rouse-the-dead howls —and she saw with a shock that the sounds were coming from the big mutt crouched in the passenger seat of Jake's truck.

The wailing shattered all the peacefulness of the night and to her horror, she heard Emma suddenly start to cry.

Crap!

Then things got worse. She heard more crying. Then a thump, which seemed to come from Austin's room, immediately followed by a piercing cry. Next Ashley started to shriek, short, high-pitched sobs.

All three kids crying? At once?

"Damn. Sorry about that." Glancing over his shoulder, Jake frowned at the baying dog in his truck. But turning back to the sexy-as-hell beauty in the doorway, he was struck not only by her obvious coolness toward him, but by the scarcely masked panic now flashing in her eyes.

She obviously wasn't too crazy about dogs,

especially ones who howled and awakened small children. And she obviously didn't have the same warm memories he did of their night together.

She tried to close the door in his face yet again, but he stuck a booted foot in the threshold and placed one strong palm against the door. "Sounds like you have your hands full here . . . this is my fault, let me help—"

"You've done enough. Help me by leaving— and take that dog with you! Just go!" Spinning around, Carly darted back into the living room, accompanied by more deafening howls from the truck.

Emma was screaming at the top of her lungs.

What if she fell off the sofa? Maybe she's hurt! Carly thought, panic clutching at her chest, but as she neared the sofa she saw with relief that Emma hadn't fallen at all. She was sitting up, sobbing, her face soaked with tears—probably because she didn't know where she was, and the damned howling dog had woken her up.

"Mumma!" she screamed as Carly scooped her into her arms.

"You're okay, Emmy. You're fine. Mommy's right here." Forcing her voice to a low, calming pitch, she smoothed Emma's damp hair back from her face. "Go back to sleep. You're fine, baby. Everything is fine."

But Emma didn't seem to believe her and actually, Austin and Ashley didn't *sound* fine.

They were both crying to raise the roof and she took off up the stairs with Emma still sobbing, cradled against her shoulder. She reached Austin's room first. The seven-year-old was sprawled on the floor beside his bed, tears pouring down his cheeks.

"I f-fell out of bed," he wailed. "Mommy!" He stared wide-eyed at Carly. "Where's *Mommy?*"

"Sweetie, Mommy had to go meet your daddy. She'll be home soon. Tell me where it hurts. Did you hit your head?"

Holding Emma against her shoulder, she knelt and tried to hug Austin with her free arm, but he twisted away from her, still sobbing inconsolably.

Ashley was yelling her little head off from her bedroom.

Great. Three crying kids. Jake outside the door. *I might start crying next,* she thought grimly, gently stroking Austin's back with her free hand.

At least the dog had stopped howling.

A moment later she saw why.

Jake wasn't outside. Neither was the dog. They were both in the house, standing ten feet away, in Austin's doorway.

"How can I help?" Jake asked.

"Leave!" she ordered. Her heart was pounding. Jake and Emma. In the same room.

This couldn't be happening. . . .

"Go. Now!" she snapped. But Austin had seen the dog and magically he stopped crying. She knew the little boy had been begging Karla and Denny for a dog the last few months, and now, seeing the big mutt wagging its tail in the doorway, he just stared at it, his mouth wide open.

"Whose dog is that? Did M-Mommy and Daddy get him for me?"

"No, honey. It's Mr. Tanner's dog. Mr. Tanner is . . . um, a friend of your daddy's. How about this—you stay with him for just a minute and you can pet the dog. I need to check on your sister."

Emma's sobs had finally subsided and she leaned her head against Carly's shoulder as Carly whirled, dodging right past Jake Tanner and his dog without a word, bolting toward Ashley's bedroom. The little girl was just tumbling out the door of her pink and purple bedroom, dressed in Hello Kitty pajamas.

"I want Mommy!" she gasped, followed by a hiccup. Tears slid down her cheeks.

"Your mommy will be home real soon, angel. Everything is fine." Still holding Emma close, Carly knelt and hugged Ashley with her free hand. Then she gently stroked the little girl's damp hair back from her face. "Ashley, do you . . . do you want to see a doggie?"

"I heard a doggie . . . it woke me up. It was crying!" Ashley leaned against her, snuggling. "Why was it crying? Why is Emma here?" she asked suddenly, and a smile broke across her face. She sniffled and stopped crying, then leaned toward Emma and kissed her cheek.

Emma peered at Ashley. Reaching out, she poked one tiny finger against the side of the little girl's nose. Ashley laughed, and so did Emma.

"Okay, how about everyone goes back to sleep?" Carly suggested, surging to her feet.

"I'm thirsty." Ashley gazed pleadingly up at Carly with huge teary eyes.

"Okay. One glass of water coming right up. You climb back into bed now, honey, and I'll bring it to you."

The next few moments rushed by in a blur as she brought Ashley water, then tucked her into bed, holding Emma all the while. Emma thankfully was falling back asleep, her head on Carly's shoulder, her eyelids fluttering.

Carly took deep calming breaths as she carried her daughter back to the sofa, laid her gently down on the makeshift bed, and pushed the protective cushions into place once more. She covered Emma with the blanket, stared at her a moment as her own heartbeat finally slowed, and then spun back toward Austin's room.

But she froze on the spot because Jake was standing in the hall watching her, and the big, now-silent mutt sat quietly, innocently, by his side. *That dog's just pretending innocence,* she thought.

"Sorry about all the commotion." His eyes alight with both apology and amusement, Jake came toward her.

Toward Emma.

Carly felt her blood turn as cold as river ice. She knew she had to try to appear casual. Normal. Calm. But she didn't feel any of those things.

Jake was here in the same room with his daughter, breathing the same air, less than ten feet away from his own child, and he had no clue. *All because of me,* she thought grimly. *Because I never told him.*

She'd made the decision two years before that she wasn't going to tell him anything about the baby, not ever. For his own good, as much for him as for Emma, she reminded herself now as she met those steady blue eyes.

What he didn't know wouldn't hurt him. And it wouldn't hurt Emma, either—not the way it would if she knew she had a father who didn't want to be a real part of her life.

"Is Austin okay?" she asked quickly, praying she didn't look as freaked out as she felt.

"Probably sound asleep again by now." Jake's voice was quiet, even. "I let him pet Bronco—" He nodded toward the skinny mutt, who now looked as docile and well behaved as a prize-winning poodle at a dog show. "Then I promised him we'd come back tomorrow so the two of them could play fetch in the backyard." He gave

91

his head a shake. "Whew, you sure had your hands full. That was my fault. Sorry."

It took every drop of willpower she possessed to keep from stepping instinctively between him and Emma as he advanced toward the sofa.

Toward their daughter.

An enormous lump filled her throat as he peered down at the little girl with the wispy curls draped across her cheeks.

Emma looked like a real-life, honest-to-goodness cherub. Beautiful. Sweet. Innocent. Deeply asleep now, her tiny fingers clutched the soft peach-colored throw tucked around her shoulders.

"Who's *this* amazing little heartbreaker?" Jake asked softly. "Since she doesn't have a bed of her own in this house, I'm guessing she's yours."

"Ye-es. My daughter. Emma." Carly tried to ignore the bubble of fear and tension expanding in her chest.

"Wow, what pretty hair. She looks so much like you. I'm sure you must know how beautiful she is." His gaze lingered on Emma, and a smile tugged at his lips before he turned slowly away and fixed those disconcertingly direct eyes on Carly.

"So. You're married now. Damn. Just my luck." Even as the rueful grin split across his face, he automatically glanced down to her left hand and registered with a small jolt of surprise that she wasn't wearing a wedding band.

Or, for that matter, an engagement ring.

"Oops. Or . . . not," he added easily, with a wider grin and a shrug of his shoulders. There was neither a question nor judgment in his eyes.

"*So* not married," she answered quickly, with a shrug. But a flush crept up her neck and heated her cheeks. "Emma's father isn't in the picture."

Whoa. What kind of an asshole wouldn't be in the picture for his very own kid? Jake felt a rush of pity for the toddler asleep on the sofa—and contempt for the man who had run out on his responsibility. He noticed that Carly's voice sounded stiff, even a little bit breathless, and he guessed she wasn't nearly as cool with the father deserting them as she wanted everyone else to think she was.

"Sorry. Didn't mean to stick my nose where it didn't belong," he began but she brushed right past him and Bronco as if he hadn't spoken, heading straight to the front door.

"I'll tell Denny you stopped by."

Man, this woman couldn't get rid of him fast enough.

She looked even *more* delicious than he remembered from that night in Houston. She had a fantastic willowy body, long and lean. And that fresh, sexy girl-next-door kind of beauty—a stunning combination of naturalness and sensuality. And her lips . . . they were probably the most pouty, shapely, inviting-looking lips he'd ever seen. And he'd seen quite a few. Fact was, he still remembered just how sweet they tasted . . . how sweet *she* tasted. . . .

What really got him, though, wasn't the knockout beauty of her heart-shaped face, or her full soft lips, or even the remembered peal of breathless, slightly tipsy laughter as they got to know each other between the sheets in Houston.

It was her eyes. Those incredible dreamy green eyes, soft and rich as a summer forest. They seemed to have a way of drawing a man in. Deeply in.

When they weren't deliberately trying to block him out.

Which was what they were doing right now.

Following her to the door, Bronco at his heels, Jake struggled to rein in his attraction to her—the same heady jolt of instant attraction that had pulled him to her across the lobby of that hotel—but she sure didn't make it easy.

She was damned sexy in that scoop-necked ivory sweater, with her mass of thick red curls, simple faded jeans, and sneakers. Fact was, she looked like a million bucks. Like some slender supermodel hanging out in Lonesome Way, lying low—on vacation, Jake thought. Tall and graceful —with very distracting curves filling out her sweater and jeans in exactly the right places.

This Carly McKinnon was so much more

down-to-earth than the stunning, polished businesswoman he'd invited into his hotel room in Houston. Back then she'd been dressed in very high heels, a gold silk blouse, and a black business suit.

He remembered her kicking off those heels and sauntering toward him with a sexy little smile. He remembered her rising up on tiptoe and kissing him within two minutes of stepping into his hotel room.

And after he'd stripped off her elegant blouse and skirt, tossed aside her wispy black bra and tiny lace thong, he'd discovered a whole other side to her.

A side that was effortlessly sexy, a little bit wild, and as hot as any spark from a campfire.

The truth was, he'd actually thought about her again the next day . . . and the next. And maybe even the day after that.

Which was unusual for him.

He'd even been tempted to call her. But he'd told himself that would be a bad idea.

Jake had a sixth sense about women. And from what he'd seen of Carly McKinnon in bed and out, he'd sensed that beneath the sexiness and the smarts and the confidence, and despite her eagerness to fall into bed with him that night, she wasn't the type of woman to either take or let things go lightly.

Which meant she wasn't a good fit for a man

who never lingered long in one place—or with one woman.

His instincts had warned him to leave well enough alone and walk away. And in his long career with horses, bulls, and women, Jake had learned to trust his instincts.

He'd never expected to see her again—especially not here in his hometown. But maybe he *should* have expected it, he thought. She'd told him they'd met briefly as kids, told him that she knew Martha Davies and had visited Lonesome Way a couple of times.

Over dinner that night she'd even mentioned witnessing a fistfight while she was in town—a fistfight that involved Jake sticking up for a younger kid.

Well, that wasn't too unusual, Jake had reflected. He'd always seemed to have a zero-tolerance policy for bullies. Like Roger Hendricks, who'd always picked on the smallest boys on the playground when they were in grade school.

Jake had put an end to that quick enough. Probably because his father had always quoted old cowboy sayings to him when they were working side by side at the ranch—and one of those old sayings had stuck hard in Jake's mind.

A cowboy should never shoot first, hit a smaller man, or take unfair advantage.

Words to live by, son, Jake's father had told him. And Jake did just that.

He'd searched his memory over dinner with Carly that night in Houston, and finally, when she described the fight to him, he'd vaguely remembered it—and the older boy whose butt he'd kicked.

Gil Tucker. An ass in horse's clothing.

Gil and he had never gotten along. The guy had been a bully practically since the time he learned how to walk. He and his cousins had cornered puny Randy Taylor outside of Roy's Diner that day. Jake didn't remember all the details. He only knew Gil had grown up to be every bit as much of a loser as he'd been in his teenaged years. He was now an assistant coach with the high school football team. According to Rafe and Travis, Gil got his kicks tearing into the weakest of his players.

Some things never changed.

But Jake was far more interested in what Carly was doing in Lonesome Way here and now. How she'd come from a big-time job out east to babysitting at Denny McDonald's house on Blue Bell Drive.

"So I'm guessing you're here visiting Martha." With Bronco following right on his heels, he joined her at the door where she waited, all but tapping her foot. She looked so pretty and so damned eager to be rid of them both that he couldn't help but take it as a challenge. "Any chance you'll be sticking around a few more days? I'm thinking we could go to dinner."

"Sorry, I can't. Emma keeps me pretty busy."

"Aw. I'm sure she does." Leaning against the doorjamb, he gazed down into her eyes. They met his with a coolness that didn't bode well. He felt a ping of disappointment. But Jake was nothing if not a risk taker. "The thing is, I have a niece. She's great—fifteen, very smart, real responsible. And she babysits—"

"I know. Ivy. She's terrific. But, as I said—I can't."

Can't or won't? he wondered. Her face was set, determined. As in *Sorry, buddy, but no way.*

Well, all right, then. Don't try to spare my feelings or anything. Jake didn't know whether to laugh or go take a shower. Maybe his deodorant was failing him. He didn't usually have this much trouble getting a date. Especially a *second* date.

"So . . . I take it you know my brother and Sophie, too?"

"I know your entire family." For the first time, she hesitated a moment, then plunged on. "I . . . we—Emma and I—we live here now."

She was staring at him almost defiantly. At least that was how it seemed for a moment. Then she gave him what looked like a forced, too casual smile. "Two doors down, actually. The McDonalds are our neighbors."

"No kidding. You *moved* here? From *Boston?*"

Her shoulders lifted in a jerky little shrug.

"Sure, why not? People move all the time."

"Not to Lonesome Way, they don't." He smiled at her, but still . . . he sensed something was off. He couldn't put his finger on it. Her skin was slightly, adorably flushed and she sounded almost defensive. "We're kinda off the beaten track. Seriously, how the hell did you end up here?"

She hesitated only a fraction of a second. "Martha, of course. She's the closest person I have—*we* have—to family. I wanted to be near her. She's Emma's godmother but she's actually more like a grandmother to her. And this town . . . Lonesome Way . . ."

She paused again, then met his gaze squarely, speaking more slowly as if she really needed him to understand. "Since the first time I visited here, I haven't been able to get Lonesome Way out of my mind. I always thought it was the perfect small town, the perfect place to grow up. Then, a few months before Emma was born, I suddenly realized I wanted to raise her here. Not in Boston or any other big city. I wanted her to grow up in a small town. In *this* small town. To put down roots . . . I didn't really have any roots when I was a child. And my foster mother had died two years before . . . so," she said, flushing a little bit more, "I quit my job so Emma could have this. A place where she belonged. I wanted her to have family close by—*Martha,*" she added swiftly.

Suddenly she put her hand on his arm and gave

him a little push. "Look, I really do need to check on the kids. Thanks for all your . . . um, *help.*"

A smile tipped the corners of his mouth. He hadn't missed the subtle sarcasm of that last word—or her speaking glance at Bronco. But the touch of her hand on his arm—he swore a tingle ran through his blood where her fingers touched.

"Seeing as it was this big guy who caused all the problems, it's the least I could do. But maybe I'll see you around." He gave her his best grin.

"Sure. Maybe." *But not if I can help it!* Carly eased the door closed.

This time he didn't try to stop her, and she pushed it firmly shut until the latch clicked. Then she sagged against it, her heart still racing. With relief she heard the sound of an engine growling to life, saw headlights flash through the living room window as his truck rolled away into the night.

God, her hands were trembling. Like leaves in a summer storm. She pressed them to her cheeks.

What a freaking *disaster.* Her mind whirled as she strode up and down the living room, reliving every moment of Jake staring down at Emma, of that smile in his eyes when he looked at her.

She'd felt too many emotions roiling through her in that moment—the terror that somehow he'd recognize Emma as his daughter, the guilt at having kept her from him all this time. Even though she knew he didn't want the responsibility and he was better off—they were all better off—with him not knowing, she couldn't quite block out the whispers of her conscience.

Jake had the soul of a nomad. He was not father material. Not even close.

Biting her lip, she paced across the patterned living room rug. And reminded herself yet again that Emma would be happier without any father than one who would feel obligated and potentially resentful.

When Karla called a scant twenty minutes later to let her know that they were on their way home, that the hospital wanted to keep Denny's father overnight for observation but his condition wasn't serious, Carly managed to tell her in a steady enough tone about Jake showing up at the door.

"Oh, damn. Denny *told* me he was coming by tonight! I totally forgot. The two of them have some business deal to discuss. We both completely blanked on it after the accident. We were so worried about Sam—*Denny,*" Carly heard her call out, *"Jake came by to talk to you about his project! We forgot to reschedule!"*

What project was that? Carly wondered after Karla assured her they'd be home within the next half hour. Not that it mattered to her what Jake did or didn't do.

But she found herself thinking again about that handsome face she could barely tear her gaze from. About that superbly muscled body, and how surprising it was to see the gentleness of his expression when he'd looked at Emma. He'd been good with Karla and Denny's kids, too, she acknowledged.

And she couldn't help wondering if the decision she'd made two years before to keep the truth from him had really been wise and unselfish.

Or self-serving and the easy way out.

She bit her lip and reminded herself she'd reached the decision for all the right reasons. And by the time Karla and Denny returned, and she scooped Emma up into her arms once more to carry her home, she had almost completely convinced herself again that she was right.

She was so immersed in her own thoughts and worries that she didn't even notice the dark-colored truck parked across the street from Willa Martin's driveway. Or see the man watching her from the driver's seat, sitting very still, sheathed in darkness, the engine turned off, and only his gaze following her as she strode with Emma across the two front lawns to the door of her home.

Chapter Six

Madison's eyes drifted closed. Pleasure flitted over her as she sat facing the street at her corner table in A Bun in the Oven the next afternoon and bit into her freshly baked cinnamon bun.

So delicious, she thought, trying to concentrate on the gooey sweetness, the drizzle of icing, the fragrant smells of dough and chocolate drifting through the bakery—and not on what Delia Craig was saying.

"So I'm going to wear this one-shouldered red shimmery dress. And wait 'til you see my shoes. *Killer shoes*. Also red. Stilettos. Does the name Jimmy Choo mean anything to you? I bought them online. On sale! What are *you* going to wear?"

"Don't have a clue. Trying not to think about it." Madison took another bite of the cinnamon bun. But her stomach was starting to knot up and ache a little. Not from the cinnamon bun, but from the way Delia was looking at her. As if she was from another planet because she wasn't psyched to prance and pose her way across the stage at the Double Cross Bar and Grill on auction night.

"You know, you really need to give this some thought. The auction's coming up soon. Less than two weeks."

Surrounded by what seemed like a quarter of the town of Lonesome Way enjoying an early lunch in the bustling, sunny bakery, Madison shook her head.

"Shhh. Don't remind me."

"We could go shopping in Livingston," Delia suggested. "At Sequins and Swirls. It's the cutest shop with lots of sparkly party dresses and jewelry and stuff. It's your day off from babysitting—why not take advantage of it?"

Delia Craig had never known a moment of stage fright. With her pert face, long, honey brown hair, nose sprinkled with freckles, and a high, soulful singing voice that melded perfectly with her boyfriend Eddie's deep twang, she positively ate up being the center of attention onstage, any stage, like a seven-year-old digging into a marshmallow-topped hot fudge sundae.

"I'm *not* wearing a party dress," Madison said firmly, licking a bit of icing off her finger. "I'm not wearing a dress at all."

"Then what will you wear?" Delia swallowed another bite of her gooey caramel brownie and stared. "Sweatpants? Jeans?" she asked jokingly.

"One or the other, probably. Yes."

"Come *on*." Delia laughed. "It's one thing to dress like that when the Wild Critters perform. You're always in the back, in the shadows anyway. But for the auction, you want everyone to see you. You want as many guys as possible bidding on you, don't you? Guys go nuts for a girl in a tight, sexy, shimmery dress. Especially one with your figure. You'll raise a ton more money for the shelter if you go with the sexy vibe."

Madison knew she was right. But the idea of wearing a dress practically made her itch. She'd worn enough dresses in her pageant years to last her two lifetimes. Sweet dresses, sexy dresses. Long swirly dresses and pink heels, white diaphanous dresses with tulle and silver slippers that made her look like a stupid miniature Cinderella doll.

And she could still see her mother's face, squinched critically as she looked Madison over before pushing her off down the runway.

"Don't slump, Madison. Shoulders back, sweetie. Way back! *Smile*. You look like you just fell down and skinned your knee. You need to look like a *princess*. A happy princess who's smiling and waving to all of her subjects. Like in a storybook. Do I need to buy you a storybook with pictures? Smile *more. Bigger* . . . that's it. A great big smile, that's the way to *win!* No more of this finishing fifth or eighth. Show them you want to win!"

With a shudder she tore herself from the stroll down memory lane hell and all of a sudden, just like that, she saw Brady Farraday walk past the bakery window.

Her chair squeaked as she shoved it back.

"Sorry, Dee, be back in a minute."

Madison had to dart around a couple of teenaged girls trying to enter the bakery. She managed to spot Brady's tall figure right before he entered Benson's Drugstore, and hurried after him.

Slightly out of breath, she burst into the drugstore and scanned each of the aisles before she finally spotted him in the back, near the refrigerated section. He already had a six-pack of beer in one hand, and he was grabbing a package of hot dogs in the other. He wore jeans and boots and, despite the cool fall day, no jacket. Just a short-sleeved blue-gray T-shirt that revealed tanned skin and hard, ropy muscles.

"Brady." She skidded to a stop before him. "I'm sorry about Cord. Are you all right?"

He stared at her, close to six feet of strapping, good-looking cowboy going very still. His thatch of thick sandy blond hair tumbled over his brow as he looked her over slowly, then shrugged.

"Saw your note. I'm fine," he said curtly, but she didn't miss the flash of skepticism in his eyes. She guessed the words *and you care* why? were flashing through his brain.

Fair question. Especially since the two of them hadn't spoken a word to each other in years. But Brady had lost his brother. And his way. Long ago, as children, Madison thought with a tug of sorrow, they'd roller-skated down her street together, holding hands. Climbed on the monkey bars in the schoolyard, racing every day to see who could reach the top first.

How many times had they sprawled together, side by side in the treehouse he'd built, eating Cheez-Its out of the box and munching on his mom's peanut butter cookies and groaning over their never-ending homework?

In middle school they'd talked endlessly on the phone every night about who liked who, who was a snob, a brat, who smoked, who drank, who was a total jerk.

And when her mother wasn't dragging her off to compete in some pageant on the weekend, Brady had come over nearly every day to hang out. They'd listened to music in Madison's bedroom, dreamed about how he was going to be a race car driver someday, how she was going to write songs and sell them to top country and pop artists all over the world.

When Dylan Hunt, a seventh grader, had pestered her to be his girlfriend for a whole week after she'd told him no, then began calling her with taunting phone calls and telling everyone in school she was a stuck-up bitch, Brady, who'd been skinny and half a head shorter than Dylan back in those days, had pushed the other boy up against a locker and warned him to lay off. Dylan had never bothered her again.

Even Madison's mother had liked Brady, because he always, unfailingly, called her ma'am.

"That Farraday boy, now *he* has nice manners. Those folks of his brought him up right."

But Brady's father drank too much, and now his folks were both dead. So was Cord. And ever since his brother got trampled by that bull, the good-natured, easygoing boy she'd known long ago had taken on a tough edge. A go-to-hell-see-if-I-care attitude that glinted out like polished steel from his narrowed gray eyes.

He's not letting anybody in, Madison realized. *Especially not me.*

For a moment, her throat ached. Sometimes she still found herself missing the old Brady so much. Wishing her best friend would come back.

But even the old Brady had stopped speaking to her in seventh grade. And who could blame him? She'd betrayed him all those years ago, shattered his trust.

"We were friends once, Brady," she said suddenly. "Maybe we could be friends again—if you want to be." She was making a mess of this, she knew it. But she plowed on anyway. "I'm pretty worried about you. And I'm not the only one—a lot of people in town care what happens to you. Everybody wants you to be okay."

Brady's jaw clenched tighter. He didn't believe her, not for a second. Not after the way he'd screwed up. He knew what people were saying.

The same thing her grandfather, the town sheriff, must be saying.

That one-time so-called hero punched my deputy in the face. Quit his job. Landed in jail. He's nothing but a loser. Like his drunken dad. Like his brother. A loser . . .

He could hear the words. They rolled endlessly through his head. He hadn't a clue why Madison was trying to hand him all this crap, but he knew it was a bunch of b.s.

"No one in this town needs to waste their time worrying about me." Brushing past her, he smacked the beer and hot dogs down on the checkout counter.

But Madison stuck around, waiting while he paid for his purchases, then she followed him outside. She grabbed his arm as he started to turn away down the street and he glared at her in surprise.

"Brady, come on, give me a chance. Don't you remember the way it used to be? I'd like to—to—"

"To what? Be my friend?"

He stared down at her in the cool afternoon light, even as a wicked September wind rustled down from the Crazies. He saw her shiver despite her oversized bulky tan sweater and jeans. But in his short-sleeved T-shirt, no sweater, no jacket, Brady felt impervious to the weather, as impervious as he was to the people skirting around them down the street. As impervious as he was to her.

"You really want to be my friend again, Madison? Sorry to tell you, but that's not going to happen. I don't have anything against you. I just don't need a friend right now. I need a job. I need work, and money to pay my bills. I need something to think about besides—"

He stopped, his mouth tightening, wondering if she knew what he'd been about to say. *I need something to think about besides Cord being dead.*

"Well, to tell you the truth, I need something, too. A favor." The words flew out of her mouth. She lifted her chin in a stubborn way that, oddly, he remembered.

"If you'll . . . help me out with something, I'll pay you." The words tumbled out seemingly before she could stop them.

Suspicion narrowed his eyes. "You're gonna pay me? For what? And just how much are you willing to pay?"

"You know about the charity dating auction next week at the Double Cross Bar and Grill? Well, I agreed to be part of it. Actually I was pressured to do it—not that I don't think it's a good cause, but—well, you know how I . . . I don't like parading up onstage."

"So?"

"So I swore to myself after my last pageant

that I'd never get up on a stage again. But—"

"Get to the point." Taking hold of her arm, he eased her nearer to the drugstore window and out of the path of a bunch of teenaged boys jostling each other as they stampeded down the street.

"The point is . . . I don't want to be on that stage any longer than I need to be. So I'll pay you to bid on me. Immediately. Just as soon as I get up there."

"Bid on you?" He repeated the words as if she'd spoken them in a foreign tongue.

"Yes, bid on me." Color flooded her cheeks. "I agreed—under pressure—to go out on one date with whoever bids the highest. But I'll be damned if I'm going to stand up there getting ogled for one more second than I need to. I swore I'd never put myself through anything like that again. So if you bid on me—and I mean if you bid *a lot*—and win the date right at the very beginning . . ." She took a breath and rushed on. "Then I'll pay you back. I'll pay you whatever it takes to get me off that stage as soon as possible. Then I'll also pay you one hundred dollars *over* your bid."

"One hundred dollars more? A date with you could go for a lot of money, Madison." The words came out a bit rougher than Brady intended, but Madison just shrugged dismissively.

"No way. I'm not dressing up like the other girls, and I'll barely put on any makeup. I'll wear my hair in a *bun* if I need to. Just tell me you'll

111

bid on me, like maybe fifty dollars, right at the outset. Then I'll pay you one hundred and fifty and you'll be a hundred dollars richer. And I'll be done with the stupid auction."

She obviously didn't have a clue what she looked like, what effect she could have on a man. Even with her hair wrapped in an old lady bun, wearing bulky dull clothes and a frown on that oval face, Madison's wide-set doe eyes and her simple beauty would just shine through, Brady thought.

Even standing beside her was enough to make a man a little crazy. Those full, voluptuous lips begged to be kissed. Her delicately shaped nose and caramel eyes would draw any man's gaze across any room.

Add it all up and Madison exuded an indefinable earthy sexiness without a whit of trying. . . .

She was five feet, five inches of luscious brunette dynamite.

"And what about the *date* part of what I'm buying—my taking you out somewhere. Is that part of the bargain, too?"

"We'll grab ice cream cones at Lickety Split— or something." She shrugged, worrying her lush bottom lip in the innocent way he remembered, the way she used to when they did homework in the treehouse. "That would make it legitimate, you know? And it'll be quick—quick and painless for both of us. That is, *if* you can endure my company for the time it takes to eat an ice cream cone."

"For a hundred bucks, I reckon I can handle it."

"Be careful, all this sweet talk might go to my head." The words came out tart. She moistened her lips, cleared her throat. Spoke carefully. "Listen, Brady, I know it's all my fault we stopped being friends. But seventh grade was a long time ago. Don't you think that one of these days you could just *try* to get over it?"

For a moment he found himself caught up in the earnestness of those wide eyes that were searching his face. He remembered how she'd stared at him in the same wistful way back in seventh grade, when he learned she'd told Margie Shane about the crush he had on her, how he couldn't stop thinking about Margie and dreamed about her every night—something he'd confided to Madison and to no one else, not even Cord.

After she spilled the beans to Margie, it had gone viral around the entire school.

He'd been twelve, a stupid, unsure, self-conscious kid, furious at the betrayal. He'd yelled at Madison that they were done. Swore to her they'd never be friends again. When tears poured from her eyes and she tried to apologize, he'd turned his back on her and stalked away, even though she'd been his closest friend since kindergarten.

Even a few months later, when her mom had suddenly married some trucker and dragged Madison off with her and the new guy to live in Missoula, he hadn't forgiven her or even said a word. Not before she left Lonesome Way and not when she moved back a few years ago on her own to live near her grandparents.

He'd always figured they'd grown apart too much to ever be friends again.

And now the idea of trying to bridge that gap was more than he wanted to handle. So he skirted her question and changed the subject, trying to wipe the hopefulness from her face.

"If you can afford to pay me a hundred bucks to get you off that stage, you must be making a fortune babysitting these days."

"Not a fortune, but you'd be surprised." She drew herself up, and the top of her head almost reached his chin. "I have a standing gig at the Spotted Pony two nights a week that pays pretty well. And I've saved some of my pageant winnings. So don't worry, I have the money. You don't need to lose any sleep thinking I'll cheat you out of your hundred dollars."

She started to spin away, but he caught her arm and tugged her back. "Look, I never said I was worried, Madison. I just want everything spelled out. One hundred dollars and an ice cream cone and you have yourself a deal."

"Done." She stuck out her hand and he shook it,

trying to ignore the spark of something hot that seemed to run like jagged lightning up his arm as his rough palm enclosed her delicate one.

The dignified, set expression on her face made Brady feel about two inches tall. He was just about dead broke right now, but there was no way in hell he was taking a penny from Madison. He just didn't want to tell her that yet. He didn't want her thinking he felt sorry for her or anything. He knew how intensely she'd hated being in all those pageants over the years and how much she must be dreading the dating auction.

"Meet me at the Double Cross the night of the auction, right before it starts, and I'll slip you the cash," she instructed him, dropping her hand to her side, rubbing it against her jeans.

She seemed about to say something more, but then she paused, shook her head, and whirled away from him. He watched her hurry back up the street toward A Bun in the Oven without another word.

Even if he'd wanted to tell her he wasn't interested in her money, she hadn't given him a chance. The truth was, he didn't mind helping her out. It hadn't mattered for a long time that she'd told Margie about his seventh grade crush.

He hadn't been angry with her for years now, but he'd never gotten around to telling her that. Or to picking up their friendship again.

Because once something's gone, you can't get it

back, Brady thought. And besides, he didn't see why anyone who'd grown up to be as drop-dead gorgeous and smart and hardworking as Madison would care to be friends with him anymore.

He was a loser. And too many years had gone by. They weren't kids now. They were two adults who lived in the same town but breathed in different worlds.

And yet . . . she'd taken the time to run after him into Benson's. To tell him she was sorry about Cord.

Funny how people can surprise you now and then, he reflected, then heard the harsh slam of brakes. Turning his head toward the street, he saw Jake Tanner sitting in his truck, with a large skinny mutt taking up the seat beside him.

"I went looking for you at your place last night," Jake said.

"Guess what. I wasn't there."

"Yeah, I got that. Don't be a jackass." Jake shot him a cool, level glance. "Need to talk to you about a job. You interested?"

A job. Brady had to force himself to swallow down the shot of hope that surged through him. "It better be at least a hundred miles away because no one in this town's going to hire me."

"Don't be so sure. Meet me at the Lucky Punch. Twenty minutes. And leave the attitude behind." Then Jake hit the gas and was gone, roaring up Main Street.

Brady stared after him.

A job.

Against his will, he felt again that small stirring of hope. Ever since he'd punched Deputy Mueller and walked out on his construction job with the McDonalds, he'd been certain everyone in Lonesome Way hated his guts.

And he couldn't blame them.

Punching the deputy had been a stupid-ass thing to do. And it had been a sucker punch, too. Mueller, a nice guy, had only been trying to offer a word of condolence about Cord and find out if he was okay. Brady had been drunk. Stupidly, idiotically drunk—weaving his way through the streets between the Double Cross Bar and Grill and the Lucky Punch Saloon . . .

But he knew his excuses didn't amount to a hill of beans. The truth was, he was ashamed of himself.

Head down, Brady loped in the direction of the park where he'd left his bike. Before going to the hardware store and then into Benson's, he'd wasted a few minutes sitting on a bench under a cottonwood, watching some high school kids picnicking on the grass during their lunch hour.

Remembering better times, and feeling sorry for himself. Because he was on his own now, his folks gone, and Cord, too. He was used to his parents being gone, of course. But he missed his brother with a raw open pain. Even when Cord had been on the circuit, away for weeks, months at a time, he'd never felt this alone.

Nothing to be done about that, he thought, throwing a muscled leg across the Harley.

By the time he was roaring toward the Lucky Punch, he told himself that maybe things were starting to look up. After all, he had a date with the most beautiful girl in town, even if they had nothing to say to each other anymore. And he had a possible lead on a job.

Could be my luck is starting to turn around, he thought. Then he reminded himself to hold the hope in check. Better not to count on it. Better not to count on anything.

Denny McDonald studied Jake incredulously over a beer and a steak in the Lucky Punch Saloon. "Let me get this straight. You want us to fix up your three cabins, build four more, a barn, and a corral, *and* renovate your private cabin *again*— turn it into a guest lodge? For a bunch of bullied kids?"

"And their families," Jake corrected him with a grin.

"Well, okay, yeah, but you sure about that last part, Jake? We just expanded and remodeled your place for you a couple of years ago."

"You did." Jake sipped at his beer. "And I've stayed there under that big old roof maybe a week, ten days total since you put in all that work, Denny. I'm always on the move. Now I've found a way to put my land to much better use. And when I come to town, which, as you know, isn't very often, I can always bunk in one of the new cabins if they're available—or stay with my family. No big deal. It's not as if I'm here in Lonesome Way all that much—"

He broke off as Brady stepped inside the Lucky Punch, halted just inside the doorway, and squinted around through the noisy dimness. Brady spotted him quickly, then his gaze shifted to Denny. Even from this distance, Jake saw him flinch.

"Suck it up, kid," he murmured, both sympathy and amusement glinting in his eyes as he took another bite of his own steak.

"What'd you say?" Denny looked baffled.

"Brady. Just came in the door. Looks to me like he'd rather jump off Coyote Cliff than come over here and look you in the eye."

Denny twisted around and saw Brady staring at him. He looked like a sturdy young calf with a rope tightening around his neck.

"I hope you know what you're doing, hiring him on for this, Jake. Not that I'm against giving him another chance, because personally I like the boy, but . . . you sure he's up to it?"

"I'm sure." Jake settled back in his chair as Brady started toward them.

Both Jake and Denny went silent as the younger

man reached their table, tucked twenty feet away from the long mahogany bar and directly across from the jukebox, where Blake Shelton's "Hillbilly Bone" was playing.

"Have a seat," Jake suggested when Brady merely stood there, a flush rising up his neck.

"You heard him," Denny added, pleasantly enough. He'd been shy all of his life and had never even really dated until he was forty-five and met Karla. Everything about his life had changed on that day.

Now he and Karla were married, Denny was a father of two, happier than he'd ever been in his life. And he had come into his own. More and more, he was taking over the daily management of McDonald Construction. His father had always been the one in charge of the business, but his dad was slowing down—and Denny, at forty-nine, was sliding fairly effortlessly into a leadership role. Still, he knew his father liked to pretend nothing had changed. Sam still had a hard enough head that he was out of the hospital already today and raring to get back to work, despite the docs telling him to take a good five, six days to recover from the accident.

"Got a business proposition for you, Brady." Denny squinted up at the good-looking young man who'd been his best employee in years.

Until the day he walked off the job without a word.

Brady Farraday had left McDonald Construction one man short, and up a creek with a hard-ass client pushing for a home remodel deadline to be met. Denny would be lying if he didn't admit he'd been pissed and furious at the kid for months.

But Brady's brother had died. And the boy had always been responsible up until then. Yeah, he'd give him one more shot.

But if he ever bailed again . . .

"What's this all about?" Brady stared warily back and forth between Jake and Denny.

"Sit your butt down and find out." Jake pushed a menu toward a space at the table where there was an extra chair. "Hurry up," he said in an even tone. "Denny and I are ready to jump with both feet into a new project and we need to know if you're in or out."

"A new project? You mean you'd hire me again?" Dazed, Brady stared at his former boss.

"Depends. Jake's willing to vouch for you, to guarantee you won't leave me in a bind again. So if you give me your word—"

"I will. I mean, I *won't* . . . run out on you, that is."

"Order yourself some lunch, then," Denny told him gruffly. "And let's get down to business."

A half hour later Jake took off for Travis and Mia's place. The more he reflected on the plan to turn his land and cabins into a part-time haven for bullied kids and their families, the more he felt like this was what he was meant to do.

He intended to have at least a quarter mile of open land in between each of the cabins. Plenty of space for people to sit out on a porch and take in the staggering mountain view, to watch wildlife right in their own backyard, to appreciate the scope and wonder and beauty of the Montana wilderness. To simply breathe.

There could be riding lessons and group activities at the main lodge, possibly even some low-key, upbeat counseling sessions. A guide to take guests on hikes or fishing trips up to Blackbird Lake or one of the other lakes in the basin, a chance to hone new skills and make new friends.

During most of the year, he could rent the cabins out to tourists, along with the three bedrooms on the second floor of the main house, making them available to vacationers, hikers, and fishermen, but he'd block out the summer months —and maybe two weeks of the school year's winter recess—for the kids who needed a real break.

Something to put a smile back on their faces, build up their confidence, and allow them to share the sheer joy of the outdoors—of campfires and marshmallows, horseback rides, and a night sky brimming with an explosion of stars.

It would be good for the city kids, good for their

parents, and good for Lonesome Way. The tourists who came to hike, ride, hunt, or fish the rest of the year would boost the town's economy. And hey, he thought as he parked, let Bronco out of the truck, and looked on in amusement as the dog followed him to the door of Travis and Mia's sprawling cabin, Sophie's bakery would likely have way more business than she could handle once the tourist folks got a taste of her cinnamon buns, her chocolate velvet cake, and her array of wrap sandwiches and country side dishes.

Rafe's wife might even need to expand her business.

"That was a really nice thing you did for Brady," Mia told him a few moments later as Bronco snored in the corner of the huge kitchen and Jake sprawled on the hardwood floor with Zoey, handing the little girl colorful foam blocks as she piled them on top of each other and then, shrieking with laughter, knocked them down.

"Denny's the one who gave him his job back." Jake shrugged as Zoey picked up a block and hurled it toward his face. He caught it one-handed and pulled her up onto his lap. Her fairy blond hair wisped in her eyes as she laughed innocently up at him, a tiny vision of dimples and deviltry. "This little one is going to break a thousand hearts," he announced and planted a kiss on her cheek.

"Look who's talking. The heartbreaker king."

Mia laughed as she strolled to the granite counter-top to put up more coffee. Travis was taking a meeting at his office, and Mia, who had taken a leave of absence from teaching after Zoey was born, had been decorating the house with streamers and posters for her daughter's first birthday party this coming Saturday.

"So who's the current woman in your life right now as of . . ." Mia peered at her watch and then turned to Jake. "As of three p.m. today, that is."

"Her name's Miss Zoey Tanner," Jake retorted easily as his niece nestled up against his chest. "And she's a knockout."

Zoey appeared completely oblivious to the compliment, though, as she began drifting off to sleep in his arms. He leaned back, studying her tiny delicate face.

Something about her utter relaxation and innocent drowsiness stirred a memory in his mind.

He suddenly realized what it was. She reminded him of that other little girl. The cute red-haired one he'd glimpsed last night at Denny McDonald's house. Carly McKinnon's daughter. She'd been deep in this same sort of blissful sleep when he'd made his way to the sofa and peered down at her.

"Carly McKinnon and her little girl—they invited to Zoey's party?" he asked suddenly.

"Of course." Mia glanced up from her cook-book. She'd been searching for a recipe while the coffee was brewing, hunting for her grand-mother's potato salad recipe. She was fixing that, as well as chicken fingers, pasta salad, fruit, mini hot dogs, and tuna roll-ups for the birthday lunch. "Carly's become a good friend ever since she moved to Lonesome Way and she's very active in Bits and Pieces, our quilting group. We've even had a few daytime meetings and speakers at her quilt shop on Spring Street. Zoey and Emma have playdates, too, now and then—even though Emma is six months older. They've hit it off." Mia's brows rose. "But I had no idea *you* knew them."

"Nothing much gets by me in this town," Jake tossed off with a grin.

"Uh-uh. Especially when there's a beautiful woman involved." Tilting her blond head to the side, Mia eyed her brother-in-law curiously. "And Carly is definitely beautiful. Emma is, too. So . . . *how* did you say you know them again?"

There was more than casual interest in her tone. And she had a speculative light in her eyes that Jake recognized.

Mia must have caught the matchmaking bug from my sister, he decided in amusement. Lissie and all the women of his family—hell, all the women of Lonesome Way—seemed always to expect love to bloom around every corner of this town.

"We met a few years ago in Houston, had dinner together," he said nonchalantly. He didn't intend to tell his sister-in-law that he and Carly McKinnon had also spent a smoking-hot night in his hotel room. A memory of Carly kissing her way down his chest, of her soft burnished hair brushing his skin, and her long legs twining around him as they made love, sprang into his mind, but he pushed the images away.

"I bumped into her over at the McDonald place last night. It was kind of surprising to find she's living in Lonesome Way. And yeah," he added as Mia started to say something, "I know all about her connection to Martha Davies. But still. Boston to Montana is one major move."

"And a good one for this town. Believe me, everyone in Bits and Pieces was thrilled when she opened Carly's Quilts. Now we don't have to drive all the way to Livingston for our supplies. Needless to say, she was welcomed with open arms. She's an amazing quilter, too—she used to be a big-time number cruncher with Marjorie Moore and gave up a very lucrative position to move here. She really wanted to be close to Martha since she's Emma's godmother and all. Martha and Carly's foster mother were cousins."

Foster mother, he thought. Had she ever mentioned over dinner or in his hotel room that she'd been in foster care? He didn't think so, but he didn't really remember either of them doing much talking that night.

"Why don't you give this sleepyhead to me."

Mia broke into his thoughts as she strode around the counter. "I'll take her upstairs and put her down."

"So what's the deal about the baby's father?" Rolling to his feet, Jake transferred his niece carefully into his sister-in-law's arms.

"The father?" Mia shrugged. "No one knows anything about *him*. Carly never mentions him, except to say he's not in the picture. Her exact words. I don't think she's ever been married, though. And she doesn't date, either . . . at least, she hasn't since she moved here." The glance Mia flicked him was a hopeful one as she reached the bottom of the staircase, Zoey snug in her arms.

"The theory around town is that Carly either had a boyfriend who walked out on her and Emma—or a one-night stand with some jerk who didn't sign up for daddyhood. Luckily she's a great mother all on her own. But still . . ." She paused, one foot on the lowest step, Zoey tucked sleepily in her arms. "It can't be easy. I can't even begin to imagine what kind of a man would turn his back on his own daughter." Mia shook her head. "It's just sad."

But Jake barely heard that last part. Just as he scarcely noticed his sister-in-law whisk up the steps and disappear into the nursery with Zoey.

He stood frozen. Stunned. As if he'd been gut-punched, or thrown from a bull and had hit the dirt hard. As if something had been knocked loose in his head.

Three short words Mia had said reverberated through his brain.

One. Night. Stand.

He and Carly. Hell. *They'd* had a one-night stand. Damn it, how long ago was that?

Jake rapidly calculated. He'd gone to Houston to host the charity bash shortly after he won that bull-riding championship in Cheyenne. So that night he took Carly to dinner—and to bed—was slightly more than . . . two years ago . . . around twenty-four months. . . .

No, that was wrong. Actually, he realized with a jolt of shock ripping through him, it was more than that . . . closer to twenty-six or twenty-seven months. . . .

And Emma McKinnon is six months older than Zoey. . . .

His stomach dropped through the floor as he did the math. Then redid it. Every muscle in his body seemed to turn to ice.

For one instant, the cowboy with the lightning reflexes and nerves of iron couldn't move or speak.

Then he raced to the door, his boots smacking against the hardwood floor.

"Jake, wait! Where are you going?"

Mia, puzzled, peered down at him from the top of the stairs. "Coffee's ready. Travis will be home any minute and Grady wants to show you his new telescope—"

"Sorry, Mia, but there's something I have to do. Right now."

"Jake, can't you—"

But he was gone, bolting from the cabin before she could get out the next word. He was only vaguely aware that Bronco had trotted to the screen door and was whining, staring morosely after him. A moment later, tension searing through his shoulders and neck, he wrenched the truck into gear and tore out of Travis's driveway, speeding east toward Blue Bell Drive.

His stomach churned. His hands clenched the steering wheel so tightly his knuckles turned white. He barely noticed turning sharply onto Carly McKinnon's street. He did remember that she lived two doors down from Denny and Karla. . . .

Two doors to the right or to the left?

That question was answered when he caught a glimpse of nosy old Willa Martin in high-top sneakers and a pink housedress, sweeping her front porch, two doors down from the McDonalds'. Willa had been a school secretary when he was in junior high and had given him the evil eye every time he was sent to the principal's office.

Which was a couple of times a week. . . .

He rolled right past her house, then past Denny and Karla's, braking sharply two houses down at the well-tended white Victorian with a pink-and-yellow-cushioned swing on the front porch.

And a toddler's swing set in the backyard.

Vaulting from his truck, he took the porch steps two at a time, his heart hammering way more than it did when he swung out of the chute on the back of an angry bull. But though he pressed Carly McKinnon's doorbell again and again, no one answered.

He couldn't hear a sound from inside the house.

Quilt shop. Spring Street.

Grim faced, Jake leaped off the porch and sprinted back to the truck.

Ten minutes later he swung into a parking space across the street from Carly's Quilts, vaulted out of the truck, and hurried toward the door.

Chapter Seven

In the back room of the quilt shop, Carly set aside the pile of invoices she'd been reviewing for the past half hour. Standing, she stretched for a moment, then walked over to get more coffee. She had just refilled her cup when the bell over the quilt shop door pealed.

In surprise she glanced at her watch. It was nearly closing time.

She didn't usually get many customers this late in the day, and Laureen had left an hour earlier with a migraine, after apparently enduring the date from hell last night.

According to Laureen, the man she'd been set up with took one glance at her when she arrived at the Lucky Punch Saloon and suddenly looked like someone who'd just been kicked in the kneecaps.

He'd ordered a beer for each of them, and a lone platter of nachos, but had excused himself after only a half hour of conversation, mumbling that he didn't have time to join her for dinner because he just remembered a work project he had to finish.

"Believe me, he was no prize himself," Laureen had told her emphatically.

But the jerk had left her feeling mortified and angry. He hadn't even bothered to go through the motions of having dinner.

"Am I that repulsive? Really? He couldn't have run away any faster if I'd had horns and a tail," she'd exclaimed as she paced back and forth along the shelves of fabrics and crafting supplies. There'd been no trace of the red lipstick on her mouth today, only her usual pink lip gloss and a frown.

"Forget about him. He's a toad. When you meet the right guy—"

But there Laureen had cut her off, insisting there *was* no right guy for her, and that she was never letting anyone set her up with a man again.

After Laureen had sunk into a chair that

afternoon, closing her eyes from the pain of the migraine while Dorothy Winston deliberated on fabric for a pinwheel quilt, Carly had quietly ordered Laureen to go home, lie down, and take the rest of the day off.

Now, alone in the shop, Carly hurried out of the back room wondering if she'd returned.

"Laureen, I thought I told you to—" She stopped short.

Jake stood just inside the quilt shop door.

Her heart gave a small jump. He looked every bit as tough, dark, and handsome as he had at the McDonald home last night—but instead of a smile, today his mouth was set in a firm hard line.

"Anyone else here? I need to talk to you. Right now." He strode toward her, not bothering with any of the conventional niceties.

A flutter of premonition sent her pulse racing. *No, it isn't possible. He can't know,* she told herself.

"What's going on? Don't tell me you lost your dog. I promise you, he's not here. You'd notice the howling." She strove for a flippant tone, but it was a struggle to stay calm as she walked past the pattern books, past the shelves stacked with fabric, past the array of quilts displayed on the walls, even right past Jake until she reached the small sitting area at the front of the shop with its two-seat lavender sofa and a comfy armchair upholstered in a cheerful old-fashioned rose and yellow pattern. If she was going to have to talk to him, they were going to do it on her terms, in her favorite, most relaxing area of the shop.

But instead of following her he moved swiftly to the window blinds and closed them with a quick yank of the cord. Carly's green eyes widened.

"What's this all about?" She planted her feet, willing her hands not to clench at her sides.

Jake advanced, halting only three feet away from her. "Is she mine?"

"What . . . did you say?" Carly's mouth went dry. Oh, God, no. She must have misunderstood him. He couldn't have said . . .

"Emma." He bit out her daughter's name, *their* daughter's name, a dangerous light in his eyes. "Is she my daughter? Tell me the truth, Carly."

Carly didn't know what it felt like to faint, but she knew the ground was swaying a little beneath her feet. And she definitely knew the sensation of pressure building in her chest, squeezing out all the air in her lungs . . . she knew that all too well. . . .

Drawing in the deepest breath she could manage, she braced herself to stand perfectly still, to face the angry glitter in his eyes. They reminded her of blue sky lit with lightning from a storm. The tension in his shoulders and the tautness of his jaw told her he was exerting a fierce effort at self-control.

So, she reminded herself, she must do no less.

One resolve threaded through the pounding that had begun in her head. *Don't tell him, don't say the words. If he doesn't know, nothing will change. He can't know. There's no way, not unless you tell him.*

"What would make you think something so ridicu—"

"Don't. Don't bullshit me, Carly." He spoke even more quietly now, looking into her eyes with a sort of controlled desperation—and absolute determination. "I did the math. I need the truth. Don't you think you owe me that much?"

Of course she did. He was right. She'd lied about it for the past two years. Her palms felt damp as she pressed them against the sides of her dark jeans. A spurt of nausea churned through her.

Well, perhaps she hadn't lied exactly, but she'd hidden the truth. He was asking now, though. Straight-out asking.

He deserves to know, a tiny voice whispered inside her even as the tight, breathless sensation rolled back again, more intense than before.

This hadn't happened in over a year. Not since she'd received that nasty phone call out of the blue from her cousin Phil. That day the panic had rushed back, swamping her with a sense of suffocation, of nausea churning like acid through her stomach.

Phil Beaumont, the son of her mother's half

sister, the boy who'd long ago gotten his kicks locking her in a closet, had done a search for her name online and had come upon a link to an article about Carly's Quilts. The story had been published in Lonesome Way's daily newspaper back when she first opened the quilt shop. No sooner did Phil read it than he called her at the shop, telling her he needed money.

He'd just been released from prison after doing time for aggravated assault and insisted he needed something to start over with. He said she *owed* him, since his mother had taken her in, given her a roof over her head when Carly had no one and nothing.

He wanted five thousand dollars.

Carly told him no and hung up, shaking. The phone call, the sound of Phil's rough voice, had triggered a full-blown panic attack. It came on so suddenly it nearly knocked her off her feet. The rush of breathlessness, the faintness, the overwhelming sense of being closed in . . .

It had lasted for hours—thank heavens Emma had been asleep—but she hadn't had a single attack since. And she hadn't heard from Phil again.

So she'd thought her panic attacks were as much in her past as he was.

But now, with Jake standing right before her, demanding to know the truth, she found herself struggling for breath.

Go away, she told the cramping tightness in her chest, cursing the reaction and her own inability to cope. She fought to breathe, to steel herself. She tried to remember how to draw air into her lungs. She did it every day . . . why couldn't she do it now?

Opening her mouth, she gave a little gasp, sucked in a breath, then another.

She wouldn't tell him the truth. She couldn't. It would ruin Emma's life and his—and her own. He wouldn't be there for Emma; he'd only hurt her, make her miss him, wonder why he was always gone and not around to help her with homework or carry her around on his shoulders or teach her how to print her name. . . .

Breathe, she told herself desperately as a warm wave of dizziness washed over her. *You can do it. There's plenty of air. Just breathe it in.*

"Hey. Carly. Carly, what's going on? You all right?"

His voice had sharpened. Not with anger, but with concern. Still, it sounded distant . . . and the nausea circled up in her throat. . . .

"I'm fine," she managed, but it came out as a gasp. "I just . . . want you to . . . leave."

"You should sit down. Then you can tell me the truth—"

"She's mine. My daughter. *That's* the truth." Carly used every ounce of her concentration to focus on him. She needed to get through this. For

Emma. She struggled to ignore the lack of air in her lungs, the erratic racing of her heart. "Emma's father is none of your business. My *life* is none of your business. . . . I—oh!"

She broke off as he reached out, caught her hand in his big palm. His fingers felt cool. Strong. His grip was careful, and unexpectedly gentle considering the determination in his eyes. She'd expected him to yank her forward, to try to intimidate her, but he didn't. He merely enclosed her hand within his strong one, his expression concerned as he stepped closer.

"You don't look so good. I'm not going anywhere until you feel better. And then you can tell me—"

"Tell you what . . . to leave? I'm telling you . . . right now. Just because we spent one . . . n-night together you think you have a claim on . . . m-my daughter. G-get over yourself. I . . ."

Her voice faded. She felt her chest tightening like a vise from lack of air.

"Whoa!" With lightning reflexes, Jake's arms swept around her waist as she swayed forward and began to gulp, one desperate shallow breath after the other.

"Come on, you need to sit down," he said quietly. "Right now. What can I do?"

She was too busy trying to breathe to answer him.

He drew her carefully to the chair, eased her

into the seat. The next instant he was kneeling beside her, gently rubbing her palms, the backs of her hands, her fingers, even as his concerned gaze searched her face.

"You eaten anything today?"

"I . . . yes . . ." Through the panic clawing at her lungs, her stomach, and filling her head with a swirly sensation, Carly fought her guilt. Miserable, overwhelming guilt.

"This . . . just . . . happens sometimes. Well, it hasn't . . . h-happened for a long time. I just need to . . ."

"What? What do you need? Maybe I should take you to the hospital."

"*No!* No *hospital* . . . it's just a p-panic attack. It will . . . pass. I want you to . . . to . . . leave me alone. . . ."

"Not going to happen. You should get checked out by a doctor—"

"Once you leave . . . I'll be all right." She fought for air.

"You don't look so good. I'm taking you to the ER right now."

"No!" Frantically she clutched at his arms as he drew her up from the chair. Even through her panic she felt a jolt of heat as her fingers touched rock-hard biceps.

"Are you this upset because I asked you if Emma is my daughter?"

She shook her head.

"It sure seemed that way."

"I . . . I just . . ."

"I know it isn't fair to ask you when you can barely breathe," he said softly, "but just keep in mind that I need to know."

Carly couldn't tear her gaze from his eyes. Those mesmerizing deep blue eyes. Guilt stabbed at her.

"I'm sorry," she whispered. "I really am . . . sorry."

Then she froze in horror. What was she saying? The panic was freezing her brain. Or maybe it was only that a part of her was cracking in two, torn between protecting Emma at all costs and telling the truth. She was an honest person. She tried to be honest whenever possible, except when it came to . . . *this.* To Emma.

But the pressure of keeping the secret sometimes weighed on her—and never more than right now, looking at Jake, lying straight to his face . . . that strong, handsome, concerned face. . . .

He studied her for a long moment before he eased her back into the armchair and left her sitting there as he strode across the quilt shop to the sink at the back and filled a glass with water. When he returned, he placed the glass in her hand, his fingers closing around hers to make sure it didn't slip from her grasp. "Drink."

She obeyed, sipping, letting the cool water trickle down her throat as she told herself to get a grip. The first burst of panic was easing finally . . . but it could come back . . . it used to come in waves, rolling in and out, eventually building . . .

She wished he didn't seem so concerned about her. That upset her more than anything.

"You doing okay now? Better?"

"Please don't be nice to me." She closed her eyes and wished she hadn't said that aloud.

"Why shouldn't I be nice to you? I like you. And right now," he added, rubbing her fingers with a gentleness that stunned her even through the haze of panic, "I'm plenty worried about you."

"No . . . reason to be. I'm fine. You should leave."

"Carly, I'm not leaving. Not until I'm sure you're all right. Let me drive you home."

She looked up into his eyes. They were the same vivid blue as Emma's and her throat closed up again, and she felt all the air evaporating from her lungs. He wouldn't give up. Not him—not this towering, quietly powerful cowboy.

He wasn't wearing a Stetson, but in his Wranglers and black polo shirt and boots he looked rugged, exceedingly muscular, and ready for anything—to ride a bull, to herd cattle for days on an open range, to unload fifty-pound bags of feed off a truck—or to find out that he had a daughter he'd met for the first time last night, a daughter who was almost two years old.

He was crouched beside her, watching her as if

he expected her to pass out at any moment and he needed to be ready to catch her and rush her off to the ER. It made her feel worse than ever. If only he was yelling at her, demanding she tell him the truth, she wouldn't feel so guilty.

It didn't mean he was giving up, she told herself. He could turn to his brother, to Travis. Travis Tanner was former FBI and now owned a security business in town. He could trace Emma's birth certificate, learn the date she was born.

And then Jake would know. . . . Everyone would know. . . .

Who was she kidding? He somehow already knew. Or suspected. There was no putting this genie back in the bottle.

She swallowed. Gasped in a little more air as the nausea skimmed through her again.

She wasn't a coward. She had to face facts. It was going to come out. Whatever had made Jake come here in the first place to ask if Emma was his daughter wasn't going away.

If the truth was about to burst over her like a dam, she'd rather have it come from her than from anyone else.

Take control of the fear, Dr. Worthing had always told her. *Don't let it control you. You can control* it.

Through the tightness in her chest she peered up at him. Bit her lip. "I want you to know . . . I don't expect or want anything from you. Not now, not . . . ever. And I'd appreciate it if you never tell . . . Emma."

She felt him go as still as a Sunday morning. She could feel his gaze burning into her and forced herself to look directly into his eyes.

"Are you saying . . . ?"

"You're . . . right. She's yours. Your . . . daughter." The nausea began to recede, just a little. *Take control.* She ran her tongue across her lips. "So . . . if you want to see her . . . now and then . . . you can. I'll think of an excuse. We'll tell her you're a friend—"

Jake surged to his feet. "What kind of a man do you think I am?" He rocked back on his heels, staring at her in stupefaction.

"The kind who doesn't . . . want a family." She pushed herself out of the chair, stood erect, as the tightness in her throat mercifully eased a fraction. "The kind of man who doesn't want . . . obligations. Commitments. I understand. I'm assuring you that you don't need to worry about Emma." She stopped to suck in a breath of air. "Or about me. We don't need you. We're fine. We're . . . g-great, actually, and—"

"I want to see my daughter. *Now.*"

Carly felt the slightest flutter of dizziness wash over her again. It was unnerving hearing him say "my daughter."

"*No.* Not . . . today. I need to figure this out and—"

"Listen to me. I need to see her." His jaw was set. There was hard determination in his eyes— and something else. Something that looked like anguish.

"I'm not saying this to upset you, Carly." He kept his tone low. "If you need a doctor, we'll go there first. But I've lost nearly two years." Suddenly he raked a hand through his jet-black hair. His expression was grim, set. Those blue eyes so like Emma's stared into hers.

"I need to see my daughter. Where is she right now? *Where's Emma?*"

Chapter Eight

Carly noticed the frown on Martha's face as she swung up Carly's driveway and parked her car behind Jake's truck.

Okay, here we go, Carly thought. Her heart pounded as she rose from her perch on the edge of her porch swing. Turning her head slightly, she studied Jake, standing on the porch behind her.

He was lounging against the wall of her house, his powerful arms crossed, trying to look relaxed, but she sensed the anger and tension coiled in his body. She watched him straighten and drop his hands to his sides as his gaze sharpened on Martha's car. Or rather, on the little girl—Emma—strapped in the car seat in the back of Martha's car.

"Just don't tell her, Jake. Not yet. Please, I don't think Emma would understand, but just in case—" she muttered for the fourth time as she started down the steps, not looking back at him.

"I won't say anything. Not yet." He spoke quietly, but firmly. "I just want to meet her. I have a lot of time to make up for."

Jake's brain still hadn't stopped spinning. He had a daughter. A little girl he'd seen the previous night for the first time while she was asleep.

He'd never even gazed into her eyes. She'd never peered into his.

He'd never held her. Touched her tiny fingers and toes.

And she didn't know him from the garbage collector.

There was a hard knot of anger in his gut because Carly hadn't told him about Emma. Just the opposite. She'd cut him coldly and completely out of the first year and a half of his daughter's life. Still, a part of him had to acknowledge that despite the panic attack he'd witnessed today, she must be one hell of a strong woman to have taken on single parenthood all alone. One thing was clear—she was fiercely protective of their daughter and obviously loved her deeply.

But she sure as hell wouldn't be raising Emma

all alone anymore. He felt a huge weight of responsibility settling like iron weights on his shoulders. Nearly two missed years' worth of responsibility. There was no way he was walking away from it.

But his brain was still reeling, which sucked right now, because there was so much he had to figure out. And a full schedule he needed to quickly rearrange.

He was supposed to leave for Wyoming and the Bighorn Bull Rodeo in a few days. And he had a commercial shoot coming up soon after that. He'd thought all he had to do was hang around Lonesome Way for Zoey's birthday party, get Brady a job and back on track, draw up some plans with Denny McDonald for his antibullying project—and then he could take off again next week.

He had a month's worth of rodeo competitions and guest appearances ahead of him after the new ad was filmed, but now it was all on hold. He wasn't going anywhere.

At least not for a few more weeks, he decided, his brows drawing together in a frown. Two weeks probably—that ought to do it. He'd have to push everything back that long and then he'd need to return to Lonesome Way again, a whole lot sooner and a lot more regularly than he'd thought.

He intended to try to see Emma at least every other week. There'd have to be a way to make that work. And he'd need to sit down and plan a schedule with Carly.

There were tons of details to work out. Like financial support for his daughter—for Carly, too, if she wanted it. But most of all, he needed to get to know that little girl, to make up for the time he'd lost.

He had to start building a relationship with this tiny red-haired stranger Carly was now unbuckling from the backseat of Martha's car.

His heart felt like it was going to shoot out of his chest as he gazed at her. Was she really his? This impish little curly-head? She had Carly's red-gold hair and it tumbled in fluffy unruly ringlets around a flushed, happy little face. For the first time he saw her eyes. Blue. Intensely dark blue. The same exact color he remembered from his own baby pictures. She had amazingly long eyelashes, dimples, small wisps of pale eyebrows.

She looked so fragile. So beautiful.

Something strange and unfamiliar clenched tight and deep inside his heart.

Emma's arms were stretched out toward her mother, eager and entreating. The way she smiled at Carly . . .

How will she react to me? he wondered tautly, stepping down off the porch.

"So what's this all about?" Martha raised her voice to be heard over the sounds of Emma's excited squeals after she caught sight of Carly.

Then the older woman shot Jake a curious glance.

"Well, now, Jake Tanner. I heard you were in town. All the single ladies who came in for manicures or cuts today are in a tizzy, thinking maybe you'll still be in town for the auction and might bid on them next week. What are you doing here?"

"Good to see you, Martha." Jake sidestepped her question and was relieved when she apparently forgot about it as Carly lifted her daughter out of the car seat.

"You know, I was supposed to keep my little miss overnight," Martha sniffed, peeved over her interrupted Emma time. "Why'd I have to bring her back so soon? We were just going to the park."

"I can't explain right now, Martha." With Emma's arms entwined around her neck, Carly started up the walk. "But I'll bring her back to you in a little while, I promise. She can still spend the night."

For the first time, the older woman noticed the strained tone of Carly's voice. She whipped a glance at her face.

"Heavens, what's wrong with you? You're pale as winter sun, child. What's this all about? Here, let me bring this big old diaper bag inside for you—"

"I've got it, Martha." Taking the bag easily from the older woman, Jake forced a smile. "Everything is fine."

But his words only drew a stare—a long one. Martha studied him, then turned sharply toward Carly, who, Jake reflected, didn't look so good. She was pale and was giving off uneasy vibes in spades. Martha's gaze shifted to the little girl in Carly's arms, then darted quickly back to Jake's face.

She drew in a breath.

"Well, I'll be going now." She spoke more faintly than Jake had ever heard her speak in his life. "What time should I come back for Emma?"

"I'll bring her to your apartment in about an hour." Carly glanced at Jake, as if expecting an objection, and when none came, she straightened her shoulders. "I'll give you a heads-up when I'm on my way."

"Whatever is going on—" Martha's voice trailed off, her gaze locking on Carly's with concern. "You know I'm here if you need me."

"Thank you. I know." Somehow she managed a wan smile before she turned toward the steps with Emma babbling in her ear, gesturing with her little arms.

It's the one thing I do know right now, Carly thought as she held Emma close. Martha would be here for her. Even if the world—meaning Lonesome Way—discovered that Jake was Emma's father and that she'd never told him he had a daughter.

Even if the Tanners and half the town turned on

her for having kept such a secret from one of their native sons.

For a moment she wished with all her heart that Annie was here, too. She was going to need all the friends she could get. *If,* after this came out, she even had any friends left.

"Down, Mumma, down," Emma ordered, squirming as they neared the porch. "Me walk. Me!"

Setting her daughter gently on her feet, she held Emma's hand and helped her up the steps. When Carly reached for the screen door, Jake was somehow there first and pulled it open.

"Hi there, Emma," he said softly. There was a smile on his face, but Carly thought it looked strained.

He wants this like a hole in the head. Her resolve tightened. *Jake has no use for a child, but he's a Tanner and he's been brought up never to run away from his responsibilities. Maybe that's why all of his life, he's avoided taking any on.*

"Emma, this nice man is Jake." Too late she realized her tone sounded forced: overbright and much too cheerful. Phony baloney, as Annie would have said. She flinched inwardly. "Jake is Mommy's friend. Can you say hi?"

Emma shot Jake a lightning-quick smile and a distracted wave, then tugged her other hand free of Carly's, darted around Jake into the house, and took off for her little playroom down the hall, just beyond Carly's sewing room, running with a toddler's wobbly gait.

"Bug!" she yelled, followed by a giggle. "Bug!"

Jake stared after her, looking dazed as she disappeared into the playroom.

There was a brief silence except for the sounds of Emma's babbling. Carly closed the front door, leaned her back against it.

"Bug is her stuffed dog. She likes the word 'Bug.' She even calls her lamb Buggy. And her doll, too. Go figure."

Every vestige of a smile had disappeared from Jake's face. He looked shell-shocked. Even more so now than he had at the quilt shop. He deposited the diaper bag on the floor.

"We have some things to discuss."

"Of course." She forced herself to move calmly, deliberately to the sofa, where she sank down. "I know that we have a lot to figure out."

She could breathe now at least, but there was still a band of tension within her chest. "We don't have to settle everything today. There will be plenty of time to sort it all out—"

"You're going to talk to me about time? I've missed two years!"

"She's only eighteen months old."

"There's the whole womb thing! The pregnancy. All of that! She heard your voice then, all those months. She could've been hearing mine. I know for a fact from my sister and Sophie and Mia—babies can hear voices in the womb."

Her gaze flew to his face, and she went very still. "You . . . you wish you had talked to her in the womb?" she asked dazedly.

Stalking over to the sofa, he took a seat beside her. His nearness was distracting. His dark, gorgeous good looks and hot cowboy vibe seemed to simmer in her cool, cozy living room with its gauzy white curtains and yellow pillows tossed across a blue and white chintz sofa.

Jake looked bigger and tougher than ever in this light, feminine room. He dwarfed her furniture, made the feminine touches look even sweeter, more delicate. But the pain in his eyes flooded her with a bone-deep surprise.

"I should have been there every step of the way," he bit out and she could see he was holding anger in check.

She could barely keep the astonishment from her voice. "I . . . had no idea you'd . . . feel that way. I never guessed. I thought I was giving you a pass . . . letting you off the hook—"

"You don't know anything about me. If I have a daughter, I damn well want to . . ." He stopped, clamped his mouth closed, then looked her straight in the eyes.

"Look, it's going to take a little time for this to sink in. But I'm telling you right now, I intend to be financially responsible for her. You've done it

151

all for more than two years; it's time to let me do my share. And if you need financial help—"

"I don't. I don't need one single thing from you."

"Damn it, Carly." He gritted his teeth. "Do you think I'm just going to go on my merry way, stop in and hand off a Christmas present once a year? I need to figure out how this is going to work—no, *we* need to figure out how this is going to work because I *will* be a part of her life from now on. In some way or other," he added tautly as she shot him a look of incredulity. "I don't know all the details yet, or how I'm going to make that happen, but I will. She's going to know me, she's going to call me Daddy—not Jake—and I'm going to spend as much time with her as I can. We'll do it slowly, gradually. You can stop looking so horrified," he added, his mouth grim. "I'm not saying I'm taking her home with me this after-noon and bringing her back to you in a couple of weeks."

Carly went pale even as he said those words.

"You and I will work this out." Taking a long breath, he grasped her hands in his own big ones, and his voice went quiet. "We'll do it together. I promise I won't do anything to shake up her life, the one she has here. And I'm not trying to shake up yours. But I *will* be a father to her, Carly. You're going to have to deal with that and make some room for me in her life. Starting now."

Her mind was whirling. "Give me a minute to

think." She pulled her hands from his grip and pressed her knuckles to her eyes. Her thoughts were in a jumble, like a ball of tangled yarn, and her throat felt so dry it was raw.

"I never imagined . . . I was trying to spare you. I came to see you once when I was pregnant and I almost told you—but I didn't think you'd want—"

"You didn't even ask me," he interrupted. "You never gave me a chance. But I'm here now. And I'm damned well going to stick around Lonesome Way for an extra few weeks while we work this out—and while I get to know Emma. You and I are going to come up with a plan, an arrangement. One that's comfortable for both of us—for *all* of us," he corrected. His jaw was clenched, no doubt with the effort he was exerting to control his temper.

She studied him with amazement. And skepticism. "Are you sure about this? I don't think you've thought it through, Jake. You can't start being Emma's father and then stop and leave for six months or so. That's not fair to her. You can't drop in once or twice a year and expect her to love you and count on you the way she—" She broke off.

"The way she counts on you?" he demanded.

She sat up straighter. Nodded. "Yes. The way she counts on me."

"I'm going to see her a helluva lot more than

once or twice a year. That you can believe." Jake's eyes had darkened to cobalt. "I may not live permanently in Lonesome Way, but I'll be here for her. On a regular basis—and anytime she needs me. Or anytime you need me, for that matter," he added in a mutter.

She shook her head in disbelief.

Then there was a loud thumping crash from the playroom and they both shot to their feet, racing down the hall. Jake sprinted ahead and through the door, Carly right behind him, her heart lodged in her throat.

There was Emma, sprawled on the floor beside the little art table and chairs near the toy chest. She'd somehow managed to pull the table over and it had crashed down on her. Her mouth opened and closed, then she let out a piercing scream just as Jake moved the table aside and knelt beside her.

"Where does it hurt, Emma? Show me where." Carly swooped over before Jake could say a word. Gently, she pulled Emma into her arms. "Shhh, you're okay, baby." She kissed Emma's forehead. "Tell me what hurts. Your head? Did you hit your head?" She tensed as Emma let out another scream—more like a wail—then began to cry.

She looks okay, Jake thought, his own heart thumping as he righted the table. There wasn't a scratch on her. The table had hit the floor, but it didn't look like it had hit Emma.

Carly was stroking her hair. "It's okay, sweetie," she said softly, easing Emma against her shoulder and gently patting her back. "You're okay. I think you just scared yourself, didn't you?"

Emma cried for about another sixty seconds, then gave a hiccup. As Carly set her down again, carefully scrutinizing her, Emma pulled away.

"Bug," she gasped. She ran toward the rocking chair, where a stuffed dog lay upon the seat. It had a goofy smile on its fuzzy brown face and was missing one floppy ear. The other ear was halfway torn off.

"Bug." Emma snatched up the stuffed dog, smiled beatifically at it, and kissed the top of its frayed brown and white head.

"I shouldn't have taken my eyes off her." Carly scrambled to her feet, ignoring his outstretched hand. She shot him a glare. It was all she could do not to order him out of her house.

If she hadn't been distracted talking to him, she'd have been supervising Emma. She usually kept an eye on her at all times.

Jake *was* a distraction. She didn't need him or his help, and neither did Emma. She certainly wasn't going to encourage him to play a part in their lives.

But now that he knows the truth, she thought uneasily, *I might not have a lot of options. What if he really wants to be involved?*

Not that she expected that to be the case once

the first wave of surprise and adjustment wore off. *He'll go back to his rodeoing life and his beer commercials and his fawning fans,* she told herself. *Oh, he'll make time for Emma now and then, but I'll be damned if I let Emma get so close to him that she'll miss him while she's waiting for him to fit her in for a visit.*

"She's a very good baby, and sweet natured," she said, keeping her tone low. "But she needs to be watched every minute, unless she's in her crib or Pack 'n Play. I shouldn't have left her alone while we were talking—"

Suddenly she sniffed the air, her nose wrinkling as she glanced over at her daughter.

"I need to change her diaper now—unless you want to do it. And then I'm taking her back to Martha's. If that's okay with you," she added tartly. She wasn't accustomed to having to check hers and Emma's schedule with anyone except Martha and Madison. Certainly not with *him.*

She expected Jake to back out of the room at the first mention of a diaper change, but to her amazement he held his ground, just staring at her steadily, and she remembered then that he was a doting uncle to a slew of kids, his sister's and his two brothers'.

Okay, maybe diaper changes don't freak him out.

And so far, actually, he hadn't freaked out at all. He hadn't looked scared at the idea of being a father. He hadn't looked like he wanted to run. It was a bit surprising. He'd only seemed upset that he didn't know.

Which didn't do wonders for her conscience.

She told herself he was just in shock. It would wear off and then . . .

Who knew how he'd feel then?

"Why don't we talk about things tomorrow and . . . arrange for another visit?"

"When?" he asked instantly.

"Well, you could see her at Zoey's birthday party on Saturday."

His jaw clenched.

"I *will* see her at Zoey's birthday party on Saturday. But there'll be a lot of kids and other people there. I'd appreciate some one-on-one time before then. How about if we meet at the park tomorrow? You can supervise while I push my daughter on a swing. Half an hour. That's all I'm asking."

She tensed even as she told herself he wasn't being unreasonable. He was trying. Trying to do what was right, she had to admit, but she had her doubts about how serious he'd be on the follow-through.

"I work tomorrow, but I suppose I can take a slightly longer lunch break," she heard herself saying. "I think short visits will be best for now, but I'll bring a lunch for all three of us. We can meet near the picnic benches."

Jake nodded. He was still in shock and trying his damnedest to hold it all together. And did Carly really think to scare him off with the threat of having to change a diaper? He'd changed a few diapers in his day. Well, maybe once or twice for his nieces and nephew.

And though the prospect certainly didn't enthrall him, it didn't scare him, either. If he could climb on the back of an enraged bull and wrestle eighteen hundred pounds of fury to the ground, he could certainly change a little diaper.

His own daughter's diaper.

But he figured it would seem petty to point that out, so instead he told her that he'd be at the park at one o'clock the following afternoon. Then he strode to the door of the playroom. His brain felt ready to explode, and Carly was sending out cautious, wary vibes. He didn't want her to go into full panic mode again. Not on his account.

She could probably use some time to come to grips with this, he thought. He sure as hell could.

His head was still spinning. But he had to decide exactly how he was going to deal with this. He'd only known for . . . what?

Less than an hour.

In that space of time, his entire world had shifted at light speed into a different galaxy.

He shot a long, appraising look at Carly. She seemed plenty steady now. Once she'd finally spit out the truth, the signs of the panic attack had ebbed. She seemed as solid as a tree trunk, but a whole lot prettier and sexier. Which was what had landed them in this pickle in the first place.

He reminded himself that right now there was something more she had to come to grips with —not only the fact that he knew about Emma, but that he wasn't running away. That she wasn't going to be raising their daughter all on her own anymore, not by a long shot.

As for his daughter—Emma had barely noticed him so far. It felt a little bit like a jagged butcher knife dragging through his gut. When he thought of how his little nieces and his nephew Aiden's faces lit up whenever they saw Rafe or Travis or Lissie's husband, Tommy, he felt a knot tightening in his chest.

He was a father. He needed to be part of his daughter's life. *It's not too late,* he told himself. *She isn't even two years old yet.* He'd do whatever he could to earn Emma's love and trust. To be there for her, the way his parents had been there for him and Lissie, Travis, and Rafe.

So much for no one depending on me, Jake thought grimly, the old ache searing through him.

For an instant Melanie's frightened eyes the last time he'd seen her flashed into his mind. And the familiar pain swept right through him along with it. He swore in that instant that he'd step up—be there for Emma no matter what. He'd never let anything get in the way. Never let anyone hurt her.

I'll take care of her, protect her.
Earn her love.

But he knew that last part wasn't going to happen in one afternoon.

"Tomorrow then. The park. One o'clock."

Drawing in a deep breath, he cast one more glance at Carly's taut face.

"You don't have to worry. I'll be there for Emma whenever she needs me. You can count on that."

When she said nothing, only stared at him in stricken silence, he turned on his heel and left, striding down the hall, quietly closing the front door behind him.

Even as he climbed into his truck, he remembered he'd left Bronco back at Travis and Mia's place—and that made him think of his brothers, his sister, and their various spouses.

What stretched before him over the next few hours made him groan.

Oh, man. He'd screwed up big-time without ever realizing it. Rafe and Travis would not be happy. And Lissie . . .

She'd go nuts.

Jake took off back toward Sage Ranch, his mouth set in a grim line. Time to face the music. He had to tell his family about Emma. Right away.

Forty minutes later in the Sage Ranch kitchen, Travis and Rafe stared at their youngest brother as if he'd just informed them he'd dropped in from Jupiter and was headed to a rodeo on Mars.

"Tell me you're joking," Rafe bit out, his face frozen in shock.

"You only found out today?" Travis, the security specialist and former FBI agent, looked skeptical and seemed intent on pinning down the facts. "Are you saying she never so much as hinted—"

"I never saw her again after that night. Not until . . . well, last night." Jake paced to the stove and back, not even noticing the platter of peanut butter brownies on the granite countertop, or the sounds of horses nickering out back in the Sage Ranch corral.

"She says she almost told me when she found out she was pregnant. She came to find me at some rodeo and then changed her mind. Damn it, all this time, I could have—"

"Stepped up?" Travis eyed him coolly. "You would have, right?"

"Of course. What the hell do you think?" Jake took an ominous step forward, his eyes narrowed on his brother, but Rafe stepped between them with the ease of a big brother who was used to calming things down.

"That's enough. Both of you." He clapped a hand on Jake's broad shoulder. "No one's saying you did anything wrong. But what happens next, Jake? You going to marry Carly?"

"I guess. If that's what she wants," he replied

tersely, trying to ignore the roiling in the pit of his stomach.

Marriage. To think that at Travis and Mia's wedding, he'd laughed off the notion, sworn he'd never walk down the aisle. And he'd believed it.

But now, here he was, ready to tie the knot with a woman he barely knew. And he'd do it, too, if he could talk her into it. It would be like swallowing a dose of horrible-tasting medicine, but he wasn't about to have his daughter grow up without a father, without every legal protection he could offer her, and offer to her mother.

"You seem to be good at getting women to fall into bed with you—now let's see how good you are at getting one to marry you," Travis muttered.

"Not helping, bro." Rafe shot him an exasperated glance.

"Look, I know I messed the hell up." Jake glared from one brother to the next, his jaw tight. "But I'm going to fix this. Carly isn't all that keen on letting me get close to Emma right now. Or to her. She's downright skittish. Maybe the most skittish woman I've ever met. I have to respect that and take things at her pace. But believe me, I'll make this work. I'll take care of both of them. You know that, right?" He shot both his brothers a challenging glance, one that had made many other men take a step back.

But Rafe just nodded and let out a sigh. "Oh, man. Wait 'til Sophie hears. There'll be no holding her back from running right over to Blue Bell Drive. And Ivy and Aiden have a cousin who's never been invited to Thanksgiving dinner—or given a Christmas gift."

"I'll fill in Mia and Grady straightaway. Zoey's way too young to understand, but she'll know Emma is her cousin in time. Now, who's going to tell Lissie?" Travis asked, taking a turn around the kitchen as he contemplated the sudden enlargement of the Tanner family.

"I'm headed over to see her and Tommy next." Jake squared his shoulders. "But Carly doesn't want Emma to know I'm her dad yet, so no one can say a word to Emma—or to anyone else outside the family—not at this point. Not that I think Emma would actually understand. I don't have a clue how much kids that age do understand—" He broke off and raked a hand through his hair.

"It will all come together," Rafe said.

But Jake paced right past the brownies and then back again, the knots in his neck tightening.

"Easy, bro." Rafe's tone remained steady. "Like Mom always said, one thing at a time."

"Yeah. Forget what I told you before. I know you'll make this work, Jake." Travis stepped in front of him, held out his hand to shake. "It's lucky you found out now—and not when Emma was any older. You have time to put things right before she even notices she was missing a father for a while there. And we'll help, all of us, however we can."

Somehow Jake managed a rueful smile. "You want to help me? You can start by saying a prayer that Lissie doesn't skin me alive."

"If you're lucky, Tommy and little Molly will hold her back." Travis fought a grin.

Jake almost smiled before he remembered that his life had just been turned upside down and inside out. There was a great deal to do, so much ground to make up with Emma. Stuff to work out with Carly.

By the time he left Sage Ranch to head to his sister's place on Old Creek Drive, he felt a little sick inside. But from somewhere came a memory . . . his father's voice, on the banks of Blackbird Lake one summer day. They'd gone fishing, just the two of them.

Life throws us a curve now and then, son, but you just have to ride it out best you can. The trail always straightens out in time and it usually leads you where you're meant to go.

The words rolled through his head and steadied him now. He thought of his daughter's face. He'd never seen anything so beautiful and sweet. A portrait of pure innocence. And she'd been completely oblivious to his existence for the past year and a half.

Then his thoughts shifted to Carly. Gorgeous, sexy, guarded Carly. She was harder to read than a book that was glued shut. As wary a woman as he'd ever met.

She reminded him of someone who'd been snakebit and wasn't about to stretch out her hand again ever—not without a very thick leather glove.

He never blinked an eye at sliding onto the back of a bronc or a bull, never felt a single thread of fear as the chute opened and the wild ride began, but he'd done both so many times he knew exactly what to expect.

Tonight, on the lonely starlit road, with a hint of winter in the air blowing through his open window, he had no idea what tomorrow or the next day would bring.

He only knew as the night and the open road flashed by that this would be no eight-second thrill ride. He needed to be all in for this. All in for the long haul.

Whether he liked it or not didn't matter. He was all in for Emma—for good.

And Carly?

He'd be here for her, too. Whether she believed it or not.

Chapter Nine

Shortly before one o'clock the next day, Carly waited nervously beside the picnic table where she'd set out a lunch of tuna wraps, potato chips, cole slaw, and fruit cups from A Bun in the Oven.

She hadn't unwrapped the chocolate fudge cookies yet.

If Emma saw them first, she might balk at eating her sandwich. There were three of everything—cookies, sandwiches, fruit cups. One for her, one for Emma, and one for Jake.

Just like any cozy little normal family, she thought as a September breeze ruffled her hair. *Except we're not any of that. Not by any stretch of the imagination.*

She had her doubts about this getting-to-know-Emma lunch. But at least she'd set a time limit on it. Any moment now, Madison would show up with Emma in tow, and then at one thirty, she'd return to take her home for a nap. Carly would go back to the quilt shop.

And Jake? Who knew where he would go? And she knew she shouldn't care. She couldn't afford to care. Her job right now was to protect Emma and keep all contact with Jake low-key and minimal until—and if—Carly became convinced he was serious about being part of Emma's life.

What she dreaded most was the possibility that Emma would become so fond of Jake she'd cry when he had to leave.

And the whole time he was gone.

Because he *would* be gone. Often . . . and for lengthy periods.

Her stomach ached just thinking about it. She had to find a way to protect Emma from expecting her father to be a real dad, one who was around on a regular basis, one who stayed put in the same town where she lived. Short, not-too-frequent visits might help keep her from getting too attached. Because after this initial, impulsive burst of fatherly duty and responsibility, the rodeo life would call to Jake. She knew it would. And then he'd remember who he really was and what he really wanted.

Freedom.

He'd start going away for longer and longer periods of time.

To be fair, she had to admit she was surprised by the commitments he'd voiced yesterday. She hadn't expected anything like that from him.

But she wasn't counting on them, either. For all she knew, Jake might have sprung out of bed that morning and decided that being part of his daughter's young life was a burden he didn't need. He might backtrack.

The only way to get through this while protecting Emma as much as she could was to take things nice and slow.

Speaking of slow . . .

She'd been keeping an eye on the time, watching the seconds tick by, and it was now three minutes past one and there was no sign of either Madison and Emma—or Jake. . . .

But just as she sank down on the picnic bench, Madison's Silverado rumbled around the corner and cruised to a stop just outside the park.

"I'm sorry, Carly. We couldn't find Bug," Madison explained as Carly hurried over and unbuckled Emma from the car seat she'd transferred to Madison's car early that morning. As always, Madison was wearing shapeless sweatpants and a sweatshirt along with high-top sneakers. Her long, shiny hair was pulled into a low, messy ponytail, but as always, she still looked pretty. "Finally Emma found him—he'd fallen between the sofa and the ottoman."

"Bug!" Emma announced proudly, waving the stuffed dog in the air. Her cheeks were pink from the cool breeze whisking down from the mountains, but she looked warm enough in her puffy little pink down jacket with the white shearling collar.

"Hungry, sweetie?" Carly asked, setting her down gently on the grass as an elderly couple strolled past them toward the park benches flanking the town square.

Emma shook her head, murmured, "No," and took off running, clutching Bug as she raced toward the baby swings. "Push, Mumma!"

"Should I come back in half an hour or do you need more time?" Madison asked as Carly started toward her daughter.

"Half an hour is perfect. I need to—"

Suddenly Jake's truck zoomed into view and whatever she'd been planning to tell Madison vanished from her mind. He drove the way he looked, and probably the way he rode those bulls—with authority and confidence and ease. Sliding into the spot directly behind Carly's Jeep, he cut the engine.

At this time of day, all of the high school kids had returned to class and the park was nearly deserted. Carly's heart jumped a little—with trepidation, she told herself—as Jake vaulted out of the truck. He wore faded jeans and a black shirt and he looked lean and strong and good . . . too damned good. To her surprise, that big scrawny dog of his leaped out of the truck after him.

Great, just great. The dog wasn't on a leash, but he trotted closely behind Jake, who waved one very ripped arm at Carly and headed toward her with long, easy strides that could make a woman's mouth water.

"See you in a half hour," she told Madison, unable to tear her gaze away from Jake.

"Got it. . . . Um, Carly, that's Jake Tanner, isn't it? Delia told me he was back in town. Everyone's hoping he'll stay for the auction. Delia says she'd die of happiness if he bid for a date with her—"

Madison's voice faded as she suddenly seemed to notice that there were three of everything arrayed across the picnic table. "Are you and Emma having lunch with him?"

"Yes. We are." Carly flushed, hoping Madison wouldn't ask any more questions. Glancing over, she saw that Emma had veered away from the swings and was now scampering toward the slide.

"Awesome. I didn't realize you had a date."

"It's not a date." She started toward Emma, but not before she caught Madison's grin.

" 'Course not. Just a picnic. Think I'll pop over and pay my grandfather a visit." Madison seemed to be trying to wipe the smile from her face. "See you soon."

"Tell the sheriff hi from me." Carly watched Emma drop Bug in the grass, then toddle to an unsteady halt and turn around to snatch him back up. "That little tornado of mine thinks she can climb up that slide," she muttered, quickening her pace.

She heard Madison laugh. "Tell me about it. She excels at keeping me on my toes every second."

As the babysitter struck off toward the town

square, Carly called to Emma, shaking her head as her daughter ignored her and continued running full tilt toward the slide.

"Time for lunch, Emma," she called again. "We'll save the swing and the slide for later."

She might have saved her breath for all the notice Emma took.

With a sigh, Carly broke into a jog and caught Emma just as she was starting to wiggle herself onto the base of the slide. Scooping her daughter safely into her arms, she turned back toward the picnic table as Emma gave a shriek of protest.

"Hey, look who's having lunch with us. It's Jake," she said casually, and Emma stared, distracted. They reached the picnic table at the same time Jake and his dog did. The big mutt might have been glued to the heels of Jake's boots.

She noticed for the first time that the animal had a sad, gaunt face, but his tail was slowly wagging, and at least today he wasn't howling.

Emma had stopped protesting, but she ignored Jake completely, leaning out of her mother's arms, enchanted, trying to grab the dog.

"Got you something, Emma." Jake pulled a soft baby doll out of his jacket pocket. He'd driven all the way to Livingston to get it at a major toy store that morning, and he handed it to Emma with a seriously hopeful look in his eyes. "Approved for one year and up," he told Carly quickly.

But Emma grasped the doll for only an instant,

then dropped it without looking at it—and dropped Bug, too—as she leaned down to pat the mutt's head.

"Bribery, Jake? Really?" Carly lifted an eyebrow, but she was fighting a smile.

He had the nerve to grin. And shrug those broad shoulders. "Hey, it usually works with my nieces and nephews. I'm desperate here. I need to learn the ropes. I'm hoping you'll cut me some slack here, Carly."

She felt the magnetic pull of that seductive cowboy charm, and against her will, some of the wariness inside her softened. "I can . . . try."

He didn't *look* like a man who would willingly break a little girl's heart. He looked surprisingly at ease and very determined. Despite all her misgivings, he did seem intent on getting to know his daughter. . . .

Setting Emma down, she listened to bubbly laughter as Emma buried her face in the mutt's furry neck.

"Emma, this is Bronco," Jake said easily, not the least bit upset that she'd ignored the doll.

"Bwonco," came the muffled sound of Emma's reply.

He knelt down beside her. "He likes it when you scratch a little bit right behind his ears. Like this."

Emma plopped her little fingers beside Jake's on the dog's fur and scratched.

"Good job. There you go."

Suddenly the mutt turned his head and licked Emma's face. She drew back, screeching in surprise, then the screech turned to a giggle.

"Bronco likes you," Jake assured her, still kneeling. He stared at her, seemingly taking in everything about her, from her pink cheeks to her eyes—the exact same color as his own—and the wind-blown curls and tiny jacket with pink hearts sewn on the cuffs of her sleeves. His expression was intent, difficult for Carly to read. But Emma was focused only on the dog.

"Bwonco Bwonco Bwonco."

"Finally. Some progress—of a sort." Jake straightened to his full six-foot, two-inch height and met Carly's gaze, a wry smile lighting his face. "She just said something to me besides 'Bug.' " He pushed his Stetson back on his head. "It's not much, but I reckon it's a start."

"Whoa, look who's here." Sheriff Teddy Hodge set down a slice of pizza as Madison breezed into his office in a one-story building in the center of the town square.

"Hey, Gramps." Grinning, she leaned across his desk, and kissed his leathery cheek. She'd had a weird feeling for a second or two as she left the park and made her way here. But once she was inside, greeting her grandfather's secretary and striding past the deputy's cubicle, it had faded away like yesterday's rain.

That same odd tingle had come over her once or twice before over the past few days. A creepy crawly chill up her back, like someone was watching her. She'd even turned around once or twice on her way here from the park just now, sure she'd find someone staring, but she didn't spot anyone except for some older guy talking on a cell phone as he settled on a park bench, near where Carly had set up the picnic lunch. She'd shaken off the crazy feeling the moment she stepped over the threshold of the sheriff's department office, though. Now she pulled the spare chair up to her grandfather's desk and eyed the open pizza box beside his computer.

"This is the best part of my day so far," Hodge said, gazing at her fondly.

"Must be a pretty slow day, Gramps." She laughed.

"You're right, nothing much going on to speak of. Matter of fact, been a slow week." He pushed the pizza box with the remaining half of the still-hot pizza toward her as she settled into a chair across from his desk.

"Few nights ago someone tried to break into the medical center, probably some kid looking for drugs. Yesterday there were just a couple of speeding tickets on Highway 19 and a domestic dispute way out on Pebble Road. And today, so far, only a shoplifting attempt at Benson's Drugstore. Henry Blakemore tried to steal a pack of condoms while Lem was ringing up candy and toothpaste for Gloria Cartright. Gloria spotted Henry snatch the condoms and yelled."

"Did Henry get arrested?" Madison reached for a slice of pizza and a napkin. Henry Blakemore was fifteen, an honor student. He and his mom, Susan, a waitress at the Lucky Punch Saloon, lived on the first floor of Madison's apartment building.

"Nope, but Zeke put him in a cell and gave him a good talking-to. Scared the hell out of him, if I do say so myself. By the time Susan got there, he was bawling like a baby. I don't think he'll try stealing anything again real soon."

"Someone say my name?" Deputy Zeke Mueller poked his head in the door, but rushed on before Madison could even say hello.

"Sorry to interrupt." His gaze was locked on his boss. "Sheriff, the wife just called. Her water broke. All over the kitchen floor. Her mom's got her and the triplets in the car. I gotta take off for the hospital—"

"Well, what are you waiting for? Get the hell out of here, Zeke! I'll hold the fort. Let me know if you need anything." Teddy Hodge waved him away and the deputy spun and disappeared at a run out the door. "Poor man. He's already got three girls and another popping out any minute now. I'm going to have to play with the budget and see if I can give Zeke some kind of a raise."

"How is he doing otherwise, Gramps? I . . . I hope Zeke doesn't have any ill effects from . . . from Brady hitting him. Does he?"

The deputy had gone down like a ton of bricks and struck his head on the sidewalk in front of the hardware store.

"Well, the concussion is gone, with no lasting effects. But I wish Zeke had pressed charges." Hodge shrugged broad shoulders. "He said he felt sorry for Brady, because of his brother and all, and that's not to say I didn't, but assault is assault and no one should get away with that."

Madison was silent a moment. Then she lifted her gaze to her grandfather's face. "I know that, Gramps, but Brady's probably very sorry. He's . . . he's not a criminal. He just went through a bad period—"

"You making excuses for him, Maddy?" Her grandfather studied her from beneath his brows.

"Not excuses—of course not. I'm saying he wasn't himself. Everyone deserves a second chance."

"Well, not everyone. Serial killers don't. Rapists don't. But . . . young Brady Farraday, maybe. Judgment's still out on that. I know you used to be friends with him, but I'd stay away from that boy if I were you."

"I *used* to be friends with him. *True*. But it was a long time ago." Madison felt her cheeks flame. She'd been considering the idea of warning her grandfather ahead of time that Brady would be the one winning a date with her at the auction next week, but now she decided it wouldn't be the best idea to give him advance notice.

Not that he wouldn't understand her reluctance to parade across the stage for any length of time.

Both he and her grandmother had opposed her mother's determination to enter Madison in every pageant within driving distance. They sympathized with her stage shyness and her desire to be a "normal" kid. And they were convinced the pageant life wasn't what their son would have wanted for his daughter. But Sergeant Thomas Hodge had been killed in Iraq during Operation Desert Storm when Madison was seven, and his widow made all the decisions for her daughter after he was gone.

She didn't care a whit that Madison's grandparents objected to her dragging Madison all over the county and even the state, even pulling her out of school some days. She just insisted that the fun and glamour of the pageant life distracted her from her "grief," and it quickly became an obsession for her. She didn't want to stop, she told everyone who would listen. Not until Madison "won."

First place or bust, she used to say, especially to her second husband, a laid-back trucker who was on the road a lot and who had no objection to her filling her time with endless thoughts of gowns and tap lessons and runway rehearsals. Madison's mother never quite forgave her daughter for never placing first—or for leaving home the day she turned eighteen, hitching her way back to Lonesome Way to live in an apartment near her grandparents. She'd consoled herself by becoming a private "coach" for girls who wanted to compete and win in pageants.

"What are you getting Grams for her birthday next week?" Madison wanted to shift the conversation away from both Brady and the auction. "I bought her a pair of opal earrings online. They're very pretty."

"I wanted to talk to you about that." Hodge cleared his throat. "I had this little idea of taking her on a trip to Junction Falls. That's where we had our first date, you know. There's a little bed-and-breakfast there that's gotten great write-ups online—figured she'd enjoy it. She always says I don't take her anyplace. And while we're there, I'm having something delivered to the house."

"Something delivered? What?" Fascinated, Madison leaned forward. As far as she remembered, her grandfather always gave her grandmother the same gifts every year—a bottle of Joy perfume, a sweater from a knit shop in Livingston, and a new winter scarf.

He grinned at her, eyes twinkling. "It's a piano. A good, high-quality American piano. Brand-new." At her gasp, he beamed with pleasure. "That one she's been playing on for the past twenty years was secondhand when she got it and it's been retuned too many times to count. This is a fine, brand-new American piano," he repeated proudly. "I'm hoping you can arrange your schedule to be there when it's delivered and set up and the old one is taken away. But it means we're going to miss the big fund-raising auction that weekend—will that bother you? Should I plan on taking her away a week later, so we can be here and keep an eye on whoever bids for you in that auction? Some of the roughnecks around here who might think of it would think twice if I'm in the audience giving them the evil eye."

"No, oh, no, Gramps. I'll be fine. Believe me, I can take care of myself and I'm not the least bit worried. I'm sure someone really nice will bid on me. If anyone does at all." Her eyes sparkled in the sunlight slanting through the window behind him. "And I'll be happy to let in the delivery people. Grams will be so excited! Just tell me what time you need me to be there and I'll make it work."

A satisfied smile spread across his face as he reached for another slice of pizza. "She'll be tickled, all right—she's no doubt expecting another bottle of Joy—"

Then his desk phone rang, and he broke off, quickly picking it up.

"Yeah? Okay, then . . . hold your horses. I'll be

right there." Teddy Hodge shoved back his chair and hurried around the desk. The smile had evaporated from his face and a grim frown took its place. The warm gleam in his eyes when he'd spoken about the gift for his wife had now transformed into the chilly glint of a lawman as he reached for his gun belt and strapped it on.

" 'Course now that Zeke's tied up all hell's got to break loose," he told Madison. "Got our first assault and robbery since last winter, honey. Someone just mugged Homer out at the gas station. Cleaned out the cash register and got away with two hundred thirty-six dollars. Feel free to finish this pizza, honey. I gotta go."

Chapter Ten

That evening, after Emma fell asleep, Carly worked on her blossom quilt for the Thanksgiving fund-raiser—wondering uneasily, as she sewed, what kind of reception she'd receive from Lissie, Sophie, and Mia when they arrived at Zoey Tanner's birthday party the following day. Suddenly she heard a light, persistent tapping on her front door.

Jumping up from Annie's old sewing machine in the smallest and coziest of the Victorian's bedrooms, she hurried to answer it before Emma woke up.

Then she immediately froze in surprise as Jake's sister launched herself over the threshold. Before she even realized it, Lissie was embracing her in a fierce hug that stole her breath. Mia and Sophie stood right behind her.

"Jake made us wait until tonight to come see you. He wanted his half hour in the park with Emma first."

"We're here to officially welcome you and Emma to the family," Sophie added. She stepped inside, carrying a white bakery box from A Bun in the Oven, and made room for her other sister-in-law to follow.

Mia surged in just as Lissie finally released Carly from the hug.

"We come bearing gifts," she announced. Her fair hair glowed in the light of the living room lamp as Carly gaped at the three of them.

"There's wine." Mia held up a bottle of pinot grigio.

"And chocolate," Sophie supplied, with a glance down at the white bakery box. "Dark chocolate cake with hazelnut buttercream frosting."

"And French vanilla ice cream with pecans," Lissie added. "How's that for decadent? It's the way we always celebrate the announcement of a new baby joining the family."

"Well, with cake and ice cream, true—but

usually the one who's pregnant skips the wine," Sophie pointed out.

"Except in this case," Mia continued, "you're not pregnant anymore, so you can join us in polishing off the entire bottle."

"You're not . . . angry?" Carly swallowed. "You do know that I didn't tell Jake for all this time—"

"That's between you and my brother," Lissie interrupted. "We know you didn't have any reason to think he'd be happy about the pregnancy— especially since he's so fond of spouting his 'no one's ever going to lasso me and tie me down' crap." She rolled her eyes. "But what you *don't* know is that beneath that rough-rider exterior he's more of a softie than he'd ever let on. That cowboy absolutely loves kids, and now that he knows he has one of his own—"

"You'll see for yourself," Sophie finished for her, sinking down on the sofa. Setting the cake box on the coffee table, she lifted the lid. The delicious scent of chocolate wafted through the living room. "He's going to be an awesome dad. And we're aunts again, so we need to cele-brate. How about some wineglasses?" she hinted as Carly continued to gape at all three of them. "Unless we want to just chug it and pass the bottle around?"

"A knife for cutting the cake would be helpful," Mia suggested.

"Need a scooper for the ice cream, too. And

plates." Lissie glanced at the other three. "I suggest we take this party into the kitchen."

"So," Carly murmured a few moments later, after she'd sipped some wine and Lissie had served everyone huge gooey slices of cake and ice cream at the kitchen table, "you're not planning to run me out of town."

"We'll tell Sheriff Hodge to set up a blockade if you even think about leaving," Mia promised with a grin as she polished off the last of her only glass of wine, as she was the designated driver.

"We'll take it slow, if you like, about other people finding out Jake is Emma's dad, but—one word of warning—you may want to casually mention it to Emma herself pretty soon. This is Lonesome Way, after all, and people find out quickly about these things, don't ask me how," Sophie said with a mixture of ruefulness and gentleness.

"They find out about *everything*," Lissie agreed emphatically. "It beats me how you've managed to keep something this big a secret for so long."

Reaching across the table, Mia touched Carly's hand. "My great-aunt Winny learned the hard way how damaging secrets—especially family secrets —can be. We don't mean to rush you, and we know Emma won't really understand just yet, but for her sake, the sooner she knows she has a caring father who wants to be there for her and in her life, the better."

A shadowy image of her own father floated into Carly's mind. The father who'd never been there for her. Never come for her. Never saved her all those hours when she was locked in a closet or hiding from Phil under the bed. Or when fear was her only companion during one of her uncle's drinking binges.

She suddenly remembered the hope on Jake's face when Emma had responded to the name of his dog. How happy he'd looked that he'd made even that small a start with his daughter.

A lump filled her throat, ached so deeply that for a moment she couldn't speak.

"And here I expected you to be furious with me." She gazed in wonder at all of their faces. These women had been her friends since the day she'd moved to town. She'd set up playdates for Emma with their children and had on more than several occasions gone out to the Double Cross Bar and Grill for drinks or dinner with one or all of them when Madison or Martha could babysit in the evening.

Now here they were, once again coming to her in friendship. Despite what she'd done, they were all watching her with kindness and acceptance in their eyes.

"We know you were doing what you felt was best for Emma," Sophie said softly. "There's no question about that. Everything else . . . everything between you and Jake . . . all we hope is that you two will work it out in the best way you can."

"As of today," Lissie told her firmly, "we consider you and Emma part of the family. We're here for you, all of us."

Carly fought back tears as a flood of emotions welled in her throat. She managed a weak laugh. "I . . . I've never had so many people there for me. It feels a bit . . . strange. But nice!" she added, color rushing into her cheeks.

"Well, you had Annie and then Martha," Sophie pointed out. "Now there's just a few more of us. All the Tanners are here for you. And that means Rafe and Travis as well."

"By the way," Lissie interrupted, lifting a forkful of cake toward her mouth. "Have you told Martha yet? About Jake?"

Carly nodded. In her mind she saw again Martha's not-all-that-stunned expression the night before when she'd explained why she'd needed her to bring Emma home right away.

"I told her yesterday when I brought Emma back to her apartment, but I'm fairly sure that after she saw Jake here, she somehow guessed. Martha's pretty sharp. She actually seemed pleased when I told her Jake is Emma's father. I mean, she was grinning from ear to ear."

"Well, he *is* a catch, if I do say so. All of the Tanner men are," Mia said calmly, but there was a warm sparkle in her eyes.

"I'm not trying to catch him. That's not going to happen. And Jake definitely doesn't want to be caught," she added, spooning out one more scoop of ice cream onto her plate.

"What man does?" Sophie laughed. "Rafe used to be the bad boy of Lonesome Way. In high school, he changed girlfriends the way some men change shirts. But he grew up eventually and became the man he is today."

"Travis dumped me in high school. I was so hurt I never wanted to speak to him again. I never in a million years thought we'd get back together," Mia told her. "It just goes to show—you never know."

Oh, I know, Carly thought. *Because Jake and I were never in love. It wasn't like that between us. It was . . . one night. One scorching hot but very random night. I only wanted him to make me forget about Kevin. And he only wanted to pass the time in Houston. Not very romantic, and definitely not a basis for marriage. Child or no child.*

But something inside her whispered that it wasn't quite that cut-and-dried. The way he'd kissed her and touched her . . .

She still remembered how he'd made her feel that night, what he'd awakened inside her. The rush of want and need, the pleasure so deep her blood burned with it.

It hadn't just been raw sex between them. Jake

was an incredible lover. He'd taken his time. Kissed her until she was going out of her mind. Brushed her body all over with his lips and his strong, clever fingers, until lightning seemed to quiver and singe everywhere he touched.

He stroked her everywhere until she nearly went mad and then he grinned and ruthlessly tormented her a little bit more.

Jake's lovemaking was an adventure in sensation and pleasure. No, they weren't in love, but it hadn't been merely lust that had sizzled between them that night.

There'd been tenderness and heat, and give and take. Jake had made her feel something again. She remembered the texture of his thumbs on her nipples, the brush of his five-o'clock stubble across her belly. She remembered how he'd made her shiver and gasp . . . and later, when they were recuperated enough to lunge at each other for round three, how he'd made her laugh. . . .

But there was no point in remembering all that, she told herself hastily as she grabbed her wineglass and gulped the few remaining drops. It wasn't as if it would ever happen again. In fact, she had no choice but to make sure it didn't.

"To Emma." Lissie splashed the last drops from the bottle into each of their glasses. Everyone clinked.

"To family," Mia and Sophie said at the exact same time and then burst out laughing.

To family. As the wine slid down her throat and Sophie carried the glasses to the kitchen sink and Lissie gathered up the plates and Mia dug for her car keys, Carly thought: *So this is what it feels like to be part of a family.*

By the time she'd cleaned up the kitchen and checked on Emma, then slid between cool cotton sheets and an eiderdown quilt in her own bedroom, she'd come to one conclusion. It was all well and good and very welcome to be part of the Tanner family, but she still had Emma to protect.

Jake might never intentionally hurt his daughter, but his reputation as a man who never lit long in one place—that would bear remembering.

She'd allow Emma to get to know him, but only up to a point. That would be the tricky part. Keeping her daughter from getting *too* attached.

Not that Carly knew exactly how to accomplish that. But surely Jake would take off for some rodeo soon, or to film a TV commercial, and he'd be gone before he became anything close to a fixture in Emma's life.

She couldn't let him become someone like Madison or Martha, someone Emma saw almost every day—or someone like Annie, whom Carly had quickly learned to count on when she was a ten-year-old girl finding herself living with the best foster mother in the world.

It would be a tricky balancing act, letting Emma get to know Jake without starting to rely on him being around regularly.

But she'd find a balance. She had to—for Emma's sake.

And for her own.

Jake Tanner was the kind of man most women would love to have stick around. She couldn't afford to think like one of those women. She had to go into this with her eyes wide open—or she and Emma could both be hurt again.

Chapter Eleven

"Here's where I want the fourth cabin. Right here."

Jake planted his feet in an open spot of the valley, surrounded by views of aspens and the rocky shoulders of the Crazy Mountains. If he were to walk a few miles west, he'd be able to catch a glimpse in the distance of his grandparents' original cabin, set near the blue waters of Blackbird Lake.

Beside him, Denny McDonald scribbled notes on a pad of paper as wind ruffled the brilliant gold leaves still clinging to the trees.

"I'm picturing this cabin two thousand square

feet larger than the older three. Four medium-sized bedrooms, two and a half baths, wrap-around deck." Jake squinted against the sun. "Big enough for a family, with room to breathe."

Denny nodded, then scanned the valley with slow appreciation. He let out a long whistle.

Jake could understand why. It was a stunningly beautiful spot. Long, deep meadows. Massive blue sky. The colors of autumn slashing across the distant hillside.

A meadowlark flittered through the trees. Jake caught sight of a white-tailed deer drinking from a stream. Peacefulness seemed to shimmer like sunbeams in the pine-laced air.

"Gonna be a big slice of heaven, isn't it?" Denny said. "Perfect for hunters, fishermen, vacationers. Plus all those bullied kids and their families. You want the other new cabins walking distance from this one?"

"Three-quarters of a mile apart. Two of 'em will go there, off to the east." Jake pointed. "The last one a mile west of here, closer to Blackbird Lake."

"You've given this a lot of thought," Denny remarked.

"I want the kids who stay in these cabins—and the fishermen or tourists who rent them out—to feel like they've really gotten away from it all. Whether they come back at night to sleep, or simply stay put all day, they should feel like this is their own private chunk of the world. No troubles allowed."

Behind Denny, Brady listened in silence as Denny assured Jake he'd begin drawing up the plans that very evening. Brady wasn't sure why he'd been invited along this morning to scout locations for the new cabins, but he knew enough not to question his inclusion. He was relieved beyond words he had a job again—a job he was good at.

Building, construction, those were things he loved. He always had. Cord had been drawn to horses, ranching, rodeo, to action and excitement.

But Brady liked building something where before there had been nothing.

"What do you think, Brady?"

"Uh, about what?" Damn, he felt like a fool. He'd been following his own thoughts and hadn't even heard the question, so how the hell could he answer it?

Denny frowned. "What's your estimate on the timetable for this project? Rehabbing Jake's other three cabins, building the new ones. And how big a crew do you think we need to get it done?"

Brady quickly cast his thoughts back over everything Jake had said about this project from the minute they climbed in his truck until now.

"Seven months with a six-man crew, five months with a dozen. Not counting weather delays," he blurted.

Denny looked at Jake, then nodded. "Not bad. We're going with a dozen. Ralph's gonna be foreman of this job and you're going to be second in command. You report directly to him. You don't miss a day, not even an hour. Don't make me sorry I hired you back, you hear? Whatever Ralph tells you to do, you do it. No guff, no complaints."

Brady straightened and met his boss's sharp gaze. He'd always loved a challenge and he knew Denny was testing him. "I get it. You won't be sorry."

"Better not be." But Denny shot him a quick approving glance before he turned back to the truck. Jake clapped him on the shoulder before he, too, turned back.

Brady didn't say much as they drove to Jake's own cabin, where Brady had left his Harley and Denny had parked his truck.

"You want to come back to the office and talk over what kind of flooring, windows, appliances, and stuff you want?" Denny asked from the passenger seat. "All the same in each cabin, or different?"

"Different. But sorry. Can't work on it today." Jake glanced at his watch. "Got my niece's birthday party. I need to get my butt over to Travis and Mia's place pronto or both my brothers will do their damnedest to beat the shit out of me." He let out a chuckle. "I'll stop by your office Monday and fill in all the blanks."

"Yeah, I forgot. I know all about that party. Karla and the kids are there by now, too." Denny McDonald shook his head. "Birthday party for a one-year-old, with a dozen or so toddlers running around? Bedlam. Better you than me, Jake. You should check out the shindig going on next week, though. The big dating auction. That seems more your style."

"First I've heard of it." Jake steered the truck around a rabbit that had decided to skip across the road.

"Most all of the single ladies in town got roped into being auctioned off to the highest bidder. Karla's on the planning committee. It's headed up by Ava Todd, Dorothy Winston, and Martha Davies. Not that you need to pay for a date, Jake, not from what I hear," Denny added with a laugh. "But don't forget, this is for charity. Lonesome Way needs a new animal shelter bad. You should check out the auction, too, Brady. All the available women in town gathered in one spot. Should be a helluva night. If I wasn't a happily married man, I'd buy a ticket."

"Yeah, I might check it out," Brady said indifferently, leaning his shoulders back against the seat. But all the while he was wondering if Madison was nervous. And if she'd track him down to remind him to show up before the auction started.

He'd seen a flyer over at Pepperoni's Pizza—

apparently her band, the Wild Critters, had a gig at the Spotted Pony tonight. Maybe he'd head over there, see if they were any good. If he got the chance, he'd let her know he hadn't forgotten about the auction.

Just in case she was worried.

Chapter Twelve

Jake had been present at every single one of his nieces' and nephews' birthday parties, so he waded comfortably into the madness of knee-high toddlers yelling, laughing, and crying, and mommies shushing, smiling, and soothing.

Into a sea of balloons and streamers everywhere. Into the hilarious sight of Mia's little dog, Samson, racing around on the deck with Bronco, both of them intermittently barking to be let back in.

To music—a children's song Madison was strumming on a guitar. And then there was Travis, the ever-efficient dad, shooting video and pictures of the kids and of a side table piled high with gaily wrapped gifts, and kids of all ages under five running amok and underfoot.

He spotted Zoey right away, playing patty-cake with Rafe's daughter, Ivy. Starting toward them, he adroitly stepped around various tykes. But it was taking all of his willpower not to scan the room immediately for Emma and Carly. He knew damn well if he went over to greet Emma first, every woman in the room would sit up and take notice. Everyone in town would be buzzing about why he greeted Carly McKinnon's daughter before his own niece at her own birthday party.

And Carly would most certainly kill him, he decided grimly.

He did manage to spot both her and Emma as he was stepping carefully around a couple of three-year-olds chasing each other across the long, high-ceilinged living room.

Emma's pretty little face sparkled. She was wearing a pink velveteen dress and white leggings and she clutched Bug tight in her arms. Kneeling beside Madison as the young woman played the guitar, Emma was happily singing along with her babysitter to "Old McDonald Had a Farm." Several other kids were gathered around, too, joining in, yelling that Old McDonald had a "pig!" and a "cow!" and a "duck!" at the appropriate moments.

Carly stood in the hall deep in conversation with Karla McDonald. He had to keep himself from staring at her. She was incredibly beautiful. Sexy and serene in a silky peach blouse tucked into soft black pants and black leather flats. There was a simplicity and a sophistication about her that made him want to stare. Her long red-gold curls tumbled in sumptuous waves past her shoulders, brilliant as fire in the light streaming through the windows. Her low, husky laugh reached his ears just as he stopped beside his niece and knelt down to press a kiss to her cheek. Zoey grabbed for his neck. With a grin, Ivy scrambled to her feet.

"Uncle Jake, take over for a minute, okay? I need to help Aunt Mia with the cake and ice cream."

Just like that she was gone, no longer a kid herself, but a beautiful, almost grown-up young woman, a teenager, bolting past him, and Jake slid into her place, his big hands gently patting against Zoey's tiny fingers. It seemed like only a week ago that Ivy was Emma's age. A baby, racing around on barely steady, chubby legs.

His stomach lurched. Holy crap, would Emma grow up as fast?

He'd better not waste any more time getting to know her better, or she'd be a teenager before he knew it and think she was too cool to spend time with her dad.

Her dad.

Closing his eyes a moment, he felt almost overwhelmed by the sudden need to get things settled with Carly right away.

His brain clicked back to where he'd been ten days earlier—on the road between Lincoln,

Nebraska, and Sioux Falls. Alone in his truck, Carrie Underwood singing sweet and fine on the radio. No dog taking up his passenger seat. No worries. Just the open road, the call of the rodeo, his upcoming commercial shoot—and an idea buzzing in his head for a way to help bullied kids.

But now was a whole different story.

Playing patty-cake with Zoey, he allowed his gaze to shift momentarily to his daughter. Carly had scooped Emma into her arms and was headed toward the festively set dining room table as Mia sailed in with a pink-and-white-frosted birthday cake on a big turquoise platter. Carly and Emma. They looked so right together, so easy and carefree and happy. . . .

Just how did he fit into this picture? That was what he had to figure out. He needed to do this right. Mistakes weren't an option—not when his little girl's happiness was at stake. And he had to make up to Carly for her having shouldered all the responsibility for so long. Even though that had been her choice.

Still, it was a strange, heavy feeling, having responsibilities to someone other than himself, responsibilities that had crashed down on him out of the blue.

I'm going to need a solid couple of weeks before I go back on the road, he realized suddenly. He had to give himself at least that much time with Emma, but it wasn't all he needed to do. He had to work out a plan. Set things up with Carly, figure out a schedule for financial support payments, for visits.

And come to some basic agreements about how to parent Emma together while living apart.

He'd call Ron Messina from the Turner Taylor Advertising Group later in the day and tell him he'd fly in for one day only to the photo shoot in a few weeks, but he couldn't stay any longer. He'd already canceled his appearance at the Bighorn Bull Rodeo in Wyoming.

He didn't give a damn who was pissed. He needed Emma to know deep down that she was loved, every bit as much as Rafe loved Ivy and Aiden, as Lissie's husband, Tommy, loved their little Molly, and with the same dedication that Travis loved Grady and Zoey.

Just like his nieces and nephews, Emma needed to know she could count on her father anytime she needed him.

He sensed that the foundation of that trust needed to be laid, solidified, before he could return to his life on the road, to the crowds, the noise, the grit of the rodeo.

He tried not to think about Melanie. How she'd trusted him. How he'd let her down . . .

He couldn't *ever* not be there for Emma when she needed him.

His chest tightened painfully. Then he caught Carly watching him. She was seated beside Mia's great-aunt Winny at the big dining room table, with Emma cuddled on her lap. Carly's cautious smile wasn't lost on him as he met her gaze.

Jake could read women pretty well. And he knew this woman was still doubting that he'd be a good father to Emma. It would be a helluva lot harder to convince her than his daughter, he realized grimly.

It would take time for Carly to trust him. Maybe a lot longer than two weeks. But she'd eventually see he meant what he said. Even after he left town, he'd call and come back often enough to convince her—and Emma—that despite being on the road, he was in this for the long haul.

Jake had no chance to speak with Carly alone until nearly all the guests were gone. Finally he spotted her while Madison and Ivy were keeping an eye on the few remaining kids.

Travis's adopted stepson, Grady, and his friend Zane had shown up minutes earlier, and Aunt Winny had assigned them a job: gathering up all the torn wrapping paper scattered around the living room, and then scrubbing cake frosting off the hardwood floor. As Carly breezed out of the kitchen and swerved to avoid the boys, Jake had a moment to study her. She had one hell of a slender, sexy body. And an airy, almost ethereal beauty with those softly sculpted cheekbones and luminous green eyes. It all added up to a delicious combination of a very hot woman.

Quit looking at her and focus on what needs doing, he told himself almost angrily. When she glanced toward him, he gestured toward the sliding glass doors. Though she hesitated for a fraction of a moment, she gave an almost imperceptible nod and moved forward to slip out on the deck just ahead of him.

"Emma needs a nap after all this excitement," she began briskly as Bronco and Samson bounded past her and back into the house. "We're taking off any minute. Just as soon as I—"

"Can you spare me a few minutes to talk to you first?"

Careful green eyes lifted to his face.

"What about?"

"Making this situation easier for both of us. You interested?" Jake closed the sliding door and waited for her reaction.

"I guess that depends on what you have in mind."

Reaching for her hand, he led her down the deck steps. "Just a short walk so we can talk in private."

"But Emma—"

"Madison and Ivy are with her. I slipped them each an extra ten bucks to keep an eye on her until we get back. Come on, this way."

He led her down a grassy bank that sloped toward a stand of cottonwoods. Autumn leaves crunched beneath their feet as they left Travis and Mia's big two-story house behind and Carly found herself walking silently beside him along a winding, sun-splashed trail. The ground was slightly hilly and uneven here, but peaceful and quiet. She could hear the gurgle of a stream nearby and caught the scent of burning leaves in the distance. It merged with the damp smell of the earth into a pleasant woodsy freshness.

When they reached a small clearing where a few wildflowers still wavered in the wind, Jake halted. The grass grew thick here, and the cottonwoods offered just enough shade.

"Alone at last." He flashed a quick smile, as if hoping to break the awkwardness between them.

"Considering what happened the last time we were alone, that might not be the best idea."

"*Considering* that a beautiful little girl happened last time, maybe we could go for a boy this time," he replied without missing a beat. He was joking, but her face froze.

"You actually think that's funny?"

"Nope." He slanted her a cool gaze. "I don't think it's the least bit funny that I didn't know I had a daughter all this time. Or that you didn't feel any inclination to tell me. But I'm willing to accept you had your reasons, Carly. Now, though, things are going to be different. You and I . . ." He stepped closer. "We're going to start working together. And we need to start right now, before we waste any more time."

"Go ahead. I'm listening."

A squirrel scrambled noisily along a tree branch above them. Jake studied her for a moment before speaking. She looked as wary and distant as she had that night at the McDonald house. Man, this woman had *walls*.

"Let's get everything out on the table. Starting with your reservations about me. Don't try to spare my feelings. Let 'em rip."

"Fine." She searched for the right words. "I think you're who you are—and no offense—but that isn't the best thing for Emma. It's nothing personal," she said quickly when a frown darkened his face. "It's just that you're famous and busy and you don't want to be tied down. Your own words. And soon you're going to get real busy again with your own life, and if you spend a lot of time with Emma now and in the future, she's going to start missing you when you're gone. You won't always be able to make time for her and then . . . she could be hurt."

His mouth tightened and she guessed she'd just hurt *him*. She hadn't meant to, but better him than Emma, right? Avoiding his eyes, she sank down suddenly on the grass, stretched her legs before her, and drew her knees up. When she clasped her hands around them, Jake dropped down across from her.

"Is that it?"

The sun had shifted and now slanted through the thicket of trees and she found herself staring directly into his eyes. "I'm worried that she'll see other kids—her friends and kids at school—with their moms and dads." She bit her lip. "She'll see them at the park, at birthday parties, or when she goes to their houses to play—and plenty of times you won't even be around. She'll wonder why not—where you are—why she hardly ever sees you. Why her friends don't know you—"

"They'll know me," he interrupted tersely. "I'll be there much more than you think. You don't need to worry."

"That's easy for you to say, but think about it. She's just a little girl, Jake. With an open, loving heart. I don't want to see her hurt and bewildered."

He was quiet for a moment, and she waited, her chest tight.

"It's true. I never planned on settling down or having any real ties," Jake said slowly. "But Emma's here and that changes everything. I'll be around for her. She'll know she can count on me. I might not live in the same house with the two of you, but there are plenty of kids whose parents are divorced and they don't have their fathers—or sometimes their mothers—living in the same house, either. I'll be around. I'm going to make this work, Carly. You need to trust me on this."

"Trust." She met his gaze. "Not my strong point."

He nodded. "Maybe we can work on that. Together."

She studied him doubtfully. He sounded sincere, but . . .

How did that saying go? The road to hell was paved with good intentions?

"I guess I don't really have much of a choice," she muttered at last.

The wind gusted suddenly, a sweep of cooler air racing down from the mountains, and in that instant, it felt more like winter than fall and made her shiver.

Jake reached out as the blast of wind blew a heavy lock of hair across her eyes. His fingers smoothed those red-gold curls back, then dipped down to brush along her jaw. His touch sent a ping of electricity jolting through her.

This isn't good. At all. She hadn't been this close to him since the night they nearly burned up the bed in Houston and she'd forgotten how his slightest touch affected her. He smelled like leather and soap and mountain air. Those intense blue eyes seemed to pierce her soul. The calluses on his strong hand lightly scraped her skin, making her shiver in a completely different way than the wind had.

"You and I need to start working together." He spoke quietly. "That would be a whole lot easier if you trusted me. If we could become friends."

Friends? She had an instant flashback to that sumptuous hotel room. To his hard, ripped chest muscles and biceps, the flat abdomen and powerful legs. To the feel of those muscular arms around her, his hot, clever mouth roaming down her body. Slow, burning kisses and frantic gasps in the dark . . . to Jake kissing her like he couldn't get enough, plunging deep inside of her, again and again, taking her on the wildest, sweetest ride of her life. . . .

"Friends, yes, that would make things *so* much easier," she said under her breath, with more than a little drawl of sarcasm.

"You don't think I'm serious?"

"Oh, I know you are. But . . ."

"You don't believe we can do it." Shifting closer to her, he captured both of her hands in his as a flurry of crimson leaves swirled around them like confetti.

"Don't put words in my mouth, Jake." Carly knew she had to focus only on the issues before them. But Jake's hands, warmly enclosing hers, distracted her. They were big, powerful, callused from riding and work. They were big enough to dwarf her slender fingers, strong enough to crush them. Yet they felt protective and comforting at the same time.

She remembered the feel of them exploring all the most sensitive places of her body, giving her so much pleasure. His touch now brought that night in Houston vividly back to her, and she almost found herself sliding closer to him. But she held on to her pride and her common sense just in time and kept her butt planted firmly on the ground.

"I see I'm going to have to convince you I can be trusted," he drawled in a deep, solemn voice. But when she saw the gleam of amusement in his eyes, she suddenly had to fight back a smile.

"I can hardly wait to hear how you expect to do that."

"Well, now, let's see." A hint of a way-too-appealing grin played at the corners of his mouth. "In my line of work, ma'am, it takes patience to learn how to rope a steer, to make that loop stick on the first throw. It takes patience to learn how to stay on a bull's back, adapt to his movement, know what he's going to do, how he's going to buck by the clenching of a muscle a fraction of an instant before he does it. Patience is how I stay alive, how I make my living. I can be patient with Emma. And I can be patient with you."

"Seriously? You're comparing me and our daughter to a steer and a bull right now?"

His grin flashed in that handsome face. Oh, he was too good-looking, she thought darkly. And *way* too sexy. Not to mention all that low-key cowboy charm. It required every ounce of will-power she possessed to keep from smiling right back at him. Who was she kidding? It took all of her willpower not to *melt*.

"Seems to me you're just *trying* to take that the wrong way." Those cobalt blue eyes sizzled into hers. "The only thing I'm serious about, Carly, is making this right with Emma. And with you."

"Don't even try to tell me you're not angry anymore. I don't believe it."

"You want the truth?" The smile did fade then. "I'm sure as hell not happy that you didn't tell me about Emma, but apparently you had your reasons. I don't have a clue about the men who've been in your life before, but I sure wish you'd given me the benefit of the doubt before lumping me in with them."

The moment the words were out of his mouth, he felt her hands clench, as tight and hard as small rocks within his. Her entire body went rigid.

Man, he'd hit the mark there. Big-time. More than he'd expected.

"That bad, huh?" He couldn't help wondering who'd hurt her and how.

"Bad enough that I don't care to discuss it."

"You know, I might understand better if you'd fill me in."

He watched her hesitate, watched those green eyes swimming with doubt. It seemed for a moment that she wasn't going to answer. But she finally spoke with a shrug, and in a low tone, apparently deciding that if they were going to raise Emma with a semblance of partnership she had to give him *something*.

"It's not an unusual story. My father left and my mother died. I had a lousy childhood."

"Sorry to hear it, but what does that have to do with—sorry, go on." Jake's thumb rubbed gently against her wrist. He could almost feel her steeling herself.

"That's about it. I moved around a lot between my relatives' homes, like a piece of a jigsaw puzzle that doesn't really fit anywhere. Nobody really wanted me. My cousin . . . my uncle . . ." She drew in a deep breath. "They didn't ever hurt me, exactly, but . . . there was drinking, yelling, things were thrown a lot, and Phil—my other cousin—used to think it was fun to lock me in a closet for hours at a time. I was scared almost every minute."

She lifted her gaze to his face. "That's when I had my first panic attack. It took me a long time to get those under control. Back then, it wasn't a peaceful environment, to say the least. All I wanted, all I dreamed about, was a real home. Someplace quiet, someplace where I wasn't afraid, and then . . . I finally found it." Her eyes softened. "I got lucky and ended up in foster care."

Foster care. Damn. That's right. And suddenly he remembered her telling him something about that the night they spent together. How her foster mother knew Martha Davies—they were related or something—and they'd visited Lonesome Way together when she was still a young girl. She'd told Jake she'd watched him jump into the middle of a fight one day. . . .

Her next words surprised him.

"I lucked out beyond anything I could imagine when they took me away from what was left of my family. I got to live with the kindest person in the world. Her name was Annie. Annie Benton. She was Martha's cousin and she was wonderful. She changed my life."

Jake saw the shimmer of love and gratitude in her eyes and a wave of something he couldn't pin down washed through him. "Glad to hear it."

"Everything changed with Annie in my life. I felt safe. Cared for. Happy. Annie was the first person who recognized that I was smart. That I had . . . potential. That there was a path I could follow to make something of my life. But years later, after I graduated from college, Annie died, too. Cancer. My life by then was on solid footing—thanks to her. I had an MBA and a good job, and then . . . a boyfriend."

"Uh-huh." He waited, vaguely sensing something nasty coming.

"He was my one and only serious boyfriend. And he lied to me. Big-time."

He watched her lips tighten almost imperceptibly. Those green eyes darkened with remnants of anger.

"Our whole life together was a lie. It seems Kevin forgot to tell me a few little details about his life. Four details, to be exact. That would be his wife—and their three kids."

Jake whistled.

"Not to mention a lousy temper," she added, plucking a few blades of grass, watching them slip through her fingers.

The word "temper" made him straighten. "A lousy temper? Meaning?"

Her eyes were downcast now. "After I found out he'd been lying to me all along, I ended our relationship. In no uncertain terms. Kevin didn't like that. And he morphed into someone I didn't even know. He shoved his way into my apartment and he . . . he broke things. Including something important to me." She paused, swallowed. "It was a gift from my closest friend, Sydney. A crystal ballerina sculpture. He threw it against a wall because I wouldn't get back together with him. I wouldn't ignore the fact that he had a family, that our entire relationship was based on a lie. *He* thought we should continue as if nothing was wrong. As if we still had . . . a *relationship*. It was . . . terrifying." She lifted her head. "That was the moment I realized I'd never really known him."

"He hurt you?" Jake's blood boiled as he thought of her at the mercy of some lying, chicken-ass jerk.

"No, not physically." She shook her head, her eyes bitter. "But I realized I'd made a horrendous choice getting involved with him in the first place. Just as my mother did with my father. I guess the women in my family are cursed when it comes to men. . . ."

She broke off suddenly and drew a breath. "Sorry, nothing personal. Too much information. But you asked. And—other than that," she added with a rueful smile, "life's been peachy."

Yeah, I bet. So peachy you grew up living in fear. And then in foster care. With a pretty well-earned distrust of every man who might come into or go out of your life at will.

That didn't even count an unplanned pregnancy and raising a child alone, he realized.

Aw, damn.

"Well, I'm not leaving." Jake got to his feet and reached down to help her up. "Not for long, at least. I'll try not to be gone for more than a week or two at a time. And for what it's worth, I don't lie or cheat or break things. Don't lose my temper much, either. It's not the way I roll. When I say I'll be here for you and Emma, I mean it."

She looked like she wanted to believe him, but didn't.

"If you hurt her, I'll never forgive you."

"I'd never hurt her. . . ." Jake tugged her closer. "If I did, believe me, I'd never forgive myself."

Something strange happened in that moment as Carly stared at him. She realized she sort of *did* believe him. At least, she wanted to. She was searching for some sign of weakness or hesitation, but saw only the determined jut of his jaw,

211

those dark blue eyes more direct and piercing than the sun.

His arms went around her waist. She tried to stay relaxed. And immune. He obviously had no idea what being this close to him could do to a woman. *Any woman,* she thought. Her breath hitched in her throat and she swore her pulse was racing like a wild mustang across open range in an old episode of *Bonanza.*

"Friends trust each other; they count on each other. I think that's the kind of friends we can be." His voice was low. "I plan to spend as much time with Emma as I can. I won't be able to live in Lonesome Way full-time," he cautioned, "but I'll be here to see her a lot. And whenever you or Emma need me, I'll only be a phone call away."

"*I* don't need anything from you," she corrected him quickly. She was about to add: *And Emma doesn't need anything, either.*

But she stopped herself. Because it wasn't true. Emma deserved a chance to have her father in her life. She couldn't deprive her of that, not if Jake really wanted to step up.

But who was to say he'd follow through? His intentions might be honorable, but he could very well lose interest after the next rodeo rolled around—or after the next curvaceous blonde he met at a bar crooked her little finger at him.

Protecting Emma had to be her priority. Not to mention protecting herself. Being around Jake

Tanner could do strange things to a woman. Make her light-headed. Unsettled. Yearning for things she couldn't have.

Like one more night in bed with him.

Not going to happen, she told herself fiercely.

"I need time to think everything through," she heard herself say carefully. "I can't let Emma be hurt—"

"I'd never do that. You don't need to protect her from me, Carly. Or try to keep me out of her life. I have a right to be part of it—and I intend to be. Seriously, what kind of a jerk do you think I am? I'd never neglect or hurt her. That's a promise."

"I know you wouldn't do it on purpose."

"Not any which way."

He sounded so sure. She felt tiny holes cracking in all her defenses. It hit her full-on in that moment that Jake wasn't anything like Kevin. He wasn't a liar, a cheat, or prone to smashing the nearest thing at hand when life didn't go his way.

Jake was a wanderer, yes, but he came from a family that cherished their connections to each other. And he was promising to be around for Emma. Maybe not all the time, but maybe enough . . . enough so that she'd know she had a father who loved her. That she'd have him in her corner, too, as well as her mother.

Life could be hard. Carly of all people knew that. Emma should have all the love and support she could get in this world. She deserved that.

She gulped, realizing suddenly that she had no choice. She had to trust him. At least a little, enough to give him a chance.

"Okay. We'll try." She swallowed. "We'll try to be friends."

"What are the odds you could add in the smallest trace of conviction there?" His lips quirked up in a dazzling smile.

Oh, it wasn't easy to resist that smile. Warmth curled in her belly. "Trust me, I'm working on it," she said as lightly as she could.

Still his strong hands lingered at her waist.

It wasn't a conscious decision to inch closer to him, but somehow she did just that. Her breasts were pressed right up against his chest, and his mouth was close enough that if he just leaned down and forward ever so slightly . . .

Jake watched her eyes, wide and cautious as she looked at him. She hadn't tensed or pulled away, though, and her body felt soft and willing and inviting as hell. *God, she's lovely,* Jake thought.

She was so damned sexy, in a mouthwateringly tempting kind of way, and at the same time there was something soft and fragile about her, something that tore at a place in him he hadn't known still existed. Not since Melanie . . .

But Melanie had been scared, vulnerable. And Carly . . .

Beneath that fragile, girl-next-door beauty, Jake sensed tremendous strength at Carly's core.

A kind of fierce resolution that could only come from bravery. She was completely, ferociously devoted to her daughter. *Their* daughter. He reminded himself that he needed to be concentrating only on Emma as well.

He and Carly could be partners in raising her, nothing more. This whole situation was already complicated enough. He couldn't do anything that would make it more so. . . .

But it felt so damned good to touch her.

Don't go there, man. Don't even think for a second about going there.

Yet, when an even colder gust of wind suddenly rattled down from the Crazies, his arms seemed to draw her protectively closer of their own accord. Then—despite his better judgment—he did something impulsive.

He lowered his head and kissed her.

It wasn't meant to be a long kiss. But her lips were even softer, even sweeter tasting than he remembered. Like wildflowers and silk and sunshine. To his surprise, he couldn't pull back from the kiss, and his mouth lingered on hers for a long time.

Apparently she didn't have any objections, Jake realized, because her lips parted responsively as she kissed him back. They were the softest lips —as sweet, as decadent as candy. He almost groaned at the deliciousness of her, at the brush of her soft curves against his body.

Heat roared through him when he heard her soft mew of pleasure. And every muscle in his body tightened. He deepened the kiss still further, sliding his fingers through her thick, fiery curls, encouraged by another little moan of pleasure.

God, he knew he shouldn't touch her. Or kiss her. But she was in his arms, warm and soft and close, and something about her seemed to pull him in. . . .

Then as a twig snapped overhead, he felt her stiffen suddenly and pull back against his grip.

"Oh, God, Jake. No." Her voice was a stricken gasp. "What are we *doing?* We *can't.* . . . I *won't.* . . ."

She was right. He knew she was right. This could go south in too many ways to count unless they kept everything boiled down to a simple, businesslike friendship.

But there was nothing businesslike about that kiss. And nothing about it *felt* wrong. He had to bite back a groan as she yanked away from him, her cheeks flushed the pink of new roses, her eyes locked on his.

"This can't happen. It *won't.*" She sounded shaken and shook her head as the wind blew strands of bright curls across her cheeks. "We're going to try to be friends and friends only. Things are complicated enough as they are."

"Agreed." Releasing her, Jake took a step back and shoved his hands in his pockets. "You're one hundred percent right. Sorry about that. It won't happen again."

"It better not." Her spine ramrod straight, as if she'd had no part in what had just happened between them and hadn't enjoyed it in the least, she spun and started back toward the house with long, assertive strides. Jake watched, captivated by the sensuous sway of her hips as she walked away from him.

For a moment he couldn't stop staring, but then he dragged his mind from all the things he'd love to do to her, *with* her, and concentrated on reality.

Focus, you damned fool. None of those things are going to happen. Not a single one.

Given their new arrangement—they were all off-limits.

"So," he said after he easily caught up to her, then slowed, matching his longer stride to hers, "when do I get to spend time with Emma again? Do you have a girls' night out coming up soon? I'll babysit."

"Brave man." Carly's heartbeat was finally returning to normal. So, she hoped, was her sanity. She only needed to stay a reasonable distance from Jake Tanner and she'd be *fine*. Absolutely *fine*. "Do you really think you're ready to handle her and Bug all alone?"

"Sure. Piece of cake."

"I hate to tell you this, but you have a lot to learn."

"I'm a quick study. And very motivated."

"My next night out is the auction," she told him as they cleared the trees and his brother's house came into sight. "I happen to need a babysitter for that night, if you think you're up for it."

"You mean the dating auction?" He frowned. "I heard something about that. You running the show or something?"

"Hardly. I've been roped into auctioning myself off to the highest bidder."

"You?" His eyes narrowed just a little. "I thought you said you didn't date."

"I don't. I *didn't* . . . but I couldn't get out of this." She shrugged. "Ava Todd doesn't know how to take no for an answer. And besides, everyone I know is volunteering. Even Madison. Martha offered to stay with Emma that night if I really need her to babysit, but she's helped Ava and Dorothy Winston plan the whole event. I know she'd love to be there and see how it comes off. I was planning to ask Ivy to babysit, but she's been invited on a weekend trip with her friend Shannon Gordon's family, so . . ."

There was a small, expectant silence just as they reached the deck. Through the sliding doors, Carly could see Madison laughing as she played ring around the rosie with Emma, Molly, Aiden, and Zoey, all of their hands linked together as part of a circle.

Emma and her cousins.

She glanced over at Jake and saw he was watching them, too. Or it seemed like he was.

"How about if I hunt up another babysitter for Emma?" he suggested. "And I go to the auction instead. I'll bid on you so you won't have to go out with some strange yahoo who can't get a date on his own."

As she said nothing, just stared at him, he offered a shrug and a heart-melting smile. "I'm always happy to help a lady out of a tight spot."

"I'm sure you are." She tried to ignore the fact that her heart had just skipped a beat. Make that two beats. *Friends,* she told herself. *Only friends. That's all you can handle.* "This lady will have to take her chances, because what I really need is a babysitter for my daughter. *Our* daughter," she amended pointedly.

"Ouch. Then I guess that would be me."

The smile had faded from his face. In the late afternoon light, as the sun slid west toward the mountains, he met her gaze, his expression serious.

"All kidding aside, I'll be here for you," he told her quietly. "Whenever I possibly can. All you have to do is ask."

His steady tone made something squeeze tight inside her. Why did he have to be so nice? So naturally easy and low-key and—okay, she had to be honest here—so utterly sexy as only a strong, laid-back, "I can handle anything you toss at me" cowboy could be. One or the other or both would be hard enough, but all of those qualities combined . . .

She fought the urge to fling her arms around those broad shoulders, to stretch up on tiptoe and kiss those casually smiling lips again.

She hadn't kissed a man since the night Jake got her pregnant and here he was in her own backyard, so to speak—the only man she yearned to kiss. Just one more time.

But she couldn't. Not now. Not ever.

They'd made a deal to be friends. Nothing more. She had to stick to that and set the tone. Obey the ground rules. For Emma's sake. Or else things could go very wrong, and Jake might leave, and Emma . . .

Emma could end up devastated.

"Just remember when you get home that night"—Jake shoved open the sliding door on the deck for her and his lips quirked upward into a grin—"if the yahoo walks you up on the porch and makes some unwanted moves, I'll be there, too. Within calling-out distance."

"How would you possibly know if the moves are unwanted?"

"Easy. We'll work out some prearranged hand signals."

A huff of laughter escaped her, but she tried to make it sound like a cough. "You'll have *your* hands full with Emma. I'll fend for myself."

And with the words she forced herself to offer him nothing more than a cool smile before she brushed past him and into the house.

Chapter Thirteen

"Well, what do you know."

Surprise charged through Brady as he drank his beer in the cavelike darkness of the Spotted Pony.

The place was a dive. No doubt about that.

It was small and crowded and dark, with sticky wood-planked floors, all sorts of moose and deer antlers lining the paneled walls, a jukebox and a pool table that had seen better days—and not much else in the way of decoration.

But the music rocking the joint was a whole lot better than he'd ever expected. *They're not bad,* he thought, *not bad at all. Actually, they're damned good.*

The Spotted Pony Bar and Grill perched on a cliff twenty miles outside of town, halfway up Eagle Mountain. Tonight it was packed to the rafters—which wasn't saying much as it couldn't hold more than fifty people, tops.

The air was thick with smoke and filled with the smells of spilled beer and whiskey, greasy burgers and fries, all mingled with cheap perfume and too much aftershave clinging to the various bikers and truckers and cowboys and their women who frequented the place.

Delia Craig and Eddie Chisholm sang their hearts out front and center on the small make-shift stage, belting out a vigorous cover of Shania Twain's "You're Still the One." They sang with a gusto that had boots tapping and people humming along. Eddie was on fire with his guitar, and slightly behind them, Steve Tuck played the drums like nobody's business. Even so, Brady found himself unable to keep from watching Madison. Though it was difficult to see her clearly, he could still make out her distinctive, richly spiraling voice singing backup. He couldn't get a good glimpse of her face since she was tucked way in the back, farthest from the lights that glowed around Delia and Eddie.

It looked like she was wearing her usual dark sweatshirt and jeans, as if she were trying to be invisible, to blend into the darkness and dingy walls. But her voice, rich and low and as pure as a starry night, penetrated the darkness and made him stare.

She was better than good. Better even than Delia, who sang with verve and sass and power. Madison sang with soul. And heart. And the quiet grit of passion.

It was Delia with her long, swingy, honey-colored hair, bright tangerine lipstick, tight purple T-shirt, and snug jeans decorated with glitter who got all the hands clapping, the boots stamping, and the whistles, but it was Madison's sultry voice that gave substance to the song, that added depth and range and a touch of irresistible sexy exuberance that made it soar.

When the song ended, their last number of the night, the Wild Critters waved to the applauding, boot-stamping crowd and quickly jumped down from the stage.

Brady pushed to his feet and ambled around the tables toward the bar, where Madison was accepting a Coke from the bartender. He watched as she and Delia slid onto the only two empty bar stools in the place. Eddie and Steve were already starting to haul the drums and equipment out the door.

He noticed a couple of other men looking Madison's way, too. Several were in their twenties or early thirties, but one was a short, burly guy of about forty wearing a plaid shirt. He'd started purposefully walking toward the two women at the same time Brady had. But Brady got there first. As he paused before their bar stools, he saw from the corner of his eye that the other man had halted in his tracks, frowning.

Sorry, bud, you're a minute late and five bucks short, he thought in amusement, noting the other man's gut sticking out above his belt buckle.

The guy wore scuffed cowboy boots that had definitely seen better days.

"Great show, ladies." Brady rested a hand at the back of Madison's bar stool. He sent Delia a friendly smile, but his gaze lingered on Madison. "You got a minute?"

" 'Course she does." Delia smiled brightly and took another sip of her Coke, but Madison stared up at him in dismay.

Now, what's that all about? he wondered.

"Only a minute." She bit her lip. "We need to go help the guys load up—"

"Oh, don't worry about that." Delia's crimson-nailed hand lifted in a careless wave. "We'll handle it, Maddy. You and Brady take your time."

She hopped off the bar stool and started toward the door to the parking lot where Eddie and Steve were loading the truck, but a young cowboy with slicked-back hair swung in front of her and asked her to dance. She practically jumped into his arms as the jukebox spun out Jason Aldean's "Hicktown."

"Liked your show." Brady squinted at Madison through the faint haze of smoke in the Spotted Pony. "You're good. I mean, you're *really* good."

"Thanks." She nodded stiffly. "I'm working on writing some songs of my own. Eddie says when they're ready we'll try them out in a couple of shows."

"You know, you're supposed to smile when

someone gives you a compliment," Brady pointed out. "Not look like you're expecting to get snake-bit."

She flushed. "Well, it's not that I don't appreciate what you said, it's just that . . ."

His eyebrows lifted as her voice trailed off.

"I have a feeling there's something bad coming next," Madison blurted. "Like . . ." She lowered her tone, even though it would be impossible for anyone else to overhear with the jukebox spitting out music at full blast. "Like you can't come to the auction, or you've changed your mind about helping me." Nervously, her gaze searched his face.

"Madison, no. You've got it all wrong. I was just about to tell you that I haven't forgotten. I'll be there. A deal's a deal."

"Really?"

Seeing the luminous smile break across her face, Brady felt something twist hard inside his chest. Damn if that smile didn't make him want to move a little closer to her. Even in the baggy navy sweatshirt with her hair pulled back from her face, she was the prettiest girl in the place, hands down. Without even trying.

"There's just one thing." He tried to concentrate only on the conversation, and not on her lush bottom lip or the velvety softness of those caramel-colored eyes. "About the money—"

But before he could explain he had no intention of letting her pay him for the date, the man in the plaid shirt suddenly reappeared and tapped him on the shoulder.

"Excuse me, son. If you're done jawing, I'd like to ask this pretty lady to dance, if you don't mind."

"I'm not your son and I do mind."

The man smirked. "Well, it's up to the lady, isn't it?"

"The lady's sorry, but she's a little too tired to dance after that long show." Madison shot him a smile as she slid off the bar stool. "As a matter of fact, I was just leaving—"

"Hey, c'mon now. We're talking about one little dance." The man stepped quickly past Brady and clamped a burly hand on Madison's arm. "I've seen your picture in the newspaper. Not lately, but a few years ago. You're the beauty queen, right? And now we know you can sing, too. I'd love to be able to say I danced with a beauty queen—"

"The lady gave you an answer. She said *no*." Brady's gaze locked on the other man. "Now, take your hands off her."

"Who are you, kid? Her keeper? The lady doesn't know all the facts yet. It so happens I know someone in the record biz. She might be interested in hearing what I can do for her and her career—"

"Sorry, I'm not interested," Madison told him a little breathlessly, pushing his hand away. "Come on, Brady, let's go."

But as they started forward, the man in the plaid shirt darted around them and stepped in front of her again.

"You're making a big mistake, young lady. I know people. Important people. I could get the Wild Critters a record deal. Just like that!" He snapped his fingers. "But you and me, we have to have a private chat first—"

He got no further.

Brady gave him a shove that sent him toppling sideways into a table. He pitched forward, knocked over a pitcher of beer, then caught himself on the edge of the table as the three cowboys sitting there swore in annoyance. In a flash the man spun back toward Brady, his face red and his fists raised.

But even as Brady took a giant step forward, ready to finish what he'd started, Madison jumped between them, her face white, taut, and pleading.

"Brady, no. Don't hit him! You can't afford to get in any more trouble! Remember?"

"It'll be worth it." Brady's gaze was nailed to the other man's face. "C'mon, step back, Maddy. Out of the way."

"Are you kidding? You could go to jail for assault this time. I'm *not* letting you land behind bars on my account!"

Then Eddie and Steve ran up, their faces flushed, their arms spread as they wedged themselves between Brady and the older man.

227

"Whoa, guys, what do you say we cool things down here?" Eddie was breathing hard.

Looking worried, Steve jabbed a finger at the guy in the plaid shirt. "You need to back off, man. You, too, Farraday."

Delia spoke up quickly. "Our stuff's all loaded. C'mon, guys, it's late. Let's get outta here!"

She grabbed Madison's arm and began pulling her toward the door.

But Madison shook free. She spun back toward Brady.

"I am *not* leaving here without you!"

To her relief, he turned away from the man in the plaid shirt and fell into step beside her and Delia. No one said a word until they were outside the bar.

"Whew. You going to be okay? Want me to drive home with you?" Delia asked Madison in the parking lot as the five of them stood beneath a star-studded sky.

"No way. I'll be fine." Madison gave her a quick hug and smiled at Eddie and Steve. "You guys go on ahead. See you at rehearsal tomorrow night."

When Delia and Steve had both climbed into Eddie's truck, and the three of them disappeared down the rough, dark road leading back to Lonesome Way, she turned to Brady with a shy smile.

The cool night breeze felt good as it swept

down the mountain, blowing away the heat and closeness and noise of the bar.

"We need to get out of here before that jerk comes out the door," she told him.

"Yeah? You have no idea how much I wish he'd walk outside right now. There'd be no witnesses, except for you." Then, at her exasperated expression, he grinned. Reaching out, he brushed his knuckles gently across her cheek.

"Don't worry, I'm not looking for trouble. Thanks for keeping me from doing something stupid. I just didn't like the way he was talking to you. Touching you. He's nothing but a dirty old man."

"It doesn't matter. I can handle jerks like that. It's not worth you going to jail over!"

"It would be worth going to jail if I had the chance to give him a couple of good punches right in the face."

She rolled her eyes. "I wish you wouldn't talk like that. My grandfather already—" She broke off.

"Your grandfather already what? Hates me? Wants to throw me back in jail?"

"He thinks you're trouble."

"What do you think?"

"I think my grandfather is wrong."

"Hey, could it be? Someone actually believes in me?" He let out a low, rueful laugh that dug with astonishing force into her heart. "That would make you the only one who does."

"Not according to what I hear. Rumor has it Jake Tanner asked you to work on the new cabins he's building up near Blackbird Lake. Something about a retreat for bullied kids and their families, right? And he got Denny McDonald to hire you back to your old job."

"Guess it's true what they say. There really are no secrets in this town, are there?" But his tone was lighter as he walked her over to her Silverado and opened the driver's-side door.

"This is Lonesome Way, Brady, remember? If you want to keep secrets, move to the big city—" Madison gave a gasp as a car horn blared suddenly from somewhere on the mountain road. She jumped and nearly stumbled, but Brady's strong hands shot out, planting themselves at her waist to steady her.

"Hey, hey. It's only a car horn. What's up? You okay?"

"I guess." She felt herself flushing. "Maybe a little on edge."

"Because of that creep back there?"

"Yes . . . no. I mean, partly—but that's not the only reason."

She was all too aware that his hands were still clamped to her waist. When had Brady's hands become so firm, so strong? *It must be from working in construction,* she thought. His grip felt good. Steady. Comforting. So did his closeness.

She hadn't been this close to him since they'd

lain side by side in his treehouse when they were kids. Or on the floor of her living room when they were doing homework together in sixth grade. Only then they hadn't even been touching.

Not that she hadn't wished they were.

She forgot all about getting in her pick-up. For the moment, she simply wanted to stay right where she was, looking up into his eyes. He held her gently but firmly. She felt a breathless sensation being this close to him. It almost made her forget why she was feeling jumpy.

"What's the other reason?" His voice sounded husky. In the pale glow of starlight, his gaze was riveted on her as if they were all alone on the planet, not standing outside a bar in a gravel parking lot, with rowdy laughter and shouts streaming softly out to them from an open side window.

"It's nothing. Nothing important."

"Madison, come on. Tell me."

"I've just . . . had a strange feeling lately." She shook her head. "It's silly."

"My dad used to say if you speak a fear out loud, it goes away."

Madison swallowed. "I guess it's worth a try. . . ."

When he didn't say anything, just waited, she took a breath.

"Sometimes lately, I feel like . . . like someone's watching me. It's happened more than once."

Brady's gaze sharpened. "Who would do that?" They'd been just joking around before, but this sounded serious.

"I don't know. It doesn't make sense. And it's not as if I've seen anyone or anything; it's just a feeling. I can't explain it. Once or twice while I was walking Emma in her stroller, I was certain there was someone behind us. I kept stopping and turning around to look, and of course, Blue Bell Drive was empty, and as peaceful as always. But the other day when I took Emma to the park to meet Carly for a picnic lunch, it happened again. Oh, never mind, I'm just being stupid."

Brady pulled her closer. "Listen, we have instincts for a reason. I learned that a long time ago. Remember that time—the blizzard . . . ?" His voice trailed off.

"When you saved that little boy." Madison nodded. "How could I forget?"

"Well, I never told anyone, but I had a feeling that day. I can't explain it. I just knew I had to stay up there, keep looking for him. I knew he was out there, that he was close and I was going to find him. After that, I've always tried to remember to listen to my instincts. You should, too—you need to be careful, Madison. I think you should mention this to your grandfather."

"And worry him for nothing? No way." She shook her head, intensely aware of how close they were standing. She could feel the warmth of

Brady's strapping body and it made her shiver as the wind blew down the mountainside. Despite her sweatshirt, she felt chilled and wanted to snuggle closer to him for warmth. But that was crazy. There had never been anything like that between them—and Brady didn't want there to be.

She had wanted it, but Brady hadn't seen that, and he never would. *Down, girl,* she told herself and forced her gaze from Brady's eyes so she could concentrate on what she was saying.

"If I see anything strange, I'll be sure to tell Gramps," she added. "But it's probably nothing."

The words hung there for a moment between them.

She sounds uneasy, Brady thought. He suddenly became aware that his hands were still wrapped around her waist. Reluctantly, he let them drop to his sides and took a deliberate step back. He dragged his gaze from her upturned face, and his mind away from the direction it kept going in.

Why did he keep wondering what it would be like to kiss Madison in the bed of his truck, to strip her out of those dull, shapeless clothes, to taste her lips, brush his mouth down along her throat . . . to kiss each of her breasts and taste her with his tongue . . .

"Sorry, I've bent your ear long enough." Her soft words broke into the heat of his thoughts. " 'Night, Brady, see you at the auction."

"Yeah, sure. See you."

It came out sounding gruff. He frowned as she turned away, springing up behind the wheel of her truck before he could even give her a steadying hand. As he watched the battered old Silverado rattle away down the mountain, an empty feeling came over him.

Brady had kissed lots of girls in Lonesome Way, but he'd never kissed Madison. He'd never even thought about it, not once, until now. Now that they were on their way to getting along again after all these years, it definitely wasn't a good time to start changing things up.

Back away from the beauty queen, he ordered himself.

But, unlike the jerk in the Spotted Pony, he knew that Madison was so much more than that title she hated.

She was a lot more.

And she deserved better than him and anything he could offer her.

That thought made him curse as he climbed onto his bike, and a scowl settled over his face. He gunned the engine and tore out of the parking lot, leaving the smoke and music and scent of spilled beer in his dust.

The moment Brady's vehicle took the first curve down the mountain, the tall, muscular man with the close-cropped brown hair and stubbly beard stepped from behind a green van. It had been parked only a few dozen feet away from where the two young people had been talking.

He lit a cigarette, inhaled deeply. He was nearing fifty, and he knew some folks might think he was too old for all this.

But to hell with that. He wasn't. Not yet.

Not by a long shot.

So far, he'd come up with nada, except those pictures he'd taken at the park the other day and sent through his phone. But he hadn't gotten close enough. Time to step up his game.

That tall kid in the parking lot had talked about instincts. *Well, hell,* he thought, blowing smoke into the frigid night air. He'd been *born* with instincts. Instincts that kept him alive. Instincts that kept him in enough dough to survive. Instincts on how to get anything he needed.

And he needed something now. No more nosing around.

Time to close in on the prize.

Eyes narrowed, he began to think creatively, deciding he didn't have time to take it slow any longer. He wasn't getting paid if he didn't produce the goods. Clamping the cigarette between his teeth, he loped back to his Dodge truck and hefted his powerful frame behind the wheel.

Then he followed the other two vehicles as they snaked their way down the mountain and along the road to Lonesome Way.

Chapter Fourteen

"Please tell me it's not too late to back out."

Laureen clutched Carly's arm, her eyes wide as they waited in the back room of the Double Cross Bar and Grill for their names to be called. The dating auction had begun a few moments earlier, and the deafening roar of men yelling, cheering, whistling, and applauding out in the packed bar and restaurant area made them both stare at each other, not knowing whether to laugh or make a run for it.

Big Billy, the huge tattooed bartender and owner of the Double Cross, had stuck his fierce head in the door right before the auction began and told all the women that if anyone felt uncomfortable with whoever seemed likely to win a date with them, they should wink at him, and he'd make sure Rudy, his cook, or one of the dishwashers in back topped the bid and gave them an out.

"Nice guy, I guess, always has been," Laureen had murmured as she stood, getting jostled, between Carly and Tansy Noble. She and Big Billy usually avoided each other, and had ever since she'd snubbed him in high school. Though once he *had* offered to beat the crap out of her ex-husband when word got out that he'd cheated on Laureen and they were getting a divorce. She'd thought it was awfully sweet of him, and totally out of the blue, but she hadn't taken him up on it. Nice guy or not, there was no way she'd ask him to do her any favors.

"There's a lot of nice guys in Lonesome Way," Carly said. "Let's just hope some of them are here tonight."

"How did we get ourselves into this?" Worrying her lower lip between her teeth, Laureen fluffed out the skirt of her floaty blue-green dress, which fell to just below her knees.

"It's for the animals," Carly muttered. "Just think about the animals."

"I am. The animals out *there*." Laureen managed a weak smile as she jerked her thumb toward the main room of the bar, where "It's Raining Men" blasted from the jukebox.

Carly took a breath and tried to tune out all the noise and shouting.

She wished the auction were over already. She wondered how Jake was doing back at home with Emma and that bag-of-bones dog of his.

Hopefully Bronco wouldn't howl. Or hide Bug. Or eat Bug. If he did, Jake was going to have a pretty rough evening.

But he should be able to handle it, she told herself. He's handled crazed bulls and the fevered chaos of the rodeo, and women throwing themselves at him.

He could handle a good-natured little girl with flyaway strawberry curls.

Restlessly, she glanced around her. There were a lot of younger women in their twenties packed in the room, all of them laughing and primping, seeming more excited and confident than uneasy. They were mostly wearing skirts that barely covered their thighs, or scoop-necked, tight-fitting, sparkly tops that didn't leave much to the imagination.

Except for Madison. She looked different from all of the other girls. She'd gone in the opposite direction.

Madison wore faded jeans and black boots and a simple lavender sweater. Her sable hair was brushed, caught in a low, smooth ponytail at her nape, and her only makeup was a blush of cameo pink lip gloss. There were tiny silver studs in her ears.

But she was biting her lips. And pacing. Carly knew Madison must be dreading setting foot on that stage, and as the girl met her eyes, and started toward her, she offered an encouraging smile.

"It'll be over before we know it, right?" Carly said as lightly as she could.

"Can't be soon enough for me." Surprisingly, Madison didn't sound quite as agitated as Carly expected. Before she could ponder this, Madison's friend Delia and a couple of other young women swooped toward her and they all circled around her, chatting excitedly.

Carly glanced toward the doorway leading to the stage Big Billy had allowed to be brought in for the auction, bracing herself for her name to be called.

She felt comfortable enough in her tan suede skirt, chocolate brown boots, and sleek ivory sweater. There was a hint of frost in the air tonight and she'd dressed accordingly. If no man out in that throng wanted to bid on a fully clothed thirty-year-old mother dressed for the chilly fall weather, so be it.

She figured her outfit must look pretty good, though. Jake had seemed to like it.

"You looking to cause a stampede in that bar?" he'd asked her with that slow smile of his when she opened the door to admit him and his dog. Against her will, her heart had fluttered at his words and the appreciative light in his eyes.

The compliment didn't mean anything, though, she told herself. Jake Tanner was a man who probably flirted easily and instinctively with every woman he encountered. He'd have told Laureen or Madison or even one of his sisters-in-law the same thing. Laid-back cowboy charm and politeness came as naturally to him as breathing.

Or riding.

Or lovemaking.

Just as she pushed that last, pulse-quickening thought from her mind, the crowd suddenly went quiet. Then she heard Ava's voice, calm and sweet as always, announcing Laureen's name.

"Go!" She met her assistant's frozen stare. "You're up! It's going to be okay."

But Laureen stood frozen, her face panicked.

"Laureen, honey. You go on out there now." Dorothy Winston, the former school principal and one of the architects of the auction, materialized suddenly. "Hurry up. We have a long ways to go and Big Billy wants us cleared out of here by eleven."

There was no arguing with that authoritative tone, which had been used to deal with everything from tardiness to spitballs to swearing, not to mention cheating, whispering, and scuffling in the classroom.

"Crap crap crap!" Laureen muttered under her breath. She looked like she wanted to bolt out the back door, but, with a grimace, she squared her shoulders, then marched out into the madness. Carly drew a breath of relief and grinned to herself as cheers erupted from the crowd.

Dorothy slipped out and disappeared into a seat in the audience. When Laureen stumbled back-stage a few moments later, she looked more than a little dazed.

"Well, what do you know? Three guys bid on me. One was a ranch hand from the Wild Hills

Ranch. Kind of cute, too! The other was Andy Ford, the mayor's nephew. The last man was someone I didn't recognize. Martha came over and whispered that he's a rancher from Livingston in town buying some horses from Rafe Tanner and decided to stick around for the auction. Guess they all must be blind, right?"

"Oh, please, will you stop? Just tell me who won the grand prize." Carly's stomach began doing crazy flips as she half listened for her own name to be called.

"The rancher. His name is Cal Meeks. He's kinda handsome, too. I guess he's going to call me to set up the date." She shook her head as if she couldn't quite comprehend it. "Holy cow, it's over with. And it wasn't even a total disaster!"

Here's hoping I can say the same, Carly thought, and at that moment Ava announced her name.

"You're going to raise enough money to build the whole shelter!" Laureen squeezed her arm.

Carly relaxed her shoulders right before she stepped out onto the stage. For a moment all she could take in was a massive sea of men. What seemed like a hundred cowboy hats waved in the air. There were some piercing wolf whistles.

Great, just great.

She noticed Big Billy looming behind the bar, his hugely muscled arms crossed over his massive chest, his gaze watchful.

Then all of the men either grinning, whistling,

or cheering as they stared at her on the stage suddenly swirled into a blur.

I may have to kill Ava, she told herself as she sashayed across the stage, pivoted as Dorothy had instructed before the auction began, then returned to the center of the stage, her heart hammering.

A Kenny Chesney hit rocked from the jukebox.

In the front row, she spotted Martha and Dorothy watching her eagerly. Ava was doing the same from the podium at the far left of the stage.

Their eyes were lit up like jack-o'-lanterns, and smiles of pure amusement beamed from their eighty-something faces as the single men of Lonesome Way applauded and whistled and stamped their feet.

Here we go, then. Setting back the women's movement a good sixty or so years, Carly thought, trying to suppress a wry grin as she pivoted again.

No wonder Sophie was fond of calling those three elderly meddlers Bippity, Boppity, and Boo. They seemed to think their sole purpose in life, besides quilting for charity, was to serve as a trio of fairy godmothers. Matchmaking fairy godmothers.

God help us all, Carly thought, as Ava blew her a kiss from the sidelines, Martha gave a thumbs-up from the audience, and Dorothy jabbed her elbow into the stocky man in his late thirties sitting beside her.

With a little jolt of alarm, Carly realized who

he was. Roger Hendricks. Dorothy's divorced nephew. He'd been single for the past seven years and Carly had a pretty good idea why. Roger wasn't exactly a catch. He was blunt and argumentative by nature. According to Lissie, he'd been a nasty bully as a kid and still had a tendency to try to barrel right over people.

Oh, please, no. Don't let it be him, she thought in a panic as his arm shot up and he yelled out a bid. She didn't catch the amount because her brain was screaming: *Why did you ever let Ava talk you into this?*

Then she looked again at the gathered throng, and blinked. Suddenly she didn't see only Roger and a faceless throng of men. Slowly, she made out the faces of the waitresses striding around tables full of men with drinks and platters of burgers and nachos and fries set before them.

One waitress was Evie Stone, who had bought fabric for a quilt for her new daughter-in-law last week. Evie waved at her. Another waitress was Charity Morton, who also worked at Pepperoni's Pizza and was putting herself through college. She'd come into the quilt shop with her mother about a month ago—she was just learning how to quilt and needed a beginner's pattern.

Then Carly saw Luke Pierce, foreman of the Circle M Ranch, and several of the nice young ranch hands from the Tall Trees spread. She saw Adam Fletcher, the new young doctor at the hospital, and Beau Carpenter, who owned a fly-fishing guide business, and Stan Wells, who owned most of the real estate on Main Street.

She saw men she recognized. Nice men. Men she passed every day on the street, men she spoke to at A Bun in the Oven or whom she ran into on her daily errands in town.

These weren't strangers for the most part, though perhaps some of the men had come in from neighboring towns. But these were mostly men she knew.

And suddenly she relaxed.

This wasn't Boston or New York or some seedy bar in a big city. This was Lonesome Way.

It was all going to be okay.

She blanked out as the bidding began, over-whelmed by the volume of the music, the shouting, the cheers.

And then somehow it was over.

"Wash Weston!" the normally genteel, silver-haired Ava called out in a voice that pierced the bedlam.

Wash Weston. She had a date with a widower in his early fifties who owned a prosperous three-thousand-acre wheat farm, and who had once bumped into her as she was coming out of A Bun in the Oven and caused her to drop a banana cream pie, which had splattered across the sidewalk. He'd outbid some cowboys in their twenties and the new doctor at the hospital.

It could have been worse, much worse, but as Carly gave him a wave and a smile and ducked backstage, she couldn't help but grin at Jake's notion that he'd have to protect her from some unwanted overtures on the night of her "date."

Wash Weston with his grave face and slow deliberate walk seemed about as tame a man as you'd find in all of Montana. She doubted he'd try to get her into his bed—but he might just put her to sleep.

Chapter Fifteen

The knock on Madison's door came at midnight, right after she'd stripped off her sweater and jeans and pulled on a comfy pale green sleep tee that reached halfway to her knees.

The knock made her heart skip a beat as she whirled toward the door, fighting panic.

Nobody ever knocked on her door this late.

"Who's there?"

She tried to sound calm and tough, but her voice seemed shaky to her own ears. At least she got the words out through the thickness in her throat.

"Madison, it's me. Brady. Open up."

Brady? Glancing ruefully down at her tee and

her legs, bare from the thighs down, she bit her lip and strode to the door. "What are you doing here?"

"What do you think?"

His Stetson half hid his dark, unreadable eyes, and he straightened from a careless slouch as she stared at him.

"Oh. Right. Of course." He wanted the money she'd promised him. Vivid color flooded her cheeks. "I'm sorry I didn't get a chance to meet you and pay before the auction started, but I had to wait at my grandparents' house for my grandmother's birthday gift to be delivered. It took forever. And it didn't arrive until much later than I expected. It was a piano—from my grand-father—and it took almost an hour for the deliverymen to haul it inside and load her old piano onto the truck—"

"Hold on," he interrupted. "I'm not here about the money."

"You're not? But then . . . why?"

"Making sure you got home and safely inside, that's all. I tailed you on my bike."

Tailed me? On your motorcycle? Madison blinked, startled. "But I never saw you. . . ."

Brady's grin gleamed as bright as lightning. It flashed, then was gone. "I stayed back behind a few cars. You still have the feeling someone's following you? If so, tonight it was me."

"Well, I haven't felt anything too weird, not

lately. . . ." She paused a moment and gave a wry shrug. "I didn't notice you following me, so I must not be as alert as I think I am."

Brady was trying hard not to stare at her lush body, outlined so sensuously in that thin whisper of a tee. It fell to only a couple of inches below her shapely little butt. Unlike the sweatshirts she usually wore, it skimmed close to her body, revealing every sumptuous curve.

His throat went dry. His body felt rock hard. Everywhere.

It took effort, but he managed not to gape like a twelve-year-old who'd never seen a girl up close before. He forced himself to look only into her eyes when he answered her.

"Well, that's what I'm here for. To keep watch. At least until our date. I laid out good money for that date and I don't want anything getting in the way of it."

Despite herself, Madison broke into a smile. Brady had followed her home. He was standing here at her door. Was he really here only because he was worried about her?

"Thanks for sticking to our agreement." She was feeling her way now. "You want to come in? I'll get what I owe you—"

"I told you I don't want your money, Maddy. Never did."

He sauntered after her into the tiny apartment. His tall, strapping body seemed to fill the small space. He swept off his hat, tossed it on a chair, and glanced around.

"Nice digs. Everything here looks like it belongs to you." Brady paused to study the living room with its wide, comfortable-looking cream sofa and scattered bright-patterned pillows, then took in a deep rose armchair, bookshelves filled to the brim, and a cream-and-violet-patterned rug on the floor.

The white bookcase overflowed with books, and there were some pretty colored perfume bottles on a distressed wooden dresser that had also been painted white. *Very girly,* he noted. That was funny coming from a girl who wouldn't wear a dress or a skirt, or much of anything besides those sweats. He wondered suddenly if her bra and panties were as plain and ordinary as her clothes. Because beneath the facade she showed to the world, Madison was anything but dull, anything but ordinary.

Not just because of the vivid beauty she'd possessed since childhood, but because of what shimmered beneath the surface. Everything that fueled the soul and twang of her songs, the layered melodies, the words that hurt and stung and uplifted, bursting like a wound, straight from her heart.

The walls of her tiny apartment were blue, he noticed. The color of a lake. The color of calm.

Her apartment was a studio, and a small one.

But everything was tidy, except for a pair of jeans in a heap on the floor. Madison's prettily made-up bed was in the corner. It had a pale blue coverlet and white-and-yellow-striped throw pillows spilled neatly across it, with a rustic wooden headboard that boasted the carved outline of flowers.

Her guitar was propped against one blue wall, and there was an electric keyboard in a corner. A flute rested across the top of the dresser, too, alongside some textbooks with titles like *Art and Creative Development for K–8 Children* and *Early Childhood Education: Introduction to Music and Movement*.

"I'll get your money." She had lifted her wallet from her purse and was rummaging through it. Pulling out a check, she thrust it at him. "Here. Thanks for—"

"Forget it, Madison. I won't take your money."

Snagging hold of her hand, he closed his fingers around it, just tightly enough to keep the check imprisoned.

"But we had a deal!"

"Truth?" A smile touched Brady's lips. "I had my fingers crossed. I never cared about the money. I was only trying to help you out—get you down off that stage real quick, like you wanted. It's no big deal. Just don't tell anyone. It would damage my sterling reputation as a total jerk."

"Nobody thinks that," she said quickly. "And

you know I don't. But I still don't understand why you won't take the money."

"Maybe I just wanted to help an old friend."

Madison searched his face. "So are you saying we're friends again, Brady? Really?"

"You want to be friends with me, Madison?"

"I guess I wouldn't mind." A saucy little smile curved her lips. Then, suddenly, she yanked her hand free and punched him in the arm. "You jerk! It took you long enough."

Brady laughed, snagged her hand, crumpled up the check she'd written. "You know Margie Shane got married four years ago. She moved to Big Timber last year, with her husband and two kids."

"I heard about that. So when I was gone all those years—did you ever get the chance to kiss her? That's all you used to talk about wanting to do."

"Sure, I did. When I was a stupid kid. And no, I never kissed Margie. She's the one that got away."

"What a shame." Madison slanted an amused glance up at him. "So I guess you'll never know what it's like to kiss the incredibly beautiful, irresistible—let's see, what other things did you say about her? Gorgeous, hot—"

"I think I'll live without kissing her," he drawled. And a grin lit his face as he took a step toward her. She took a step back, and he advanced one more. Then he yanked Madison close, up against his chest.

"But I'm not at all sure I can live another minute without kissing you."

Her heart skidded in all different directions as she gazed up into those cool gray eyes and a moment later, she was kissing him.

She had no idea whether she kissed him first, or the other way around.

All she knew was that her arms had slid around his neck and Brady was holding her tightly, so tightly it felt as if he'd never let her go without a crowbar to pry them apart. Their bodies pressed together, fitting perfectly, and Madison had never felt such heat. Such a storm of need.

She'd had two short-term boyfriends before, and she'd lost her virginity with a third one when she was nineteen, but she'd never felt anything rock her the way Brady's kisses did. He kissed her and kissed her, with a deep hunger that seemed unquenchable. It was as if he was searching some-where inside her for the very center of her soul. His kiss tasted like moonlight and danger and fire. His tongue explored her mouth as if it was hidden treasure, summoning something deep inside her as he waged a sweet teasing battle that left her utterly defenseless. He smelled of saddle leather and spice.

Brady . . .

She was actually, finally, kissing Brady. . . .

The room seemed to spin in slow circles as his big hands stroked her breasts and his mouth burned against hers. She was shaking at the intensity as her lips parted and his tongue went on a search-and-engage mission with hers. Her heart raced as Brady's tongue swept inside, as the taste of him filled her. Her body ached for him in places Madison had never ached before and Brady's stroking hands knew exactly how to fuel the fire jetting through her.

"Maddy," he groaned against her lips. She felt his need, his entire body pressing against her. How many times had she sprawled beside him doing homework, wishing this would happen? She'd only been twelve then and it had never happened, but now it was. . . .

Clinging to him, she traced his lips with her tongue as he eased her backward, back, back, toward her bed. Fire seemed to sear their lips together as they sank down on the comforter and he pulled her onto his lap.

"You've been driving me crazy since the moment you followed me into Benson's Drugstore," he grated as he drew back for a second, his eyes glinting into hers.

"Good," she gasped. "I'm . . . glad." *Because you've been driving me crazy since the moment I met you,* she thought, but she managed to stop herself from saying the words.

She then lost all power to think or to speak as Brady's cool hands skimmed down her hips, hitched up her T-shirt, found the tiny thong she wore, and, as he kissed her, slipped a finger inside the pale peach silk. "Oh, God, you've been driving me crazy ever since you built that treehouse and . . . Brady . . . I don't know why I'm even speaking to you, you were so mean to me. . . ." Another long kiss that made her dizzy. But not dizzy enough to stop telling him everything pent up inside her. "And all because I told Margie—"

"Shhh, baby. I know. I'm sorry about that." He drew back, a remorseful smile on his face as he stared into her eyes, his body tensed and hard with need. "I was a stupid dumb kid back then," he muttered in between kisses. He began to slide that thong down her thighs. . . .

And then her cell phone rang.

Madison jumped. Brady froze, then let out a groan.

"It's . . . probably my grandfather," she gasped, still in his lap, staring at him, caught between longing and obligation. She pulled slowly away, then hopped off Brady's lap, her cheeks burning. "He said he'd call me . . . after the auction. . . ."

"You mean, you're going to *talk* to him? *Now?*" Brady looked like a kid who'd just had his new Christmas gift snatched away.

"He'll keep calling if I don't. He worries about me. He's a sheriff—he imagines all kinds of terrible things if I don't answer my phone!"

Brady realized the ringing of the phone was

coming from the pocket of her jeans. The ones she'd tossed onto the floor before she changed into the tee, which had fallen again now past her hips. He leaned down, snatched up the jeans, yanked out the phone, handed it to her.

"Gramps, hi," she exclaimed brightly.

He sighed, watching her flushed face, listening half in amusement and half in frustration as he sat there on the edge of Madison's bed, frowning as she struggled to talk naturally to her grandfather.

The man who'd arrested him for punching out the lights of his deputy.

The man who'd raise holy hell if he knew that his only granddaughter had been about to get naked with a no-good kid from a family of losers. Brady's father had driven drunk and killed both his wife and himself. Brady's brother had wasted his own life chasing a dream and finding only injury and frustration and ultimately death beneath the bruising heels of an enraged bull.

And Brady had been locked up, at least for a while, in her grandfather's very own jail.

"No, everything went fine with the delivery," she was saying a little breathlessly. "They were late getting there, but Grams's piano is in place and it looks awesome. Grams will be thrilled. Oh . . . yes, the auction. It wasn't too bad. No . . . not at all. Who . . . *won the date with me?*"

Her voice cracked on the word "date."

Brady watched with raised brows as her wide eyes locked on his.

"Well, um . . . actually, Gramps, it's Brady who won the date with me. No, he wasn't the only one who bid on me, but . . ."

He watched her eyes close for a moment. Watched her wince as she listened carefully. And something tightened in his stomach.

"No, Gramps, it's nothing like that. You're wrong. Brady and I—we're friends again now. And I'll be perfectly all right. Brady bid on me out of kindness because he knew I didn't want to . . ."

Brady didn't hear the rest. He was already at the door, yanking it open, bounding into the hall. He turned back and met her startled gaze for one instant before he pulled the door shut and took off down the hallway, his boots thumping on each step of the single flight of stairs.

He'd be damned if he could listen to any more.

Madison didn't deserve grief from her grandfather because of him.

He had to get this under control. Right now. Whatever *this* was. He'd never intended to kiss Madison or touch her or end up anywhere near her bed with her when he'd gone to her room.

All he'd wanted was to make sure she was all right. That she hadn't sensed anyone following her over the past few days. To make certain she wasn't scared.

But why should she be scared? She had

Lonesome Way's sheriff to protect her. Maybe he was out of town right now, but he'd be back. And Teddy Hodge wouldn't need any help taking care of his granddaughter.

Madison didn't need him. Just the opposite. He'd only cause trouble for her. Hodge would give her an earful of grief about why associating with him was bad for her. And he'd mostly be right.

Madison had already gone through a terrible breach with her mother. She didn't need to have Brady come between her and her grandparents now. Teddy and Joanie Hodge were basically the only family she had left.

His jaw hardening, he slipped out of her building and strode toward his Harley. Just because he'd messed up his own life didn't mean he had a right to mess up hers. As he swung a leg over the bike, he tried not to think of how sweet she'd tasted when she kissed him, how her lips seemed to melt into his. Or of how soft and eager she'd felt in his arms. Or of what might have happened next, if the phone hadn't interrupted them.

Her thong might have been on the floor alongside her jeans in another second. Her T-shirt would have gone next. . . .

Brady grimaced and accelerated down Coyote Road, leaving the town behind in a blinding blast of dust.

He'd spent a lot of time alone since his parents died and even more after he got the news that Cord was dead. But he knew he'd never felt quite as alone as he did now, roaring off on his bike, the first bitter frost of winter snapping through his leather jacket. It chilled him deep to the bone as he tore through the vast and starless night.

Chapter Sixteen

Two weeks later, Carly stood beside the racks of colorful fabric in her shop, trying to focus as Professor Penelope Andrews, a member of Montana's Circle of American Masters, spoke about unified quilt design for nontraditional quilters.

Every available space in Carly's Quilts was packed with folding chairs, women, handbags, and refreshments. All of the quilters in Bits and Pieces—and a few others from neighboring towns with their own quilting groups—were crowded in to listen to the seminar by one of the most popular speakers in the state.

Penelope had donated her usual speaker's fee to the animal shelter fund-raiser and Sophie had supplied the refreshments, which would be served after the talk, free of charge. The quilters would be offered a choice of sandwiches from A Bun in the Oven—roast beef or tuna with melted cheddar, plus creamy potato salad and cole slaw for each attendee, along with a big tray of caramel brownies. Carly was supplying the paper plates, napkins, coffee, and tea, along with pies—two of Annie's specialties, which she'd baked early that morning. A luscious peach-raspberry pie and a lemon meringue.

So far the event was going well. But as the professor reached the end of her talk and began taking questions from the audience, Carly noticed Wash Weston stride past the quilt shop window and she suddenly lost the thread of the talk as her mind began to wander.

Her date with Wash had gone off without a hitch. Well, without too much of a hitch. Wash had been a perfect gentleman the entire time they were at dinner at the Lucky Punch Saloon. They'd talked about his farm, and how his son was studying agriculture in college, and how Wash hoped to turn things pretty much over to him by the time his son graduated. Wash looked forward to being able to kick back and see a bit more of the world.

He told her how he'd always wanted a daughter, but instead he had three boys. He asked her about Emma. Hinted that it must be hard raising her alone. His wife had died when his youngest boy was twelve so he knew what that was like.

He seemed lonely and was a perfect gentle-man—until they returned to Blue Bell Drive and he walked her to her door, then leaned in to give her what she'd expected would be a chaste good-night kiss on the cheek.

"I enjoyed our date, Carly. Wouldn't mind doing it again sometime," he said in a grave tone.

"It was a very nice evening." Carly smiled non-committally. Wash wasn't the most exciting man in the world but he was pleasant, and unfailingly polite, and it didn't seem necessary to explain to him that she didn't really date—or why.

Maybe he wouldn't call her again. If he did, she'd just say she was busy.

Which was the truth. She *was* busy—with Emma.

Though Jake was watching her daughter tonight, in a few days he was leaving for Salt Lake City to shoot that commercial.

Besides, she and Wash had pretty much exhausted every avenue of conversation by the time he drove her home. Not to mention the fact that he was nearly twenty years older than she was.

But the quiet, gentlemanly farmer had a surprise in store for her. After that quick, chaste cheek kiss, he suddenly grabbed her waist with both beefy hands and tried to plant his mouth on her lips.

Carly thrust her fists against his chest and pushed him away before he could.

"Good *night,* Wash." Her tone was firm, but she forced out a brief smile to take the edge off.

"Honey, you know there's more where that came from," he told her with a mixture of hopefulness and eagerness. She was so taken aback she froze for a moment, and then he reached for her again. Instinctively, she stepped back.

"No, Wash," she said quickly. "There isn't." And at that moment the door opened. Jake strolled onto the porch.

And he wasn't alone.

Bronco squeezed out, too. The formerly down-on-his-luck mutt didn't look nearly as emaciated these days, and his tail wagged happily as he ambled toward Carly.

But aside from dropping one hand to his golden head for a little absentminded pat, she barely noticed. Her gaze was locked on Jake.

"Evening, Wash." The smile on his face was cool. A glint of steel hardened his eyes.

"Jake Tanner?" Wash's gaze had sharpened. "What are you—"

"Babysitting Emma," Jake interrupted him, hooking his thumbs in the pockets of his jeans.

Wash appeared at first stunned, then puzzled, as his hands fell from Carly's waist. "You two . . . uh, the two of you . . . Are you . . ."

"Yep." Jake nodded. "We are."

Carly felt herself flushing. *We are what?* she wondered in annoyance. She didn't know what

260

the hell Jake thought he was doing, but she had to admit he'd made his appearance at a propitious moment.

Still, after Wash was gone she'd need to set him straight on a couple of things. . . .

"Thanks again for dinner, Wash. Good night." She started toward the door, but not before catching a glimpse of the farmer's crestfallen expression.

"Yeah. Guess I'll be seeing you around." It was a disappointed mumble and on the words, Wash turned away and trod heavily down the steps.

"I suppose I should thank you, but was that really necessary?" she demanded once she and Jake and Bronco were alone inside her cheerful hallway and the front door was firmly closed.

And locked by Jake.

"Thought I'd give you a hand. It was obvious you were having trouble getting rid of him. You're too nice—at least to *him*. Wash didn't seem to be getting the message that his one-shot deal was over and done."

"I'm perfectly capable of getting my own messages across by myself." She led the way across the hall and into the living room. "Did Emma go right to sleep? Did you have any problems?"

"Aside from throwing peas all over the floor for Bronco to eat while we were having supper and making me read her five stories about Bitsy

Bunny before I could turn out the light, it was a snap. Oh, and she kept asking me to sing some song but I didn't know it."

" 'Five Little Monkeys'?"

"Yeah!" Jake raked a hand through his jet-black hair. "You'd better teach it to me. She kept waving her arms, trying to sing it, and getting very frustrated that I wouldn't participate."

"I'll loan you the CD." But Carly was having a hard time holding back a laugh. She could just picture big, tough Jake Tanner, the bull rider, trying to sing "Five Little Monkeys Jumping on the Bed."

"Emma's definitely a girl who knows what she wants," he informed her with a touch of pride as she sank down on the sofa and kicked off her black pumps.

"You think?" Carly grinned. "Don't get me wrong, she's as sweet as Sophie's cinnamon buns, but she's a munchkin with a mind of her own."

"I'd expect no less." He moved toward her with his lithe cowboy gait and dropped down beside her on the very feminine sofa, stretching his long, jean-encased legs as far as he could with the coffee table in the way. Instantly, her heartbeat revved up.

Damn, why did he always have this crazy effect on her?

"She looks just like you, Carly. You gotta know that. Soft, sweet, beautiful. I'm not trying to sweet-talk you here," he added matter-of-factly. "Just stating the truth."

"Actually, she has your eyes. That deep, dark, amazing blue . . ." Carly suddenly became aware how close together they were sitting. He was less than a foot away. She could almost feel the heat and strength radiating off his powerful body. In a tan and black flannel shirt and faded jeans, he certainly looked unlike any babysitter she'd ever used since the day Emma was born.

She had a quick, distracting flash of that intense, intoxicating night that Emma had been conceived, seeing in her mind's eye the spectacularly muscled chest beneath that shirt, the powerful forearms and tanned glisten of his skin as his mouth slid with excruciating slowness down the entire length of her body . . . the feel of him pumping inside her . . .

And then . . . and then . . .

Carly blinked. Someone had said her name. It was Penelope Andrews. She had finished speaking and the women gathered at the quilt shop were now out of their chairs, chattering enthusiastically and helping themselves to coffee and sandwiches, pie, and brownies throughout the shop.

"Professor Andrews." Jolting back to the present, Carly focused on the woman's round, pleasant face as conversation bubbled everywhere throughout Carly's Quilts. "We all enjoyed your talk very much." She spoke quickly, a flush climbing up her neck. "It was fascinating. And we so appreciate your taking the time to come today."

The words were the truth. The woman was well-spoken and informed. The part of the talk Carly had actually listened to had been quite helpful as well as entertaining, but somehow . . . somehow . . .

Jake had taken over her brain.

It wasn't like her to tune out that way. In high school and college she'd learned to focus and to channel her attention to whatever task was before her. In her previous life, she'd delivered complicated financial reports to the entire board of directors of Marjorie Moore without losing her train of thought or breaking into a sweat.

But now—all she seemed able to do was focus on Jake and Emma.

It amazed her how good he was with her. Better than good, he was great. She had to admit he had more patience even than she did and was the most laid-back, easygoing man she'd ever met.

He let Emma muss up his hair, pull his ears, play with the buttons on his shirt. She'd gotten into the habit of climbing onto his lap with Bug in tow every time he dropped by to see her. As long as she wanted, he held her on Bronco's back as if the dog were a pony, and the mutt's tail never stopped wagging as he walked around the house or across the backyard with Jake holding Emma in place as she yelled, "Ride 'em, cowwoy!"

He'd promised Carly he'd teach Emma to ride for real in a couple of years. His first pony, Dakota, was now eighteen, gentle as a puppy dog—and in retirement at Sage Ranch. "By the time Emma's four, I'll have her riding like a rodeo queen," he'd told Carly and she wasn't sure whether to be pleased or alarmed.

"Something I need to tell you." Ava's whisper interrupted her thoughts. Suddenly Carly glanced up and realized that nearly all the quilters had left. Only a few remained, along with Laureen, Ava, Martha, and Dorothy, and they were all busy dividing up and packing the leftover brownies and pie and washing off platters and plates and cups.

Ava jerked her regal chin toward the front of the quilt shop, farthest away from where the other women were working, and, mystified, Carly followed her to the parlorlike sitting area of comfy chairs.

"I *know*," Ava whispered. Her eyes danced with a conspiratorial gleam. "About you and *Jake*."

Her heart stopped so fast she thought she was going to fall over. "You know *what* exactly?"

"Why, that he's Emma's father." Ava's dimples popped out as a wide smile spread across her face. "And I'm awfully glad to hear it. It's time that boy quit running here and there and finally settled down."

"He's not settling down anywhere—and how

did you know?" Carly demanded in a low tone.

"Well, now, honey, how do you think?"

Carly closed her eyes with a sigh. "Martha," she muttered, opening her eyes to study the other woman.

"Of course it was Martha. She only told me the other day, though. You see, while I was working the cash register at A Bun in the Oven a few days ago, Willa Martin came in to buy some cupcakes and she happened to mention that Jake had been spending quite a bit of time over at your place. She's seen that dog of his in your front yard a lot, not to mention Jake's truck in the neighborhood nearly every day." Ava's smile widened even further as Carly drew in her breath.

"So," Ava continued, "I simply mentioned it to Martha, and she got all flustered. Now, we've been best friends since grade school and she can't lie to me, so I finally got it out of her. But don't worry, dear, the only other person we've told is Dorothy—and she's tickled about it. We won't say a word to anyone else. Still . . ." Ava shook her head and whispered a warning. "Word is bound to leak out sooner or later. This is Lonesome Way, after all, and it's nearly impossible to keep a secret in this town. Willa will surely tell someone else that Jake is always around—"

"That's ridiculous. He's *not!*" But Carly knew her protest was futile as Ava patted her arm gently, looking amused.

"Of course he isn't, dear. Not that it's anybody's business. It certainly isn't mine. But I'd be lying if I didn't say that the three of us agree that the three of you—you, Jake, and Emma—would make a lovely family—"

"Ava!" Martha hissed suddenly and both Carly and Ava jumped.

Martha had materialized out of nowhere, exactly like a fairy godmother, Carly thought, but she could only stare at this particular godmother with narrowed eyes.

"You told her, Ava, didn't you?" Martha scowled at Sophie's silver-haired grandmother.

"I merely wanted Carly to know that all three of us are aware that Jake is Emma's father and that we're behind her one hundred percent no matter what happens—"

"Shhh!" Carly gasped as Dorothy suddenly appeared right behind Martha.

"No matter what happens about *what?*" the former principal inquired softly, with a glance toward the back of the shop. Then she saw the expression on Carly's face.

"Oh. *That.* We're talking about *Jake.*" She nodded sagely. A grin widened her chipmunk cheeks. "No worries, dear. None at all." She waved a hand in the air. "We know you had your reasons for not telling him the truth way back then." Her whisper grew to a stage whisper and had Carly's spine tightening in alarm.

Carly's glance flew to the back of the shop again, but thankfully that sharp-tongued Gloria Cartwright, on a prolonged break from her shift at Lickety Split, was busy poring over a pattern book, and the other women were mostly chatting among themselves and paying no attention to what was being discussed in the front of the shop.

"But now that Jake is here," Dorothy continued, "and spending so much time with you and little Emma, someone's bound to notice and put two and two together. It's not much use trying to keep secrets in a town like ours—"

"Apparently it's futile." Carly whipped a glance at Martha, who blinked guiltily, then shrugged.

"Well, I didn't mean to tell. But Ava wouldn't stop pestering me. Willa Martin had gone on and on about the amount of time Jake and Bronco have spent at your house—and about how Jake babysat Emma the night you went on your date with Wash. She happened to have her window open that evening and she claims she heard him tell Wash flat-out that the two of you were . . . were . . ."

"Together," Ava filled in helpfully. "That's what the young people say now."

"We're not together! We're not . . . anything . . . of the sort. . . ." Carly caught herself, and bit her lip. It was true. Jake hadn't so much as *touched* her any of the times he'd come over to spend time with Emma since the day of Zoey's birthday party.

Not that she didn't want him to.

Every time he was within ten feet of her, hot little licks of desire trembled along her skin. But he was sticking to his end of the bargain and she would, too. For Emma's sake. And for her own.

It wasn't in the cards for her to be with a man. Any man. Especially a loner of a cowboy who answered only to the call of the rodeo and the open road.

And who would soon be taking off for months at a time, risking his life on a near daily basis while he rode enraged bulls until they bucked him off and possibly stomped him to death. Dancing and drinking beer in rowdy bars at night with pretty, scantily clad women all too eager to fall into his arms, into his bed. . . .

As *she* had only a few years ago. . . .

Her stomach clenched.

Now, a man like Wash Weston, she told herself, would be perfect. He was older, settled, and he wanted a daughter. But she'd felt only a desire to pull away when he'd reached for her, tried to kiss her.

On the other hand, all Jake had to do was walk into a room and her heart started bouncing around like a pinball in her chest and she ached all over for . . . for what? For him to kiss her? To wrap her in his arms, carry her off somewhere, and make her forget that she was now a sane, stable woman, no longer that heartbroken girl, trying to banish the memory of a lying, cheating jerk?

She had a home now. A sweet, beautiful child. She had a business, friends, a town where she belonged. She didn't need anything or anyone else. She didn't need Jake Tanner stirring up her life, stealing away all the calm and peace of mind she'd worked so hard to come by.

Suddenly out of the corner of her eye she noticed Georgia Timmons thumbing through a pattern book only a few feet away. And glancing sideways in their direction.

The girl who'd been voted in high school as Most Likely to Take Over the World wore skinny pink jeans, boots, and a glittery denim jacket. Crap. Had Georgia overheard any of the conversation? All of it?

Her heart sank as Mrs. Pretty in Pink met her eyes, closed the pattern book with a snap, and drifted over, smiling.

"I'm sorry, I couldn't help overhearing. You're not what, Carly? And with who?" she inquired with a smirky kind of smile. Her blond hair fell in flawless waves to her shoulders and her eyes flitted over each woman in the little group.

Georgia liked wearing pink almost as much as she liked being in charge of everything. She was the refreshment chair again, as always, for the town's upcoming fund-raiser. She *had* been every year for as far back as Carly—and Martha— remembered. And she would be, Martha had told

Carly once privately, until she was lowered into the ground and a pile of earth heaped atop her casket.

"Come on, now, what secrets are you ladies keeping? Carly, is there something we should know?" she asked in a tone that was at once teasing and suspicious.

"If there was, you'd be the first person I'd tell." Carly managed to pull off a breezy smile just before she changed the subject. "Georgia, I'll need to know how many cakes, pies, and whatever else you'd like me to bake for the fundraiser. Since it's just before Thanksgiving, I thought pumpkin pies would be appropriate. Or pecan pies. And I have a recipe for a maplewalnut tart that is heavenly—"

"Oh, my! Is that Annie's recipe?" Martha's eyes shone. "Her pumpkin pie was the best! My cousin, Annie, she had a way with a pumpkin pie like no one else," she told Georgia fondly. "And I bet she gave you all her secret recipes," she added, turning toward Carly with a smile.

"As a matter of fact, she did," Carly murmured. But as several other of the remaining women streamed past them, calling out good-byes, and Georgia Timmons followed them out the door, her mind was already drifting.

The Lonesome Way fairy godmothers were so far off it was almost laughable. Oh, she knew the story about how Ava had believed Rafe Tanner would be the perfect man for Sophie after she divorced her husband and returned to Sage Creek. Ava had put Rafe right at the top of her list of eligible men in town. The number one man for Sophie.

And in that case, she'd been right.

Within weeks of Travis Tanner moving back to Lonesome Way, everyone had guessed that he and Mia would get back together. And they had.

But they were wrong in her case, all of them, very wrong about Jake. He and Carly and Emma weren't ever going to become a real family.

True, he'd postponed his trip to Salt Lake City for another week to squeeze in a little more time with Emma. But he hadn't touched Carly or tried to kiss her, or shown any inclination to do so. He'd been a perfect gentleman.

She, on the other hand, had scared herself with how many times she'd wondered what would happen if she leaned in and kissed him after Emma went to bed, or reached for him all those times she said good-bye to him at her front door.

If she let herself touch him just once, wrapped her arms around his neck, allowed herself to give in for even a moment to the intense longing to be close to him . . .

Damn it, she wanted to kiss him again. To see how it felt to taste those firm, warm lips. She wanted his arms around her. To feel all that rugged power and strength and cockiness mixed in with an unexpected gentleness that never ceased to surprise her.

She wanted what she shouldn't want—and couldn't have.

She and Jake needed to remain friends. Only friends. For Emma's sake.

But whenever she saw him, her heart did a crazy little dance.

It'll be better when he goes off to Salt Lake City, she told herself. Then she'd find some peace.

She wouldn't stare at her ceiling every night, remembering the deep timbre of his voice as he told her some new story about what Emma had said or done. Or thinking about his easy, gentle way with their daughter. Or the way Emma had begun to look for him when he wasn't there, asking where he was, when he was coming to see her, babbling about him and Bronco as Carly made her bed, straightened up the house and Emma, dragging Bug, toddled after her from room to room.

In a strange way, Jake was part of their household now. Somehow he had become an almost daily fixture of their lives, entertaining Emma while Carly made supper. Washing the dishes while Carly got Emma ready for bed.

It had seemed to happen so naturally. But he was still hands-off. And apparently that was fine with him because he hadn't once tried to touch her, much less kiss her.

His manner at all times was kind, direct, considerate.

Screw that, she thought bitterly.

But she knew it was for the best. She only had to hang on for another week, then he'd be gone for the commercial shoot, and then a rodeo, and who knew when he'd come back?

Once he hit the road, returned to the vibrant thrum of the rodeo, saw the glare of lights and heard the excited roar of a crowd chanting his name, he might not come back to Lonesome Way for a very long time.

She tried to ignore the hard knot tightening in her chest every time she thought about it.

Emma would ask for him. But, after a while, she'd forget. Wouldn't she? She was still so young. . . .

Only a few days before, all three of them had driven over to Sage Ranch in Jake's truck and he'd introduced her and Emma to Dakota. His once frisky paint pony was now a placid senior who wickered long and loud in greeting when Jake appeared, carrying Emma on his shoulders into the barn.

After he'd saddled the pony and led him into the paddock, he'd lifted Emma up into the saddle and held her there.

She'd looked a tiny bit uncertain at first and as if she might cry.

Carly had taken a few steps forward, but Jake

spoke offhandedly. "Hey, Emma, you're riding Dakota, Daddy's first pony. He's the best pony in the world."

"Ponee!" Emma's tiny fingers had grabbed onto Dakota's mane and tugged. Jake instantly enclosed her hand in his. "Soft, Emma. Soft and gentle . . . like this."

He showed her how to rub Dakota's neck, held his hand lightly atop hers as she smoothed her tiny fingers along it.

"Wide!" She stared at Jake, her lower lip pushed out with determination. "Me wide. Me."

"Sure you can ride, Emma. It's easy." Holding Emma in the saddle, he walked Dakota around the paddock. Emma squealed with excitement as Carly leaned against the corral post and watched, her heart filling her throat.

When Jake finally lifted Emma off the pony, he turned toward her with a grin. "Two years from now, I'll start her on some real riding lessons. My dad taught me before I turned four."

Two years. A long time from now, Carly thought, knowing she couldn't allow herself to count on Jake being around much by then. His schedule could be even busier, he could meet some woman—get distracted for a while—or get bucked off a bull and stomped to death. . . .

Her throat constricted and she said a quick fervent prayer that the latter would never happen. But she had to prepare herself to continue raising Emma alone. And to keep Emma from feeling abandoned.

We'll both forget what it's like having him around, she assured herself as she finally locked up the quilt shop and headed for her Jeep.

Me and Emma—and Martha—we're the three musketeers. In this together, all for one, one for all. And all we really need is each other.

Once Jake was gone for a few weeks, or a month, Carly was almost certain Emma would stop asking about him. And so would that pesky whispering voice inside her own heart.

Chapter Seventeen

While Carly was driving home from town, Jake sat in his truck thirty feet from his huge cabin in the woods. He watched through the trees for several moments as Brady and a crew of four other men demolished the crumbling back wall of one of his fishing cabins, a scant three hundred yards away.

The harsh rumbles of hammering, machinery, grunting, and swearing broke the peace of the isolated clearing not far from Blackbird Lake, but Jake knew that tomorrow silence would reign again in the thick woods leading to the lake.

Tomorrow was the start of the weekend, and the crew would be off.

His gaze shifted to Brady, who was hauling lumber from a flatbed truck, sweat sheened on his face despite the chilly wind racing through the brush.

Cord's brother had been working hard, tirelessly. He hadn't once complained and he was stepping up. Denny was pleased with his work ethic, and Jake allowed himself to feel a measure of relief.

Brady seemed to be headed back in the right direction—working and on track. Working damned hard, as a matter of fact. Jake had driven over to the Farraday house once or twice and noticed that Brady had fixed up the old place in his off-hours.

The broken floorboards on the porch had been repaired. There were a couple of fresh coats of white paint on the shingles of the house.

It seemed as if Brady had finally dislodged that chip from his shoulder.

Jake thought of Cord, a lingering sadness filling him. He missed his old friend. So he could only imagine how Brady must feel.

But at least it seems like he's going to get through this. He'll be okay.

Hearing a whine, he glanced down at Bronco, who'd shifted closer to him, seemingly disturbed by all of the construction noise.

"Come on inside, partner. Let's do a walk-through."

He opened the door and led the way into his huge two-story house. The dog pattered through the door after him and curled up just outside the kitchen.

Soon enough, the crew would be tackling this cabin, too—all six-thousand square feet of it.

He'd had the place built impulsively after his first burst of big wins and his first sports endorsement contract. But now, as he crossed the high-beamed entranceway, gazed at the high-beamed oak ceiling, the hardwood floors, the sweeping expanse of rooms, he wondered what the hell he'd been thinking.

The place was far too huge and empty for him. Hell, it was too huge and empty for *ten* of him. He had a much better use for it, for all the big bedrooms, the library, sprawling kitchen, and game room, and for the rugged land surrounding the house.

As a guest lodge with five bedrooms and three bathrooms available on the second floor alone, and a massive dining room, first-class kitchen, and a living room easily converted into a lodge lobby and office on the main floor, the "cabin" would be serving a much better purpose. He didn't need all these soaring ceilings and vast spaces.

And what was more, now that the novelty had

worn off, this huge fancy cabin in the woods didn't mean anything to him.

He was accustomed to much less. A motel room with a flimsy mattress, or a five-star hotel suite with a massive king-sized bed and all the trimmings—it was all the same to him.

None of it was home. He didn't need a home. Just a place to park his boots and a pillow to rest his head between gigs.

Yet for some reason a big Victorian on a quiet, tree-lined street popped into his head. A bright-eyed little toddler with a dazzling smile. And a stunning, sexy redhead with mile-long legs and a way of looking at a man that made something inside him clench so hard and deep it was almost painful.

He forced himself to shake those alluring images of Carly loose as Brady spoke suddenly from the doorway.

"Got a minute?"

Jake swung toward him. "Sure. What's up?"

The younger man took a few steps into the cabin. "First, thanks for getting me another shot with McDonald Construction." He cleared his throat. "It's a great opportunity. I know I don't really deserve it and that you probably did it for Cord—"

"Wrong," Jake interrupted. "I did it for you. Granted, Cord would want me to help you out— he loved you more than anything, Brady. He only wanted the best for you. He hoped you'd have a better life than he did. But I've known you for a long time, too, and if I didn't think you had the potential to be great at whatever you set your mind to do, I'd never have gotten involved. From here on out, kid, it's up to you."

"Yeah. I get that." Brady grinned. "And don't worry, I won't make you look bad for going to bat for me."

"Better not or I'll kick your butt," Jake said cheerfully. "Denny's told me some about the job you're doing. He's more than satisfied. So what else you got on your mind?" Jake watched as Brady crouched down to scratch Bronco behind the ears.

"I made some sketches . . . ideas I had for a new layout for your place here. I heard you're turning it into a main lodge for the kids and their families." Brady rose, and Bronco pattered over to the rug by the empty fireplace and settled down again.

"So I thought about how we could make maximum use of the space. I have a few ideas to bounce off you. I showed them to Denny—he seemed to like them but told me to run them by you. I thought we could review them, if you have time."

"Sure, we can do it right now."

"Great, but . . . there's something else I need to ask you first."

This is what it's really all about, Jake thought as he observed the tension in Brady's neck and jaw. *He got the other stuff out of the way, but this is what he's working up to.*

"Let's hear it."

"I want to know if you've seen Madison around—and how she's doing. Does she . . . seem okay to you?"

What the hell? That came out of left field. Jake's eyebrows lifted. "According to Carly, you're the guy who won a date with her. Don't you know?"

"We haven't gone on that date yet," Brady said tightly. "I'm just asking your opinion. She seem all right to you? Not . . . jumpy or . . . scared . . . or anything?"

Jake's inner radar switched into high alert. He hadn't seen all that much of Madison, but when he *had* seen the girl, he hadn't noticed anything odd about her behavior. Brady was the one who looked like he wasn't okay.

"I think you'd better tell me what this is all about."

"Madison thinks she's being followed." As Jake's gaze narrowed, focusing on Brady with complete, razor-sharp attention, he added, "She's never actually *seen* anyone, but—"

"When did this start? Where was she when she first thought she was being followed?"

"I'm not sure. I went to her gig one night at the Spotted Pony and she mentioned getting a weird vibe every now and then. She didn't explain it much—except she told me about a day she brought Emma to the park for a picnic with Carly. She didn't *see* anyone actually watching her, but she was pretty freaked out."

Tension sliced through every muscle in Jake's body. Hell. He didn't like this. At all.

If someone *was* following Madison, that meant at least part of the time they were following Emma, too. If his daughter's babysitter was in any kind of trouble, Emma could be at risk of getting mixed up in it, too.

"Does Madison have any jealous old boy-friends—any enemies?" he asked sharply, think-ing of all the wacky secret admirers a former beauty pageant princess might attract.

"Not as far as I know. Madison doesn't date." Brady shrugged. "Most of the guys around here don't really get her. And she's busy a lot of the time with school, her job taking care of Emma, and her music. She has all these gigs at night with her band—and then there's rehearsals. I don't like her being scared," Brady added darkly. "I want to know if she has anything to really be scared about."

"I'm going to make it my business to find out," Jake told him grimly, then shot Brady a long look. "But if you're so worried about her, why aren't you going on that date with her—talking to her about it yourself? Or tell Teddy Hodge what's going on. He'd be pretty interested in the fact that his granddaughter believes she's being followed."

"He sure as hell doesn't want to hear it from me." Brady snorted. "The sheriff might just have a heart attack if he finds out I know more about what's going on with Madison than he does. And she doesn't need any grief from him on my account. So forget it. Forget I mentioned anything."

"Afraid I can't do that." Jake sent Brady a level glance. "I'll keep an eye out for her every chance I get, but if you're worried, you should talk to her yourself."

Brady's mouth tightened. "That's not exactly an option. Having me involved in her life will only make things worse. Her grandfather hates my guts. He thinks I'm bad news. Her grandmother probably feels the same way."

"But you know better, don't you? And so do I." Jake held his gaze. "Why don't you give Hodge a little time to get used to you? Show him you're not the hothead he thinks you are."

"It won't work. Everyone in this town knows Madison deserves better than me." Brady's eyes held a bleakness and a steel that Jake had never seen before.

"Maybe you should let her decide for herself. If you have feelings for her, don't run from 'em, man. Don't run from her. *Tell* her. Look, you punched out Hodge's deputy when you were

283

down, at your very lowest point. But you're a better man than that and you're back on your feet. You showed it when you apologized to Mueller. You just have to keep going forward and be the best man you can be. The man who saved that kid on that mountain. That's what Cord would want you to do. Hold your head up. Stand up. Whether you know it or not, everyone in this town is pulling for you. I bet deep down, Hodge is, too. You make his granddaughter happy, he'll give you a chance."

Brady looked incredulous. "You think the sheriff's going to let me within ten feet of his only granddaughter?"

"Only one way to find out." Jake stared him down. "If you don't care enough to give it a try, that tells you something right there."

Brady fell silent. Then took a deep breath. "You ready to talk about those plans now?"

"Nope, changed my mind. It can wait until tomorrow." Jake started toward the door. "I just remembered someplace I need to be."

"You know where to find me." Brady followed him to the hall and glanced outside, toward the noisy construction site. "For what it's worth, I think it's a really cool thing you're doing down there. For those kids."

Jake paused. Studied him. "I've learned that everyone in this world needs a break now and then," he said evenly. "And I do mean *everyone.*"

Chapter Eighteen

After dropping Emma off at Martha's for her sleepover, Carly let herself into the house as the sun glimmered in a dusky lavender haze over the peaks of the Crazies.

The weather report promised a warm-up for tomorrow. The temperature would hit the upper sixties, and there would be plenty of sun. It might be one of the last gold-tinged days of autumn before winter came blasting hard and fast through Montana.

Maybe she'd ask Martha to bring Emma to the shop at lunchtime tomorrow and they'd all walk to the park for one final picnic before the first snow came.

For tonight, she planned on paying some bills, emailing Sydney, and getting to work on the Tinkerbell costume she was sewing for Emma to wear on Halloween.

She hung her jacket in the hall closet and made a beeline for the kitchen. As she began sorting through the stack of mail on her writing desk, she noticed Annie's pumpkin pie recipe paper-clipped to a message pad beside her laptop and suddenly remembered she needed to write a list of ingredients she'd need for the pie.

Annie had also served a special Thanksgiving punch, she remembered. That might be nice for the big fund-raising dinner dance to be held in Lonesome Way High School's gymnasium. Of course she'd have to run it by Georgia Timmons first.

The fun never stops, she thought wryly.

She was just about to get to work at her writing desk when she paused, noticing that the kitchen felt cold. Much colder than the front of the house and the hall.

Odd.

She swung toward the sliding door leading out to the wraparound deck and yard, and froze.

The door was open. Not wide open . . . but several inches open. So was the screen.

A prick of fear stabbed her. That door had been closed when she left for work that morning, and it was closed when she checked again a short while ago before bundling Emma into her jacket and driving her to Martha's apartment.

Now as she moved toward the open space her breath seemed trapped in her throat. Chilly air wafted into the room. She shoved the door shut, fastened the lock, then whirled around to glance uneasily around the kitchen.

Had someone broken in? Was anything missing or out of place?

Her desk drawer was closed. Nothing looked disturbed. She hurried into the hall, checking each of the downstairs rooms, then rushed up to Emma's room, the third bedroom, her own bedroom . . .

Her bureau drawers were all closed. Her nightstand drawer . . .

Open.

Only a few inches, but she always closed every drawer tight, worried that Emma might accidentally catch her fingers in one.

And that wasn't all. . . .

She suddenly noticed the overhead light glowing in the small closet Denny McDonald had built for her in the corner of her big, airy bedroom.

She was certain the *only* lights on when she'd left with Emma had been the living room light and the porch light.

Her heart thumping, she edged toward the closet and peered inside. *Calm down. Everything is in order. . . .*

Except . . . it wasn't.

The vintage hatbox on the top shelf. A gift from Annie. It was where she stored scraps of fabric, photos of quilts she loved, notes Annie had written her while she was in college, and poems she'd collected over the years, copying favorites onto stationery and storing them in the box to keep. The hatbox was now turned sideways on the shelf, the front portion of it nearly teetering over the edge. Seizing it with cold fingers, she took it down and peered inside.

On first glance, it didn't seem as if anything was missing.

But someone had been here and moved it. Had they been searching for money?

Only one name popped into her mind.

Phil.

Icy fear slid through every inch of her body as she tried to fight off panic.

It had been over a year since he called. Was he so desperate for cash that he'd actually tracked her down after all this time, come after her, all the way to Montana? Had he broken into her home, trying to grab whatever cash she had lying around, figuring she wouldn't call the police on him, that she'd still be that scared, timid little girl who didn't want to cross him, who cried and begged him to let her out of that tiny hall closet?

If that's what he thinks, he's dead wrong. Taut with anger, she left the hatbox on the closet floor and darted back into the hall and down the stairs toward the tiny room—an alcove really—that served as her sewing room. The childproof hook at the top, which she used to keep Emma from wandering in there alone, was unlatched.

Bursting inside, she pushed the oval embroidered rug in the center of the little sewing room aside, then knelt and curled her fingers around the single loose floorboard.

Beneath that floorboard was the metal box where she kept five hundred dollars cash hidden in case of an emergency. Copies of her passport and driver's license were stowed there, too, as well as her birth certificate and Emma's, a copy of her will, and the title papers to her home. The originals were in a safety deposit box at the bank. In Annie's old neighborhood in Boston, there had been occasional break-ins, and Annie had taught her to store her personal valuables and copies of her really important documents beneath the floor and to cover it with a beautiful rug.

Everything's here, Carly realized with relief, still kneeling beside the box.

But everything wasn't all right.

Someone had broken into her home.

They'd invaded her privacy, her peace of mind, her safe, calm life here with Emma. For a moment her throat closed up and she felt panic bubbling from deep inside, but she pushed it back and raced toward the living room where she'd left her purse and her cell phone.

She had to call Jake—

No. *No.* Skidding to a stop, she drew in a shaky breath. What was she thinking? She needed to call the sheriff, not Jake. She couldn't let herself start turning to Jake whenever something—anything—happened. She couldn't let herself think she could rely on him—

Suddenly someone banged several times on her front door, and she gasped.

But immediately she realized that whoever had

broken in would hardly come back and knock for admittance. Even Phil wouldn't be that stupid—

Or would he?

Hold it together, she told herself as she peered cautiously through the living room window on her way to the door. That was when she spotted Jake's truck parked in the driveway.

Relief made her knees tremble. She practically tore the door from its hinges as she yanked it open and there was Jake, standing on her porch, his hand raised to knock again. Bronco waited alongside him, his scraggly tail wagging with pleasure.

"Thank God!" It came out as a breathless gasp of relief and his gaze sharpened on her.

"What's wrong? Carly, you're as pale as the damned moon—"

Clutching his arm, she pulled him inside and Bronco followed as always, right on his heels. "Someone broke in. My back deck door was open when I came home. I had just dropped Emma off for her sleepover at Martha's and it was closed when I left—I know it was," she explained in a rush as Jake shut the door behind him and studied her with a frown. "Several things look out of place. Someone's been in here."

"They take anything?"

"It doesn't seem like it so far, but I . . . I'm not sure."

She must have looked as distraught as she felt,

because he caught her to him and gave her a reassuring squeeze. Leaning against him, Carly felt her breath come a little slower and easier as the burst of panic eased.

"It's going to be okay. Are you . . . having a panic attack?"

"No . . . I don't think so. Maybe a little, but . . . this is just so crazy," she muttered, shaking her head. "We don't have many home invasions in Lonesome Way. I don't understand who would break in—but we should call Sheriff Hodge—"

"Let me do it. You sit down."

When she was settled on the sofa, he yanked out his cell. He didn't take his eyes off her while he spoke to the sheriff, and after setting his cell down on the coffee table, he took both of her hands in his.

"Do you have any idea who would want to break in here? I won't touch anything, but I'm going to take a look around. But first there's something I should tell you. It's about Madison."

She went still. "What is it?"

"It's the reason I came by. Madison thinks someone might be following her."

Fresh shock bulleted through her. "She never said anything to me. Do you . . . think this break-in could be about *Madison?* Why on earth . . . ?" A chill rushed all through her body.

"I don't have a clue. Yet." Jake's tone was low, tense.

He must have seen the alarm in her eyes, because he suddenly tucked her close to him again. His arms felt so good. So strong and firm and safe.

"Listen, Carly, I promise you, everything's going to be fine. I'll be with you until we find out what's going on and whoever broke in gets arrested. In the meantime, you and Emma are stuck with me."

She drew back, stared up at him. "What do you mean? You're . . . moving in?"

"Unless you've got a problem with that."

She drew a breath and smiled up at him.

"No problem. If you think I'm going to argue, I'm not."

"Good. Because this is one argument you can't win."

Slowly she relaxed in his arms, her head resting against his chest. Bronco sat on the rug, watching them a moment, then eventually stretched out and closed his eyes.

As a siren sounded in the distance, Jake stroked her hair.

"I just hope you don't get sick of me before Hodge catches this creep," he said. "Because until he does, I'm sticking to you like Elmer's."

Stick all you want, she thought and then excised the very idea from her mind. *We're friends,* she reminded herself. *Emma's parents and . . . friends. Be smart for once and don't mess it up thinking crazy thoughts about anything else.*

Chapter Nineteen

At four a.m. Carly jolted up from her pillow. Thin beams of grayish moonlight seeped through her bedroom window. Shoving her hair out of her eyes, she realized she was shivering.

Of course she was. She'd dreamed that someone was crawling in through that window. She couldn't see the man's face . . .

But as she peered through the dimness, she could see that the window was closed. And the house was silent.

Then she remembered. Jake. Refusing to go home and leave her alone tonight. He was sleeping on the pullout sofa in the third bedroom. Just down the hall from her.

Despite everything, her heartbeat slowed. She felt almost calm. At least, calmer than she'd ever expected to feel tonight, after spending two hours going over every detail of the break-in with Teddy Hodge.

The sheriff had dusted for fingerprints, warning her that if whoever broke in had used gloves, there wouldn't be any prints to be found.

If it's Phil, she'd thought, something hard and determined knotting inside her, *he's going to be sorry he ever came near my house.*

Her thug of a cousin was dead wrong if he believed he could still frighten her out of her wits. Or extort money from her—or anything else.

She'd been shocked to find someone had searched her home, but he wasn't going to scare her again. Or push her around.

And she wouldn't give him so much as a penny. Not a single one. Not ever.

Determination was one thing, but falling back asleep was another. She wasn't thinking of the break-in any longer. She was thinking about Jake. After several torturous moments of staring at the ceiling, all wound up, listening for any sound, she sat up suddenly, swung her legs over the side of the bed, and padded barefoot to the door.

She wanted to see him, she told herself. Just make sure he was really there. And then she'd go downstairs and make coffee, since she was never going to fall back asleep again.

A moment later she was in the hallway, tip-toeing past Bronco, who looked up at her for a moment, tail beating against the floor, then went back to his snoring. Just as she reached the open doorway of the third bedroom, a floorboard suddenly creaked beneath her feet. And Jake—bare chested—sat up.

Through the shadowy darkness she saw the outline of his powerful body and the hard thrust of his jaw. "Carly. You all right?" His deep voice sounded as alert as if it was five o'clock in the afternoon and not five in the morning.

"I couldn't sleep." It was an effort but she forced herself to stop staring at that broad, muscled chest. Taking a steadying breath, she stepped into the room, only to remember, too late, that *she* was wearing only a long pink tank. And a wisp of lacy ivory thong.

A flush surged through her cheeks. Why hadn't she thought to toss on a robe?

She didn't allow herself to linger over the question. Or the answer.

"I . . . was going to put on some coffee." Liar, liar, pants on fire. "No way am I falling back asleep," she murmured, even as she inched another step closer to the dangerously handsome cowboy watching her from the pullout bed.

It should definitely be a felony for any man to look that sexy, she decided, her heart thudding. All muscles and hotness and manly five-o'clock-in-the-morning stubble. It just wasn't fair.

"I've been tossing and turning most of the night," she heard herself say. "Sometimes I don't sleep well when Emma is at Martha's. I miss her. Little troublemaker that she is." God, she was babbling. She never babbled. But she'd never had Jake Tanner half naked in a bed in her house, either.

"Careful. That's my kid you're talking about." He grinned and raked a hand through his hair.

297

"I don't take kindly to anyone calling my daughter a troublemaker."

The glint of humor in those midnight blue eyes made her heart skip, oh, three or four beats. Okay, maybe six. Enough so it was hard to breathe.

"She definitely takes after you—in a lot of ways. And she's not even two yet." Carly almost succeeded in keeping her voice steady, just this side of sarcastic—all the while thinking that she should really back up and walk away—no, *run* away—down the stairs and straight into the kitchen. She needed coffee. Not Jake. So why wasn't she going?

"Yeah?" He slanted her a look that shot tingles down to her magenta-painted toes. She forced herself not to stare at the breadth of those shoulders or the taut muscles of his chest. The lower part of Mr. Sexy's body was covered by the bedsheet, but what she could see above it was just as she remembered from that long-ago night. Wide muscular chest, rock-hard abs, every inch of that gorgeous body gleaming in the moonlight that floated through the curtain.

Not that she was looking or anything, she told herself. She was only glancing now and then.

His face. Look at his face, a voice inside instructed her.

But that was an equally perilous option. That rugged, darkly handsome face, the strong nose, the sexy little cleft in his chin. That whole rugged alpha male thing he had going on was enough to unnerve better women than her.

He was studying her right back as she hesitated only a few feet away from him. The intensity in his gaze had her shivering again—but this time for a whole different reason.

"Why don't you come over here and tell me exactly how Emma takes after me?" he drawled in his deep voice.

"Sounds like a dare."

"It is."

She met those challenging eyes, darker, bluer, deeper than an ocean at sunset, and her gaze shifted once more to his chest, lightly matted with dark hair. Of course she couldn't help glancing at those wide cowboy shoulders. Though the sheet still hid the lower half of that tall, lean body, she could well imagine . . . actually, she *remembered* . . .

And she edged closer.

"Sure you don't want to go back to sleep?" she asked. A little flame caught inside her at his ear-to-ear grin.

"Trust me, sleep has never been further from my mind."

Leaning forward so suddenly she gasped, he reached out a long arm and snagged her hand, tugging her toward the bed and right down on top of him. Her breasts were pressed against his chest, her legs splayed across the blanket covering his thighs. When her breathless yelp turned into a laugh, he smiled slowly, then tightened one arm around her and, with his other hand, stroked his fingers through her sleep-mussed hair.

Uh-oh. Trapped on a bed. With the sexiest cowboy this side of the Rio Grande. *You're in trouble now, girl.*

She knew she should pull back, way back. Right now. But her reflexes didn't seem to be operating properly. . . .

"*How* is Emma like me exactly?" Jake asked casually, as if they weren't lying almost naked together on his bed. As if lust—*her* lust, at least—wasn't gobbling up all the air between them.

Before she could summon up any coherent words with which to answer him, he leaned forward and began nibbling his way gently down her neck. Oh, she was in real trouble now. Jake knew just how to nibble . . . and *where.* . . .

She needed to put an end to this. Wriggle away from him. Tell him to stop right now. But roaring need pulsed through her as he trailed those warm, delicious kisses across her throat. Caressed his way seductively along her jaw. And melted every rational and cautious instinct she'd ever possessed.

So instead of pulling away, she nestled closer. And he brushed another kiss along the shell of her ear.

"She's . . . um, adventurous . . . reckless . . .

d-daring . . ." Carly managed to say. She couldn't think clearly. Not when his mouth blazed hot against her skin. "Her . . . eyes are the same color as y-yours—"

That was as far as she got.

Her brain closed down completely as he slipped his hand beneath her tank and began stroking her breast. Rubbing his thumb over her nipple. Driving her crazy. He knew *exactly* how to touch her—everywhere—and his lips . . . they tasted of heat and fire and spice. With a moan she gave up any thought of pulling away and instead slid her arms around his neck and parted her lips, inviting him in, needing to taste more, feel more. . . .

She wanted him. All of him. . . .

A shudder of pleasure shimmered through her as his tongue swept inside her mouth, stroking, flicking. Instinctively she closed her lips around it and sucked. He gave a groan and she felt the entire length of his body, every hard inch of muscle and sinew, tighten and clench. The next thing she knew, he'd captured her in his strong arms and was kissing her back, openmouthed, with a deep, slow possessiveness. Lingering, deep kisses that suddenly changed, in a heartbeat, into something more.

Something wilder, hotter, needier.

Too late to escape now, Carly thought happily, her hands stroking through his thick dark hair.

Whatever measly willpower she once might have possessed had turned to mush.

All his fault, she decided as their mouths and tongues stroked and licked, as a thrill of heat spread like a wildfire inside her, leaving no space for anything else.

"You have any idea how beautiful you are?" His hands were exploring her slowly, no rush. "I couldn't take my eyes off you when I saw you in Houston that night. And I still can't."

"You're just trying to get me into bed," she breathed against his lips, as her fingertips slowly explored all the scars and muscles and sinew that defined his body.

"Here's some news for you, girl." His hand slid over her bare bottom and squeezed. "I've already *got* you in bed. And you're even sexier than I remembered."

She got lost in his words as much as in the way he was looking at her, the way he was touching her. A few moments later the bedsheet and the blanket and quilt all ended up in a heap on the floor as they frantically kissed and cuddled and tousled some more. He'd been sleeping in his jeans, but they were about to be gone, she promised herself as she rubbed her hand against his thick erection. Her breath was coming in short, happy gasps. How could it not, when he was sliding those clever hands up and down her body, slowly stroking her, arousing her everywhere?

A sane little voice in her head tried to tell her that they should stop now. That she wasn't thinking clearly, that she should push him away, bolt down the stairs, brew some coffee. Or mop the floor, for heaven's sake!

She should do something sane and normal and *safe,* like she always did, but somehow she was still kissing Jake, touching him. Frantically flicking at the button of his jeans and trying to slide the zipper down past the enormous bulge of his erection.

And he was still cradling her against him, his mouth drawing at hers with a growing urgency that made her forget everything else but this room, this bed, *him.*

They kissed and stroked and touched in the dark, locked together—sharing long, hungry, delicious kisses—before she suddenly was struck by an instant of sanity. She froze.

"Jake, we're crazy, aren't we? What the hell are we d-doing?" She was hot with lust, but also suddenly unsure.

"Do we really need to stop so I can explain it all to you?"

"Don't you *dare* stop anything . . . if you even think about stopping . . . I might have to . . . to hurt you," she gasped, her hands gripping his shoulders, sliding down his back.

"Wow. Scared now." He laughed. "Do your worst, baby." And then, in one smooth move, he yanked her pink tank over her head and tossed it aside.

"You know we're both acting crazy." She pulled him closer as he stroked her breasts. "We . . . made a bargain to be friends . . . just friends."

"Hell, if this isn't friendly, Carly, I don't know what is." Jake caught her lips suddenly in a kiss so strong and deep and slow that it didn't end until there was no breath left in either of them. She ached with pleasure when his tongue slipped inside her mouth again and she gave herself up to the dark, musky taste of him, to his leather and spice scent.

When he turned his full attention to one of her nipples, his tongue playing, circling, teasing, and then shifting gradually to the other, she closed her eyes and moaned. She was almost too distracted by quickening tingles to notice him making short work of sliding her thong down her thighs.

Excitement beat through her when he tossed it across the floor. But when he slid a condom from a pocket of his jeans, then stripped the wrapper off with ease, her head cleared enough to murmur, "We tried those once and they didn't work, if you remember."

"And we're damned lucky they didn't," he said huskily. His eyes gleamed as she took over, eagerly sliding the condom in place.

Then he moved with the grace of a leopard,

covering her body with his own, bracing an arm on either side of her to protect her from his weight. His voice thickened in the faint amber-pink light of dawn now stealing through the window.

"Maybe we'll end up two for two." The smile on his face made her heart somersault and her brain whirl.

Are you kidding me? was what she was going to blurt, but before she could get the words out he was kissing her again, kissing her mouth, her throat, her breasts, licking the hard, exquisitely sensitive peaks of her nipples. His hands were clever and wicked as only an All-American cowboy's hands could be, and the way he touched her made her gasp with pleasure and burn for more. His mouth scorched its way down her body before, with slow, deliberate strength, he finally eased himself over her, fitting himself inside her, going slow and deep, then deeper still, into her center, filling her, pumping and thrusting as she clutched him to her.

She held on, tight, small, wild cries bursting from her. Time and space wavered. Blended. There was only Jake, inside her. His touch, his kiss, his strength. His voice saying her name and his body hot and lean and strong, making her gasp and cry out and bury her face against the warmth of his neck as they joined together in a blur of deep, pure pleasure.

Their lovemaking was sweet and wild and intense. It was different from that night in Houston. Then he'd been practically a stranger, tough, fascinating, and mysterious.

Now . . .

Now she wasn't trying to forget someone else. She was here with him, wanting him, not just because he was her childhood hero or rock-star sexy. But because he was Jake—who'd fixed her screen door the week before, who was trying to teach Emma old cowboy ballads he'd learned from his father's foreman as a kid. Who had stayed here tonight because he cared about her and knew she needed him.

He was kind, calm, fearless, and steady Jake. The daring rodeo rider and the solid-as-a-rock man. The father who made Emma laugh effortlessly, whose face Carly had secretly longed to see in the crowd the night of the auction—though she'd never have admitted it to a soul. The man who made her heart miss a beat whenever she heard his voice or saw him standing on her front porch waiting to be admitted, his black Stetson shading those midnight eyes.

Jake.

After another bout of slow, delicious lovemaking that lasted even longer than the first, a silver-pink dawn drifted gradually into the room, delicate as a dream. She spooned against him, their bodies warm, close, somehow more intimately linked even than when they'd been making love.

Just before she slipped into sleep in his arms, she felt the brush of his lips on the back of her neck.

"I'll be here just like this when you wake up," he said quietly. "That's a promise."

And those were the last words she heard before drifting into a long, deep, untroubled slumber.

Chapter Twenty

All night long, Jake's advice had drummed in Brady's head.

He hadn't been able to stop thinking about it.

As he parked his Harley on Spring Street just before nine o'clock the next morning, and headed to A Bun in the Oven for a muffin, fried eggs, and coffee, he knew he should have been there a lot more for Madison. He never should have stayed away from her these past weeks, watching out for her from a distance. He should have had her back all the time.

He'd thought it wasn't his job, or his place. That all he'd do was make more trouble for her. That her grandparents would give her grief about him, and she'd had enough strife in her family already.

He hadn't wanted to be the cause of more.

But ever since the gig at the Spotted Pony, he couldn't stop himself from thinking about her. Worrying about her. He'd even hung out across from her apartment building a few times late at night when he knew she had gigs. Just to make sure that after parking her car, or getting dropped off by one of the members of the band, she got in the door and upstairs safely.

Not once had she even known he was there.

So now I'm following her, too, he thought. And wondered about the other guy.

Who was he? Brady hadn't seen anyone else hanging around her building late at night. Not once.

Hell, just call her, he told himself. *You owe her a date. It's a matter of honor.*

Torn between eagerness to see her and the conviction that he wouldn't be doing her any favors, he finished his breakfast and paid his tab. Shoulders straightening with resolution, he left the bakery and strode the few blocks to Madison's apartment.

He took the stairs two at a time and knocked on her door more than once, but there was no answer.

Maybe she was at work already, taking care of little Emma McKinnon.

Or rehearsing somewhere with the Wild Critters for her next gig. He'd seen a poster at the Lucky Punch, advertising the band's next performance in Big Timber.

Brady cursed himself for never having asked Madison for her cell number. So he dug a scrap of paper from his jeans pocket, found a stub of a pencil, and scratched out a note.

How about our date? Ice cream. Tonight. I'll pick you up at seven. If you can't make it, call me. He hesitated before writing the next line. *But I hope you can.*

Then he scribbled down his cell number and shoved the scrap of paper under her door.

He'd been intending to go back home and sit with his feet up on the porch railing for a half hour before he had to be at work, but he suddenly was hit by another thought and changed his mind.

Leaving Madison's apartment building, Brady turned left on Hickock Street and walked toward the sheriff's office.

Chapter Twenty-one

"All I know," Carly told Martha on the phone as sunshine poured through the kitchen windows, "is that it definitely wasn't my cousin breaking in, looking for money. It seems he's been located—in New Jersey. I can't believe it. I was so sure it was him."

She paced across the kitchen, then back toward

the table. "According to Sheriff Hodge, Phil's turned his life around. He works at a manufacturing plant now. He's been gainfully employed for just over a year. His foreman says he clocked in for the late shift yesterday and was at work during the time of the break-in, so now I don't know what to think."

Jake filled two bright blue mugs with coffee and noticed how tightly her fingers were clenched around her phone. She looked rested at least, and beautiful in sleek jeans and a soft plum sweater, but her tension was palpable—and had been ever since the call from Teddy Hodge minutes before.

He couldn't say he blamed her. If her asshole bully of a cousin wasn't behind the break-in, they were back at square one. Jake would be spending a whole lot more time making certain she and Emma not only were safe but that they *felt* safe.

"There's going to be a lot going on here today while Travis installs the security system," Carly continued, "and Madison has a three-hour online exam this afternoon, so if you're *sure* you don't mind keeping Emma at your place, I can pick her up sometime later when I head to the shop—"

Carly listened a moment. "Of course I know you *like* to take her shopping, Martha, but you weren't planning on being tied up today. Are you sure? You don't have appointments at the Cuttin' Loose? Okay, thank you, but don't spend too much money. Emma has all the clothes she needs. I'll pick her up at your apartment no later than four."

Disconnecting the call, she set her phone on the burnished wood countertop and met Jake's gaze as the smell of fresh coffee wafted through the kitchen.

"She and Dorothy are taking Emma clothes shopping in Livingston today. Martha insists on buying her a new dress to wear for Thanksgiving dinner. I think because it will be her first Thanksgiving at Sage Ranch with your family."

"My family? *Her* family," Jake corrected her. "And yours. They all love you—you know that, don't you?"

She nodded, a faint smile touching her lips. But her eyes still looked troubled. He knew she was still focusing on the break-in.

Her next words confirmed it.

"I can't believe we need a security system," she muttered for the fourth time that morning as she carried a platter of bagels to the table and set it alongside the cream cheese, raspberry jam, and apple cinnamon muffins already arrayed in the center.

Jake was opening the sliding door to let Bronco back in from the yard. "Think of it this way. You don't actually *need* Travis's system. It's only a backup."

"A backup to what?" She'd been about to slip

into her chair but she paused and stared at him in confusion.

"A backup to me. I told you, until Hodge gets this guy, and all this is resolved, I'm your full-time, round-the-clock, living and breathing security system." He lifted a brow. "Unless, after last night, you have any objections."

"Hardly." She grinned up at him. "Unless you've changed your mind."

"I'm not changing my mind."

He moved toward her, cupped her face, and brushed his lips against hers. At her instant response, a fierce fire seemed to shoot through his blood. He kissed her again, wanting to do so much more.

But now wasn't the time. Reluctantly he forced himself to let her go, and as she slipped into her seat, he took the chair beside her.

"How do you know Hodge will get him?" she asked as she spread cream cheese on a bagel.

Jake sipped his coffee. "Because Hodge is good at what he does. And so is Travis. I can guarantee you, after today, no one's breaking in here again."

She lifted her cup, then set it down again without drinking. "I really thought it was Phil. It's been a long time since he called me demanding money, but I can't think of anyone else who would break in here. It's unnerving not knowing who was in my house. You heard Sheriff Hodge say there haven't been any other reports of home invasions in town. And nothing was even stolen. So . . ."

"Someone was searching for something."

She nodded, stared bleakly into his eyes. "The question is what."

He'd been wondering the same thing, turning possibilities over and over in his mind. But so far, he didn't have a single theory. "We'll get to the bottom of this, Carly. Give it some time. But right now, I have a plan for the day."

She swallowed another bite of bagel and studied him. How did he always manage to appear so calm? Somehow, his easygoing confidence steadied her and she found herself smiling almost lightheartedly.

"Does this plan include something besides me going to work and you helping Travis install the system?"

"So happens it does. Since Laureen is opening the shop, I thought we'd wait and let Travis in, then take off while he does his thing. He can put in your system blindfolded—he doesn't need my help."

"Take off for where?" she asked, taking a sip of her coffee.

"That I can't tell you. It's a surprise."

Her spirits lifted inexplicably as she saw the anticipatory glint in his eyes. "I have to warn you, I've never been fond of surprises. I had a nasty one yesterday when I found someone broke into my house and I'm—"

He leaned forward, cupped her chin, and gave her mouth a gentle little kiss to quiet her. "I promise you this is a good surprise. There's something I want to show you. It won't take long. Then I'll get you to work and after you close for the day, we'll take Emma to the Lucky Punch for an early supper. If she's not too tired, I thought we might stop for ice cream at Lickety Split. Something tells me today might be one of the last days we want ice cream for quite a while. We'll be freezing our butts off before we know it."

She momentarily forgot about the break-in and the security system and someone searching her home. All she saw, all she knew, was Jake, tall and hunkily handsome in a black shirt tucked into faded jeans, his longish jet hair still damp from the shower, his elbows on her kitchen table as he kneaded her hands gently within his. He was talking about "we" and "us" as if he was going to be around all winter. But he was leaving soon for Salt Lake City. Did he mean that he'd be back fairly often?

Whoa. Don't count on it, a wiser voice inside her head counseled.

She leaned back and nodded.

"I'd love to see what you have to show me. Something at your cabin? The one you're turning into a lodge?"

"Not far from my cabin, but we're actually going past it—somewhere else." He pulled her to her feet, wrapped an arm around her waist. "Let's pack a lunch and head out soon after Travis gets here. Bronco can keep an eye on ol' Travis. I'll keep an eye on you."

"And where did you say we're going again?" she persisted.

"Oh, hell, I may as well tell you." With a smile, he brushed a strand of her hair from her eyes. "We're going to Blackbird Lake."

Chapter Twenty-two

The tall man waited until Tanner's pickup turned the corner off Blue Bell Drive. Then he hit his accelerator and followed at a discreet distance.

Giff Hurley had watched through binoculars as a powerfully built, dark-haired man driving a black SUV had parked in the McKinnon woman's driveway and carried a box of some sort into the house, and then a few moments later, Tanner and Carly McKinnon had headed out—only the two of them. He didn't know what that was all about but the man who'd gone inside had "cop" of some sort written all over him.

The sheriff had been there, too, the previous night. *And now this guy shows up.*

Damn. I really screwed up. Shouldn't have been drinking before I went in there. I got real careless.

His client wouldn't be too happy. The asshole had a temper and had made it more than clear he didn't want any attention from the cops. *But then,* Giff thought, *he doesn't need to know. I sure as hell don't plan to tell him. Not if I don't have to.*

Giff had started out in life planning to build a career on the right side of the law. He'd never thought he'd end up skirting the edge of it.

Hell, he'd wanted to be a cop himself, until he got kicked out of the damned police academy. All because they found out about that stupid drunk driving accident when he was fucking seventeen. They were pissed because he hadn't bothered to mention it on his application. He guessed mouthing off to his training officer hadn't helped much, either.

This career was a better fit for him, though. He worked for himself and he didn't have any dumb-ass rules to follow, except the ones he made up as he went along.

When business was good, he had plenty of dough. When things were quiet, and he hadn't picked up a case in a while, there were always the casinos.

He usually did pretty well at blackjack—except

lately when he'd been on a gawd-damned crazy-shit losing streak.

As Tanner's truck took a left on Coyote Road, he swore under his breath. Tanner and the McKinnon woman were driving *away* from town, not toward it, and he scowled at his bad luck.

He'd assured his client the woman would be going to her quilt shop like she did every day. Their plan had been to corner her there, with just her and the other woman who worked for her in the shop. Giff had observed that normally customers didn't show up until an hour after the shop opened. This little town came awake lazily in the morning—except for that bakery, A Bun in the Oven. So they'd be alone with the two women—and maybe only with Carly McKinnon —if things went their way.

Giff had done his best to make sure the other gal got in late so they could lock the door again and have the McKinnon woman all to themselves.

But now she wasn't even headed to town, not yet.

And, worse, she wasn't alone.

Where the hell were she and Tanner going?

He clenched his hands on the steering wheel as he realized he'd have to inform his client there was a little hitch in their plans. Maybe even a major change.

Reaching for his cell, he eased back on the accelerator, keeping Tanner's truck in his sights.

His employer had landed at Gallatin Field Airport nearly an hour before. He'd rented a car and was already headed to the damned quilt shop in downtown Lonesome Way. The guy was uptight and so keen to get his hands on this woman he probably hadn't even stopped along the way to piss or eat any breakfast. The bastard wanted answers and he wanted them bad.

He was already riled up and pissed as all hell that during all this time Giff hadn't managed to produce anything conclusive, nothing substantial enough to use, except a few photos that didn't prove squat.

So now that his client was finally here, the guy was pumped. Ready to tear up this town and whoever got in his way, if need be. Giff figured it would be best if the man never found out how much time he'd been spending at the casino in Billings, trying to rack up enough dough to keep his ex-wife from squawking since he'd missed three or four child support payments, all the while billing his deep-pocketed client by the hour.

Better that the boss should keep all that fury raging inside him centered on the woman, and not on Giff. His sister's husband had recommended him for this job and he didn't want any crap hurled back at his brother-in-law, or his sister would get royally pissed.

'Course he could take the guy if he had to, but

he'd rather get paid in full and finish this job ASAP with a wad of cash in his pocket. The way Giff figured it, that could happen as early as this afternoon.

He punched the client's number into his cell, then sped up a little, careful to keep a good distance back from the rodeo champ's truck as it rumbled away from the outskirts of town, headed in the direction of Sage Creek and the rolling prairie beyond.

Could be those two were headed to some nice secluded romantic spot. A good place to corner the woman, if that was where the boss wanted to do it.

But you never know, Giff reminded himself. The client might want to go a different route. He might want to go after the kid.

Giff could handle that, too. He'd followed Carly McKinnon when she dropped little Emma off at an apartment building in town, apparently for one of her sleepover dates with the old bag—that Davies woman.

Eenie meenie miney mo. Let the client choose how this will go.

One way or another, this job was gonna be finished and done. And he'd be cruising back to Wyoming with a pocketful of dough before the sun stuck its head out the next morning.

Chapter Twenty-three

Laureen was twelve miles from town and singing lustily along to Brad Paisley on the radio when her engine light flashed on.

"Oh, crap. What's *this* going to cost me?" Her heart sank as she slowed, staring at the flashing light.

This was turning out to be some week. Three days before, her clothes dryer had conked out and she'd had to fork over almost three hundred bucks for a new one—which hadn't even been delivered yet. And the night before, she'd finally had her "date" with Cal Meeks, the rancher from Livingston who'd paid good money for a chance to go out with her.

And what happened?

What always seemed to happen. Nothing.

She'd shown up at the Lucky Punch Saloon for dinner with him and never made it as far as sitting down at a table, much less picking up a menu.

She'd swept into the Lucky Punch in her new red stilettos, wearing her new red lipstick and a dress the same color, which she'd ordered online—a pretty, knee-length silky number that her sister-in-law, who viewed her modeling it on

Skype, insisted made her look five pounds thinner.

So she felt almost beautiful for once as she peered around the room for Cal—and there the bastard was—cozying up at the bar with a rail-thin brunette in tight jeans and a glittery scoop-necked top. The girl's boobs were as false looking as her eyelashes and she could barely be old enough to have graduated college.

And didn't look smart enough to get into one.

"Uh . . . Laureen. Hey."

He spotted her and sauntered over, flushing just a little, while the brunette watched, sipping her wine and eyeing the other men lined up at the bar.

"Uh, look, Laureen, this isn't going to happen."

"What do you mean by that?" she managed to bite out in a tight little voice, shock, anger, and humiliation squeezing through every pore of her body.

But he pretended not to notice. "It's nothing personal, honey. Honest. But I met someone else. It just happened. I lost your phone number, or I'd have called you. Don't worry—they can keep that donation for the animal shelter—but you and me . . . honey, it just isn't meant to be."

"Damned straight it isn't, you slimeball—" she began, but he turned on his heel and hurried back to the brunette before she could finish telling him where he could go.

Feeling like an idiot, she spun around and headed out of there as fast as she could walk in those damned shoes. But she saw Big Billy wiping down the bar, casting a couple of glances at her as she fought to keep the anger from showing in her face.

It was hard to read his eyes, but there might have been a flicker of pity there.

Laureen had ducked out faster than you could slap a tick.

Guess it's just my lucky week, she decided, staring in disgust at the red engine light on her dashboard. Now she'd have to fork over even more money at the body shop—*and* be late for work. And Carly was counting on her to open up—

Her car sputtered. Crap. Crap. And crapola.

Then it did more than sputter . . . it jolted . . . slowed . . . stopped.

Laureen choked back a shriek of frustration as she realized a tire had gone flat. Engine light, flat tire. What next? A hurricane whirling across the sky and blowing her and her piece-of-crap car into the next county? Into a sinkhole?

She grabbed for her purse and dug for her cell phone. She'd better let Carly know she'd be late opening the shop. Of course this had to happen the one day Carly said *she* was coming in late. . . .

But . . . shit. Her cell phone. It wasn't in her purse.

It was . . .

322

Laureen groaned. It was still charging in the kitchen, plugged in next to the microwave.

She'd skipped breakfast that morning, her stomach still topsy-turvy after her not-a-date date the previous night, and she hadn't even noticed that she didn't have her phone. . . .

Laureen threw open the car door, slung her purse over her shoulder, and started walking, wondering when in hell this spell of bad luck was going to change.

But she hadn't gone more than about twenty yards when an SUV came over a rise in the distance. It was coming fast, from the direction of town—a big black Explorer. The windows must have been rolled down, she decided, because some mean rock-and-roll was blasting, loud enough to waft clear up to the peaks of the Crazies.

The driver must be flooring it, she thought. It was coming real fast. . . .

She scooted to the side of the road and was startled when the driver slammed on the brakes. The Explorer screeched to a stop just as it passed her, then it quickly backed up.

The music disappeared. Big Billy leaned out the driver's-side window. The tattoos covering his thick neck gleamed like spilled ink in the sunlight.

"Hey, babe, it's a long way to town. Looks like you could use a lift."

Chapter Twenty-four

"You got an appointment, son? I'm busy."

Teddy Hodge plunked down his coffee cup and pushed his chair back from his computer. His shrewd gray eyes lasered in on Brady Farraday, but the young man standing tall in his doorway seemed undeterred by the cold-eyed stare of a career lawman.

"No, sir, no appointment, but this won't take long." Brady moved toward the sheriff's large desk, littered with files and folders and empty Reese's Peanut Butter Cup candy wrappers. He met Hodge's stare unflinchingly.

"How'd you get past Lonnie?" the sheriff growled.

His secretary was a fierce watchdog. Only his deputy or his wife or granddaughter could get in this office without her waving them through. She was very protective of Teddy's space, something he didn't always appreciate.

Until moments like this one.

"I brought Lonnie a cinnamon bun from the bakery. And a half dozen chocolate-covered strawberries." Farraday's eyes glinted. "Then I told her I needed to speak to you about a matter of the heart and I wouldn't keep you more than three minutes."

A matter of the heart. Teddy stiffened. "That's all it took?"

The sheriff's lips twisted in disgust. Lonnie was usually tougher than that. But, knowing his own wife's affection for chocolate, he reckoned the boy had hit on the one weakness a lot of women had in common.

"Well, you've wasted two minutes already, so you'd better talk fast." He leaned way back in his chair. *Matter of the heart, be damned.* The Farraday kid smiled at him, but that smile didn't get anywhere near his eyes. He looked damned determined—downright resolute.

Hodge would give him that much.

And nothing more.

"I've apologized to Deputy Mueller for that sucker punch I laid on him. But I never did apologize to you, sir. It was your officer I hit, and I had no business doing it."

Hodge said nothing, just sat as still as a fence post, with his hands clamped on his stomach.

"Mueller's a good man," Brady Farraday said. "But I wasn't one on that day. I . . . I kinda lost myself for a while. I don't even know that man who acted that way—throwing a punch at an officer of the law. And I did a few other things I'm not proud of. But that's not me, not who I really am, and I'm trying to be a better man. Trying to

325

find the best in me again. And to be a man who deserves—"

He broke off and, for the first time, Hodge saw him swallow hard, saw the tension in his body, the telltale muscle flick in his neck. And he knew what the boy was doing didn't come easy for him.

He also knew, somehow, that what he was going to say next really mattered.

But Hodge showed nothing, said nothing, giving him no help. Just glared at him in as intimidating a manner as he could muster, which, after forty years on the force, was pretty powerful stuff.

"I bid on that date with Madison because I care about her. And I believe she cares about me. It'd be nice to have your blessing before we go on that date, so she knows you won't be angry with her. Could be it's the only date we ever have—or maybe not. That's up to her. But Madison's been through a lot, sir, and she shouldn't have to lose anyone else that matters in her life. Especially not because of me—"

Hodge jerked forward in his chair. "You really think you can come between me and my granddaughter?" he asked furiously.

"No, that's not what I'm saying." Brady spoke quickly, but stood his ground. "I don't want Madison worried. I don't want her having to be torn up about anything. You and Mrs. Hodge are real important to her. So I'm telling you personally that I'm sorry I hit your deputy and—"

"You've done what you came to do, Farraday. Now get out."

Brady's broad shoulders stiffened. He frowned and started to turn away, but Hodge pushed himself heavily to his feet.

"Hold on! Just what are your intentions?" he spat out, and the younger man spun around to stare at him. "This is my granddaughter we're talking about."

"Yes, sir. And my intentions are to see where things go between us. To respect Madison—and to find out if she . . . well, if *we* . . . Actually, sir, our intentions are between the two of us, no disrespect meant."

Hodge pursed his lips. Not bad for a hotheaded young man. Farraday seemed to have a cooler head these days. *Must've come to his senses since that day he slugged Zeke.*

Madison had certainly been a whole lot less polite than this when Teddy had his wife invite her over to dinner so he could try to talk her out of going on any kind of a date with Brady Farraday. His granddaughter had told him in the bluntest of terms that she expected him to mind his own business. She said she loved him, and always would, but she could handle her own life all by herself and wouldn't have anyone telling her what to do.

To Hodge's disgust, his wife had sided with the girl unequivocally.

After that, Hodge had been so wound up, he hadn't even wanted any of Joanie's award-winning cherry-rhubarb pie for dessert. Not that she'd been too eager to give him any.

Instead he'd gone on a long walk. He'd come home good and winded and downed a glass of scotch before he had to listen to Joanie lecture him like some ten-year-old for a good half hour.

Now he looked the source of all the trouble over carefully. The boy had been unfailingly polite, but there was a mix of both youthful cockiness and manly resolution beneath the controlled surface. Hodge didn't like weakness or kiss-asses any more than he liked criminals, so his estimation of the boy slid up a notch or two.

"Where you taking her on that date?" he asked gruffly.

"Lickety Split." Brady cocked an eyebrow. "I promised her a double decker sundae. It's pretty well lit and usually crowded in there so we can't get into too much trouble, sir."

"We'll see about that. You'd better not hurt her."

"I'd never do that."

The sheriff let out his breath. "It took some guts to come in here and I respect that. But if you don't treat my granddaughter right . . ." He let the words trail off meaningfully.

"That'll never be a problem, sir." The boy had the nerve to grin as he started toward the door with long, youthful strides. "You have my word.

I'll let you get back to work now, Sheriff. Be sure to give my best to Mrs. Hodge."

He was gone before Teddy even had time to glare at his back.

Cocky young bastard. But . . . strong, too. Plenty of determination in that one.

Farraday had said all the right things. He'd better mean 'em. Because otherwise that young man might just find himself up to his ears in traffic tickets and jaywalking citations and whatever else Teddy could find to throw at him and make his life a living hell.

A satisfied smile touched his lips as he glanced down at the computer screen where a new batch of evidence reports had just popped up. He pushed the Farraday kid from his mind and got back to work.

Chapter Twenty-five

Carly stared out the window, filled with wonder as Jake's truck rumbled past a pair of mountain goats straggling along the old jeep road. The largest hawk she'd ever seen wheeled overhead, its great wings seeming to sweep in slow motion as it circled the peaks of the Crazies.

They'd seen plenty of wildlife, tall waving

grasses, and sweeping hillsides of pine and fir, but they hadn't glimpsed another soul or vehicle since leaving Coyote Road.

She, Jake, and the mountain goats might have been alone in the wild vastness of Montana.

Then they cleared a rise and she saw the valley —and the tiny cabin ahead.

It looks like something out of an oil painting, Carly thought. Small, quaint, old as the trees, and beautiful. The cabin was dwarfed by a flank of huge ponderosa pines to the right, and in the distance, the jutting crests of the Crazies. A short distance beyond it, a lake glimmered like a beautiful jewel.

Blackbird Lake.

She'd heard it mentioned many times but had never seen it before now. The sun glinting on the lovely rippling water dazzled her almost as much as the weathered cabin. So did the great open spaces stretching in all directions. Jake had explained to her that they were on private land— Tanner land—a quarter mile from the Half Moon Campground and other public access roads leading into the rugged heart of the mountains and the alpine lakes nestled among them.

"So this is what you wanted to show me," she murmured, feeling like she'd fallen under a spell, hurtled back in time to a quieter, more peaceful place.

"The lake and . . . my grandparents' cabin."

She turned to him, surprised. "Your grand-parents lived here?"

"From the day they were married. My grand-father left parcels of land to all the grandkids, but the largest was the acreage where I built my own cabins."

"Were you his favorite?"

"That's what I always told Rafe, Travis, and Lissie." He shot her a sideways grin.

A laugh burst from her. "How long did your grandparents live there?" She studied the small log structure as the truck bumped its way over the rough road.

"More than fifty-five years. They built it when they married, and raised three children there, including my father. Grandma Mae passed first, and a year later to the day, Grandpa Samuel's heart gave out. Lissie went through the place inch by inch. She catalogued and stored all of our grandmother's things and has shared them with Sophie and Mia over the years. We've cleaned out the cabin pretty much, but left some of the original furnishings. I thought you might want to see it."

"Yes, I do. Very much." Carly was fascinated by the sense of history the Tanners shared. "I don't have anything to help me remember my parents. After my mother died, my relatives must have taken whatever belongings she had. They probably felt they had it coming as payment for taking me in."

"Do you have good memories of her?"

"Oh, yes," she said softly. "I remember her brushing my hair, braiding it very gently. Reading me stories every night. Looking back, I remember we didn't have very much, but she always told me we had each other, and that mattered the most."

"A wise woman. Like her daughter."

As they rumbled closer to the cabin, awe filled her at the history of this Montana land, of this family. Not to mention this small cabin—preserved, honored, respected. It had been treasured in Jake's family for three generations.

"I envy all the touchstones you have with your past."

"We're pretty lucky that way." Jake glanced at her. "I always took it for granted. Rafe never did. Travis, either. But I always had something in me that compelled me to roam. My grandfather called it a twitch of the soul. On the other hand," he said with a smile, "for a girl raised as something of a tumbleweed, you've got a talent for putting down roots."

"Now, that's ironic," she murmured. "A tumbleweed. That's how I've thought about you. You have all this to anchor you, and yet you wander far from home. Once I found my home here, I knew I didn't want to ever leave it."

"You *made* a home here." Jake put the truck in park twenty yards from the cabin and turned to look at her. "You came here knowing only Martha, and you made a home for our daughter. You gave her a place to belong. You did it all alone, and—"

"Not all alone," she protested, blushing. "I learned about home from Annie. She taught me what it meant to be safe, loved, cared for from the time I was ten. And I wanted that for Emma more than anything. I wanted her to have those things from the very start. I couldn't bear the thought that she'd ever feel—" She broke off, her chest so tight with emotion it was difficult to find the words.

"Abandoned? Adrift?" Jake asked softly.

"Yes. That's it exactly. I never wanted her to feel unwanted. As if she didn't belong anywhere . . . or to anyone. Thanks to Martha, neither of us ever did. And Lonesome Way welcomed us with wide-open arms. From the moment we came here, I knew that if anything ever happened to me, Martha would be there for Emma and that your family would be, too. They'd take her in, love her."

Suddenly she spoke quickly, unburdening herself of the last secret she'd kept from him.

"I have a will, Jake. It explains that Emma is your daughter, that she's a Tanner. If something ever happened to *me,* I wanted to be sure she'd have Martha and your family to take her in and care about her. I wanted the Tanners to know her from the very beginning. I . . . I wanted them to care about her. After only a few weeks in

Lonesome Way it was obvious that your family sticks together, so I was sure that if something ever happened to me, and my will was read, they'd love her, accept her. Look after her, not just out of obligation . . . but . . ."

Her voice wavered, and Jake swallowed hard.

"Aw, Carly. Damn. I wish I'd known. I know that night I never gave you any reason to think I cared a damn about anyone other than myself, but I did . . . I do. . . ."

"I know that, Jake. *Now.*" Impulsively, she brought her hand to his cheek. "I knew you were a good man, but I didn't give you the benefit of the doubt when it came to Emma. It never even occurred to me. I was so convinced that the little I knew about you was all there was. But I couldn't have been more wrong."

"It's my fault, Carly, not yours. You did great. You were under stress, alone, and look at all you've done. The life you've built for Emma here, it's amazing. Now it's my turn to show you how important she is to me. How important—"

He broke off suddenly, thinking better of whatever he'd been about to say. "Come on inside. I want to show you the cabin. Then we'll have our picnic before I get you back to the shop."

But as they walked up the uneven path to the door of the cabin, she couldn't help wondering what he'd stopped himself from saying.

How important *she* was to him? Could that have

been it? But he'd changed the subject, rather than say the words. He didn't want to say them. Because he didn't mean them.

Jake wasn't a man to say things he didn't mean, or to make promises he couldn't keep. He hadn't said the words because he didn't feel them, or he wasn't ready . . . or sure. . . .

The wind blew softly through the trees as he unlocked the cabin door. She tucked away her foolish hopes, swallowed back the taste of disappointment sticking in her throat, and followed him inside.

The cabin was small and dusty, but orderly. Only five small rooms, two of them bedrooms, but the tiny home, despite the mustiness, still retained a delightful charm and sense of warmth. There was an old woodstove in the kitchen, a fireplace, and an old-fashioned hickory sofa with worn plaid cushions in the parlor. The larger bedroom boasted a rocking chair, a dresser with a music box atop it, and an old-fashioned iron headboard on the double bed Jake's grandparents had shared. The carved dresser was made of wood and there was a lovely oval mirror above it. While running her fingers across the carved wood dresser, she noticed an old brass trunk against one wall.

Some antique paintings, including a color-soaked scene of a sunset above rolling hills and one of a woman in bustled skirts and holding a parasol, adorned the parlor walls.

"It couldn't be any more charming, Jake." She tried to take in everything. The faded gingham curtains, which looked like they'd been recently washed, the old milk pitcher on the kitchen counter. "They were happy here. I can sense it."

"Yeah, they were. That's how I remember them. Real happy."

He joined her at the side of his grandparents' bed, narrow by today's standards. "There's something else I wanted to tell you while we're here."

He clasped both of her hands in his.

"This cabin will belong to Emma one day. I'm leaving it to her, just as my grandfather left it to me. And I want her to have that music box—it belonged to her great-grandmother. As soon as she's old enough to understand and take care of it, I'm planning to give it to her."

For a moment she was too astonished to speak. First shock, then happiness rose in her. She'd sensed that Jake was taking Emma into his heart, but this told her more. He was solidifying her connection to his family in the deepest way. Linking her to all the Tanners who had come before and who would come after.

Knowing that Emma would forever have that connection calmed something deep inside her. For an instant, Carly almost thought she heard the music box playing. A slow, lilting waltz . . .

"That's amazing, Jake. Thank you. I—"

"Don't thank me. I should be the one thanking you. For our daughter."

After they stepped outside, he scooped up the picnic basket and a checkered blanket from the back of the truck. "I fell in love with Emma almost from the first time I met her. Who wouldn't?"

"She is easy to love, isn't she?"

Carly's throat thickened. Jake loved Emma. A vast sense of relief engulfed her. Emma had a father who truly loved her, a father as well as a mother dedicated to her happiness. She had to blink back tears as they picked their way down the embankment behind the cabin and walked toward the lake.

While Jake spread out the blanket, she looked over at the dark, silver-edged water. The lake glimmered, cool and inviting. A sparkling gem nestled amid thick wild grasses, surrounded by soaring pines, a whirl of crimson and gold leaves, and guarded by the spectacular rocky peaks of the Crazy Mountains in the distance.

On the opposite shore another embankment rose, this one steeper, rockier, and thicker with trees and brush. She caught a glimpse of a beaver making its way to the lake to drink.

"It's so quiet here. So peaceful." It seemed as if they were a thousand miles away from every-thing. She'd almost forgotten about the break-in. Almost.

She unpacked the picnic lunch, setting out cold meat loaf sandwiches, potato salad, two apples, and half of a chocolate chip banana cake she'd baked yesterday morning before work. It was Annie's recipe and indescribably delicious. Of course, she usually served it warm, with chocolate chip ice cream, but today—well, today, she decided everything tasted as perfect as it could be.

This entire day would be perfect, she reflected, if she could only forget completely about someone sneaking through her house yesterday—and the unsettling possibility that perhaps the same person might be following Madison.

She jumped when Jake's cell phone rang.

He glanced at it with a frown. "Sorry, I have to take this."

She tried to focus only on the peacefulness of the lake and the cabin and the tall pine trees even as she heard him say firmly, "Ron, sorry, it couldn't be helped. I don't rightly know. I'm gonna have to get back to you. I'm dealing with a family crisis here."

She watched his eyes darken as he listened a moment. "Yeah, I'll do my best. Tuesday is possible. No, not definite. *Possible.* That's the best I can do. Give me a day or two and I'll let you know."

He ended the call abruptly, then scowled.

"Ron Messina. Vice president of the Turner

Taylor Advertising Group. They represent that new shaving cream I'm endorsing. I've been putting off the commercial shoot, but they need me to film in Salt Lake City next week or it'll totally screw up their marketing schedule. But I'm not leaving you and Emma unless everything here is okay. Even if I have to break my damned contract," he said darkly.

"Jake, it's all right." She touched his hand. "You need to do what you have to do. I'm sure once Travis has his system in, we'll be fine."

"Yeah, well . . . maybe." His brows drew together. "But if this isn't all settled, and Hodge hasn't caught whoever broke in, I think you and Emma should move in with Rafe and Sophie for a few days while I'm gone. Or else with Mia and Travis. I don't know if you remember, but I'm committed right after to a damned rodeo appearance in Carson City. Three-day gig. I'm not competing this time—just have to show up, wave to the crowd, sit with the announcer awhile each day. And make a few comments for the crowd." He met her eyes, his own earnest. "I'll cancel if you want me to."

"No. Don't. I understand."

"No matter what, I need to know before I leave that you and Emma are someplace safe. I'll try to be back before Emma misses me."

She forced a smile, unable to help chiding herself for her own foolishness. For getting too close, too vulnerable. Too accustomed to having Jake around.

This honeymoon period with Emma was coming to a close. He was going back on the road, back to the life he loved. And it would suck him in again.

She'd known it would happen. Jake had a life of his own and he had commitments. Sure, she realized now that one of those commitments was to their daughter and she sensed he'd do his best to keep it. But she had to maintain some perspective. She needed to protect her own heart as much as Emma's. Jake was still a roamer. A daredevil. And he always would be.

Time for you to act like a grown-up, she told herself. *Enjoy whatever there is between us—the camaraderie of being Emma's parents, maybe a friendship. . . .*

But just because they'd had some very hot, highly combustible, knock-your-socks-off sex the night before was no reason to think anything had changed.

Jake was who he was. A wanderer at heart. A cowboy who steered clear of fences. Only a fool would expect anything different. . . .

Then he shifted closer to her on the blanket and pulled her into his arms.

Oh, hell, so she was a fool. She melted against him. Wrapped her arms around his neck and held on tight.

Tomorrow she'd be sane and careful. Next week she'd do her best to forget him. Today . . .

She fisted the front of his shirt as he pushed her down on the blanket, and then drew him down to her. As his lips brushed hers, his eyes glinting, she smiled into his eyes and gave herself up to his kiss. The waters of Blackbird Lake shone and rippled, the wonderful tiny cabin sat perched on its hill, and they were alone. No one around for miles.

Heaven, Carly thought dizzily as heat licked through her. His kiss was so gentle it was almost a caress. A tease, full of promise. Then it deepened, grew more urgent. Her lips clung to the demanding contours of his mouth. Oh, yes, she wanted more.

"You taste so damned good." He explored the curve of her lips, stroked her hair, then began to rain kisses very slowly along her throat. "I think I could kiss you forever—"

Suddenly a sound broke the peacefulness surrounding them.

Not the murmur of the lake, or the whisper of wind through the pines.

The unmistakable sound of a car door slamming.

The next instant, he rolled away from her and was on his feet.

"We've got company."

Carly jerked upright, pleasure vanishing in a

blink. Her heart raced when she saw the grimness of his face.

"Who—?"

"Shhh," he warned, his voice low. "Don't know."

He pulled her to her feet. "Quick, go take cover in the brush behind those trees," he instructed softly, but even as she glanced toward a stand of pines perhaps twenty yards away at the bottom of the embankment, and her lips formed the word "no," two men appeared at the crest of the hill.

Carly froze. She strained to make out their features. One man was tall, perhaps in his late forties, with brown, close-cropped hair. He looked solid, almost as tall as Jake. The other was thinner, with fair hair and . . .

Her hands clenched in shock. Oh, God, it couldn't be.

"You're trespassing on private property," Jake called out in a hard tone she'd never heard from him before.

But neither man answered. They merely started down the embankment, coming fast.

Carly felt sick to her stomach. Though she'd never seen the older man in the scuffed jeans and plaid shirt before, he looked slightly—very slightly—familiar. Like someone she may have passed a few times on the street.

But she definitely knew the man alongside him.

The man whose fair hair was cut short and snappy in the latest style, whose elegantly toned body was immaculately clad in a black Gucci leather jacket over a gray polo shirt and dark slacks. She'd have bet a winning lottery ticket that the loafers on his feet were Pradas.

Kevin.

Chapter Twenty-six

"That's Kevin Boyd—my ex!" Carly gasped, too stunned to move.

"Is it, now?" Jake squeezed her hand, a grim look in his eyes. "It's going to be all right. Don't worry."

Swiftly he positioned himself between her and the newcomers as the men skidded to a stop at the bottom of the embankment and approached across the tall grass.

Kevin's face was frightening. His expression was hard and angry—every bit as angry as it had been that night he smashed her birthday gift from Sydney, the exquisite crystal ballerina sculpture. Her stomach dropped.

"That's far enough," Jake warned. "Both of you—hold it right there." Though his tone was low, its unmistakable note of authority had an effect on the other two men. They both halted simultaneously in their tracks. The heavier, older man eyed him cautiously, not afraid, but taking his measure.

They stood maybe fifteen feet away—close enough that Carly could see the fury ablaze in Kevin's eyes. In the still, pine-scented air, she could swear she caught a whiff of his aftershave, the private French label he'd used for years and which cost one hundred twenty-five dollars an ounce. She'd liked the scent before, but now it made her want to gag. When she was dating him, she'd thought of him as attractive, sophisticated, and appealing.

Now when she looked at him she saw only the bastard who lied to everyone closest to him. A man who cheated and deceived, who was all shine and sophistication on the outside. Without a drop of substance inside. A man with no strength of character. A hollow tin man without a heart or a conscience. Only a keen sense of his own self-importance.

And suddenly, her fear ebbed. Just like that.

Whatever was going on, it all had to do with her. With her and Kevin.

It was one thing to be afraid of the unknown, but she wasn't afraid of Kevin Boyd.

"How dare you break into my house." Furious, she stepped forward to stand beside Jake. "Whatever you were looking for, you can't have it."

"Wanna bet?" Rage lanced Kevin's words.

"Hold on a minute, now," the taller man

growled. He lifted a hand. "Let's everybody stay calm and peaceable."

Jake ignored him, nailing Carly's ex with a cold stare. "You're done, Boyd. This is over." His eyes flicked to the older man in the flannel shirt and jeans. "Who the hell are *you?*"

"Giff Hurley. I'm a private detective, hired by Mr. Boyd to help him get his daughter back."

"To . . . help him . . . *what?*" Carly gasped as if a fist had slammed into her stomach. She stared at Kevin in shock. "You are certifiably *insane.* Emma is no more yours than this lake is!"

"Save your breath, you lying bitch. You really thought you'd get away with it?"

Fury vibrated off Kevin Boyd like invisible bolts of electricity. He looked as livid as he had that night in Boston when she'd learned the truth about him having a family and confronted him. He should have been ashamed and apologetic, but no, instead he'd been enraged. Contemptuous. Now—like then—layers of wrath rolled off of him.

"I know all about what you've done," he spat out, his eyes brimming with scorn. "So you'd better call off your hick cowboy boyfriend here because I'm going to make sure you—and he—never put your filthy paws on my daughter again."

"She's not your daughter." Carly managed to speak through her stunned horror. "This is Jake Tanner and he's—"

"Stop! Stop lying! You thought I'd never find out, didn't you, bitch?" Despite his designer clothes and elegant physique, Kevin couldn't hide the savagery of his anger. "You stole my kid!" He lunged toward her, out of control, his eyes filled with a dark fury.

Jake leaped in front of her fast as a streak of lightning and slammed his fist into Boyd's jaw. Carly heard the *thunk* and her ex's grunt of pain as he reeled backward and went down, spinning like a bowling pin.

"Don't you talk to her that way. Don't even think about *touching* her or I'll break both your arms." Jake shot a hard look at the detective. "That goes for you, too, got it? Both of you better back off if you know what's good for you."

"Now, hold on a minute." Uneasily, the detective glanced down at his moaning client and reached out an arm, trying to help him to his feet. "You'll hear Mr. Boyd out if you know what's good for *you*. He's got rights in this situation and you'd best let him say his piece. You should know I have enough dirt on the woman and you to make sure he gets full custody of his daughter," he blustered.

Carly gaped at him, stunned. "What are you talking about?" she asked, her voice shaking.

"Not only did you steal his kid and not inform him he had a child," the detective continued, glaring at her with a look of triumph, "but I happen to know you take her out in the middle of the night when any good mother would keep her home and safe in her own crib. I got the photos to prove it." He looked her over with smug satisfaction as Boyd pushed slowly to his feet. "You entertain rodeo cowboys—specifically *this* rodeo cowboy"—he jerked his head toward Jake—"while you're babysitting other people's children. Not very respectable or responsible, is it? What kind of a woman are you? And most of all, why did you deny my client any opportunity to know his daughter—"

"Tell you what, buddy." Jake cut him off, his eyes slits of blue. "You promise not to say another word until the sheriff gets here, and I'll try really hard not to beat you to a pulp. Carly, call Sheriff Hodge. Tell him to get out here pronto."

She grabbed her cell phone from her purse and began punching in buttons, but suddenly Kevin dove forward again and tried to wrest the phone from her.

"If anyone calls the police, it's going to be *me.* You ruined my life. I don't believe a word out of your lying—"

Jake launched himself at the man and flung him away from Carly, ignoring the sound of Boyd's leather jacket ripping. Then he swung a fist into Boyd's jaw again and watched him crumple to the ground.

"You're crazy, Kevin." Carly watched dazedly

as he tried to push himself to his knees. "You and I were broken up for *months* before Emma was conceived—"

"Stop your bullshit lies. You think I'm an idiot, don't you? I know the truth! Miguel told me. You remember Miguel, don't you?"

Miguel? She stared at him in confusion as the wind chased through the trees. "Miguel from Los Sombreros? I haven't seen him in years, not since the last time you and I had dinner there. What in the world are you talking about?"

Maybe Kevin had lost his mind. Miguel had been their favorite waiter at the little Mexican restaurant where they'd dined at least once a week when they were together.

"I stopped going there after we broke up," Kevin spit out. "But I ran into Miguel about a month ago."

"And your point is?" Jake's eyes were specks of blue flint.

"He asked me about you." Though Kevin looked none too steady he still managed to sneer at Carly as if Jake didn't exist. His jaw was red and raw where Jake had slugged him, and he hadn't yet been able to get to his feet. "He didn't know we'd broken up. He said he saw you at the airport—just about two fucking years ago. He remembered when it was because he'd been headed to Chicago for his uncle's funeral that day. He said you didn't see him, but he passed your gate while you were in line to board, and he saw you were flying to Bozeman, Montana. He was happy to see you were pregnant, he said, and he asked me how we were doing, and how was our baby? Wanted to know what we named it—said you were so big, you looked like you were going to have the kid on the plane—"

"*That's* why you think Emma is yours?" she gasped, incredulous. "Not that it's any of your business, but I was only five months pregnant when I left Boston. Emma was conceived *months* after you and I broke up! That would have been a pretty fancy trick, if you were the father. One for the record books. And you hardly qualify for setting any records, not when it comes to sex, that's for sure!"

He scrambled up then and, with an oath, tried to spring at her again—and again Jake decked him. As Giff Hurley swore and took a threatening step forward, Jake gave him a one-handed shove that sent the big man staggering backward, nearly tumbling to the ground.

"This discussion is over," Jake said.

Carly could hardly believe she was *having* this discussion. But she wasn't done. "I'd have had to be nearly full term when I came here if Emma was yours, Kevin! And there's *no way* my doctor or *any* doctor would've let me fly that far along. That's why I moved here when I did—so I could have time to set up my home here, find an

OB-GYN, and get everything ready before my baby was born. So that she'd have a home and a mother who was settled and becoming part of this community long before she arrived. I carried big . . . it happens sometimes. You're *so* not the father of my little girl. *This man* is her father. Not you. *Never you*."

Blood oozed from his lip as he finally, a bit unsteadily, gained his feet. "You think I believe you? A filthy lying slut who—"

"Maybe you'll believe this." This time when Jake's fist shot out, it slammed into Boyd's narrow nose. The architect went down like a tree sawed off at its base. Blood spurted from his nostrils.

"That's enough!" the detective yelled. Swearing under his breath, he reached down a burly arm and started to haul his client up.

"No," Jake ordered. "Leave him right there."

Reluctantly, Hurley obeyed, releasing the other man's arm. Boyd slumped back down, dazed and bleeding as he sprawled on the grass.

As Carly punched in the sheriff's number and spoke quickly to Zeke Mueller, Jake stared down the detective.

"You're the one who broke into her house yesterday. You've been following the babysitter. And my daughter."

Giff Hurley looked panicked at his hard tone and the implacable anger in his face. "So what?"

he said defensively. "I might have followed them a couple of times, but I never laid a hand on either of 'em, never even bothered 'em. I was just doing my job. And I didn't break into anyone's house. You won't find a single print that says I did. My client claimed Ms. McKinnon stole his kid and he needed proof. I tracked her down, that's all. Told him where she lived—that was it. Told him about the kid, yeah, anything I could. I was looking into things, trying to get the scoop without drawing any attention. I couldn't even ask too many questions because I was afraid someone would tell the lady here and she'd make a run for it with the kid. But I never broke in. If I did that, I'd lose my license."

Which is why you won't admit to it, Carly thought, stuffing her phone back in her purse after Zeke assured her they were on their way.

"I swear, it wasn't me! I didn't break a single law here. I can't afford to lose my license!"

Carly almost believed him. It could well have been Kevin.

Kevin who broke in, who snooped through her bedroom. Kevin who searched her home when the detective balked at breaking the law. She wouldn't put it past him. But the detective had probably told him *how* to break in. A queasy chill ran through her, quickly followed by anger.

"Sheriff Hodge is on his way," she told Jake. Then she turned to the detective. "If someone did break in, what would they have been looking for?" The man looked formidable and scuzzy, but he didn't seem willing to get his hands dirty enough to go to jail. He shrugged at her question.

"Probably the kid's birth certificate, to see her date of birth. Look, I'm not saying whoever did it was right, but no one should keep a man from his own kid—"

"Shut up," Jake growled. "Emma's not his— she's ours. Mine and Carly's. And you're going to have to explain yourself to the sheriff and to a judge."

The detective winced. He gazed back and forth between them. Maybe he was better at reading faces than at gathering information because he ran a hand across his eyes.

"Oh, crap. You're telling the damned truth, aren't you? You're the dad." He looked stunned, as if it had never occurred to him before.

From a distance, Carly heard a siren wailing. Thank God. Sheriff Hodge was on his way. Or Deputy Mueller. Or both. The siren grew louder.

"Don't talk to her again. Not another word," Jake warned, his cool gaze shifting from the detective to Boyd. The asshole still looked dazed. He was moaning, out of commission.

Tucking Carly's hands in his, Jake drew her close and spoke softly.

"You okay? This will all be over soon."

"I know." She felt her pulse slowing as she looked into his calm, steady eyes.

"You don't need to stay here," he said quietly. "There's some rope in my truck. Why don't you get it and toss it down to me? I'll truss up Boyd real easy before the sheriff arrives. You can wait in the cabin if you like. It might be easier on you."

"I'm not going anywhere, Jake, and it doesn't look like you need any rope. I'm fine. I'll wait with you here."

Tossing a quick glance at Kevin, she saw that he still looked dazed and too weak to get to his feet. He sure didn't look so elegant and full of himself now—or capable of causing any more problems. With both his nose and his lip bleeding, his eyes bleary, he didn't even seem steady enough to lift himself into a sitting position. His leather jacket was ruined. There was blood on his Prada loafers.

"Why didn't you come ask me yourself?" she asked suddenly, taking a step toward him. Her hands were clenched so tightly her nails dug into her palms. "Why did you need a private detective? I could have explained this to you."

"Yeah? If . . . I'd called you . . . what would have stopped you from running before I could get here?" He spoke with resentment and with effort, through his rapidly swelling fat lip. "I was afraid you'd take the kid and disappear. With that damned tether attached to my ankle until my trial was over, I couldn't leave the state . . . and then my fucking trainer at the gym . . . recommended his brother-in-law." Kevin snorted and shot the detective a baleful glance.

But Carly was no longer listening. It suddenly came back to her—the article Syd had emailed. About Kevin taking his kids out of school without his ex-wife's permission. Trying to drive them over the state line to his parents' house. And when the police stopped him, he'd tested positive for drunk driving and taken a swing at the officer who pulled him over.

Of course. He'd been charged with a crime. Forced to wear a tether to keep him from leaving the state of Massachusetts until his trial. That was why he'd hired the detective to do his snooping.

"He told me his sister's husband was this hotshot private detective in Wyoming—that he was real good at his job and could come here and start building a case against you even before I got there. So, I thought Hurley would have . . . everything under control." He scowled as he glanced, narrow eyed, at the detective. Fury and frustration shone in his face, as blood continued to flow from his nose, down his chin, and onto the grass.

"I . . . flew out as soon as my lawyer got me off with community service . . . and they finally took that fucking tether off. . . ."

He let loose a string of expletives.

"You just blew up your life again for nothing," she said quietly. "There's not a drop of your DNA in Emma, thank God."

"I'm supposed to take your word for that? I want to see her birth certificate! I want a DNA test!" he yelled and attempted to push himself to his feet.

"Stay down!" Jake loomed over him in a flash. "You don't get up until I say so."

To her shock, Kevin swore another blue streak, but he stayed where he was, on the ground beside Hurley, bleeding and looking none too steady.

And as if he didn't want to tangle with Jake Tanner's fists again.

Jake slipped an arm around her shoulders as the sirens grew closer. "You sure you're okay?"

"Thanks to you." She leaned in close, rested her head for just a moment against his chest while Kevin glared at them and the detective's eyes squinted in worry.

"Damn it all to hell," Giff muttered in disgust, watching them together. Then his glance shifted to his still-half-out-of-it client.

"Stab me with a damned fork. I'm done. I went and put my money on the wrong horse. *Again.*"

Chapter Twenty-seven

Laureen watched from the side of the road as Big Billy changed her tire. He'd handed her his cell phone to call Hanson's Garage for a tow, while insisting on putting the spare on for her himself, to save her a few bucks.

"But you were headed home from the bar. You must have been working all night. I don't want to keep you," she protested. "I'll be fine waiting until George Hanson gets here."

"No way I'm leaving you stranded on this road 'til then, Laureen." He didn't look at her, just kept cranking the jack.

"But it's daylight. Perfectly safe. And this is Lonesome Way."

"It'll just be another minute or so, then I'll drive you into town. You can wait there while George tows her in." Pausing in his work, he sent her a long, quizzical look. "And didn't you say you need to open Carly's Quilts? Your boss is counting on you, right?"

"Ye-es." Laureen bit her lip. "But . . . you were headed home. I hate to put you to the trouble of turning around and going right back."

"Who said it's trouble?" Big Billy asked gruffly.

He turned his attention back to removing the last of the lug nuts and Laureen lapsed into silence, watching him work. It was impossible not to stare at the huge muscles rippling across those thick arms, at his solid, bulging chest beneath the green and black T-shirt garishly emblazoned with a whiskey bottle, a gun, and a rearing horse.

It was still hard to believe that the short, puny kid so far behind the other boys in physical development by his freshman year of high school had turned into Lonesome Way's fierce, macho giant—the rough bartender and sole owner of the Double Cross who'd served three tours in the army and who needed no other bouncer in the bar besides himself.

She'd noticed him later on in high school, sure, after he finally shot up and filled out and became a star running back on the football team. Most of her friends had dated him at some point, but Big Billy had dropped each of them, one by one.

Laureen had steered clear. She and Billy hadn't spoken more than five words to each other since that autumn day freshman year when she'd told him she already had a date for the Homecoming dance.

Even though she didn't.

She'd chosen to stay home alone rather than go to the dance with the runt of the high school.

And if Big Billy Watkins ever had a soft spot for her, it had hardened up real fast.

But over the years, the more she saw of him, the more interested—and regretful—she'd become. Big Billy might be ferocious and scary on the outside, but she'd noticed there was more to him than his tattoos and gruff voice would suggest.

He looked out for his customers. He didn't allow anyone to leave his bar if they were going to drive home drunk, and she'd once overheard him tell a customer who was complaining after having an argument with his wife that he'd better get his sorry ass home, suck it up, and beg her forgiveness before he lost the best thing he ever had.

She chewed on her bottom lip like a schoolgirl as he finished putting on the spare, wiped his greasy hands on a cloth, and surged to his feet. When he came around and opened up the door of his truck for her to get in, she shot him an uncertain smile.

"If you're sure it's no bother—"

"I look bothered to you?"

No. No, he didn't, Laureen thought. He looked remarkably good-natured for a man who resembled the leader of a biker gang, and someone she'd actually seen take on five drunken bikers at once and leave blood and destruction in his path.

Not at all like the young fourteen-year-old boy, half a head smaller than the other boys his age, who'd shyly invited her to the dance and whom she'd dismissed with a quick, airy reply, telling him she already had a date.

She hadn't. But Laureen had been hoping that Tim Larson would invite her. He was the coolest boy in school back then and she was on the fringes of the cool group of girls. She'd set her sights on Tim. So why on earth would she lower herself and go out with shy, skinny little Billy Watkins, who was four inches shorter than her, whose arms were as skinny as a couple of snakes, who still looked more like a measly sixth grader than a boy in high school?

"Come on, then, get in," Billy said.

Laureen stepped up into the truck, but the heel of her shoe caught on the floor mat and she nearly toppled in headfirst. Big Billy grabbed her just in time and steadied her.

"Th-thanks," she muttered, flushing.

"No problem."

When he'd vaulted into the driver's seat and they were headed to town, he dialed the volume on the radio up. Way up. Some crazy Kid Rock song nearly blasted Laureen out of her seat.

"Mind if I turn it down? And change the station?" she shouted finally when she thought her eardrums were going to explode.

Big Billy cast her a glance that she could swear held a flicker of amusement. "Sure, sunshine, knock yourself out."

"Don't mind if I do," she muttered, not looking

at him. She whirled the volume down. Way down. Then fiddled with the dial until she found a country station playing a Martina McBride song.

"Much better," she mumbled.

"You like the soapy songs, huh?" he grunted.

"If that's what you want to call them. I call them good old-fashioned country."

"Country's not bad. But I'm a little bit rock-and-roll."

"A little bit? That's all?" She couldn't help it. The words just flew out of her mouth before she could stop them. She'd been having a really terrible day and, sure, Big Billy had helped her out, but . . .

Suddenly she heard something she'd never heard before. A laugh. *Big Billy's laugh.* It was surprisingly soft and humorous, filling the truck like music.

"You're all right, Laureen, you know that? Not nearly as stuck up as you pretend to be."

"S-stuck up?" She was shocked by the words.

"Yeah. Stuck up. That's what I said."

"I am *not!*" she protested hotly.

"You got a friendly word for everyone in town, you go out with all these other men, you *meet* 'em all right in front of my nose at my own bar, and you never even say so much as 'hey' to me. Even when you come in with your girlfriends."

"I . . . I . . . didn't know you . . . wanted me to say hello to you. I thought . . ."

"What? That I'm still stinging from that time you turned me down in high school? Honey," he told her with a chuckle, "I got over that. Long time ago."

"Well, of course you did. I never thought—" Laureen broke off abruptly, a hot pink flush coloring her cheeks.

There was silence in the truck for several moments, except for Martina McBride's lilting voice and the rumbling of the truck's heavy tires over Coyote Road. Then Big Billy glanced sideways at her.

"There's one thing you don't know, Laureen. Maybe it's time you did."

"What's that?" She couldn't imagine what was coming next.

Big Billy, huge, tough, successful bar owner, bartender, and biker, cleared his throat.

Laureen waited, wondering what in the world he was going to say. She felt all of her nerve endings shiver. She was intensely aware of everything about the man sitting beside her—the fringe of coarse black stubble along his massive jaw, the muscles bulging in his thick neck and tattooed forearms, the shaggy blue-black hair that looked surprisingly clean and combed. One powerful hand rested on the steering wheel, while his right arm stretched along the top of the seat back behind her head.

For some reason, her heart was beating faster

than it had in a long time, faster than it had ever beat with any of the men she'd been fixed up with since her divorce—or gone out with on a date.

"I've come a long way since freshman year, honey." Big Billy's voice sounded matter-of-fact, but she detected a hint of huskiness in it. He seemed to hesitate just a moment.

"Fact is, a hell of a lot of things have changed since then, but not everything. Not these two things. The first one is . . . I always thought you were the prettiest girl I'd ever seen. And the second . . ." He cleared his throat. "I may have gotten over you turning me down when I asked you to that dance—but, oh, hell, Laureen, I never did get over *you*."

Chapter Twenty-eight

That evening Madison did something she hadn't done before.

At least, not since her last pageant appearance. And not willingly.

She put on a dress.

No one forced her. She actually wanted to do it. She didn't know how she'd feel once she had it on, because she always associated dresses with pageants and with her mother's slew of compliments and criticisms—poking at her hair; correcting her posture and her walk; scolding her that she turned around way too fast or too slowly. Studying her smile and *grading* it on a scale of one to ten.

It had been years now since her last pageant. Years since she'd seen her mother, who now had a whole crew of little pageant princesses to primp and torture.

So she wanted to see if she was finally over it. If she could wear something besides jeans every day and not feel like . . . like the girl who was someone else. Not herself—but only her mother's little dress-up doll to push onstage and show off.

Could she wear a dress now and still be Madison?

She'd bought the dress off the rack the day before at Top to Toe. It was a simple dress—long-sleeved flowy silk, in a sophisticated deep oxblood red, that ended a good few inches above her knees and made her look tall and slender. She hadn't even tried it on yet, had merely guessed at her size and brought it home, hanging it in her closet. She *still* wasn't sure she was ready to put it on.

But she had to meet Brady at Lickety Split in a half hour for their "date." He'd written her a pretty nice note, but she didn't have a clue if he was merely getting the obligation of this date out of the way or if he really wanted to spend time with her.

Or if he'd give up and run again if her grandfather happened to call while they were together or if they somehow bumped into him on Main Street.

She wanted Brady to know she wasn't upset that her grandfather didn't think too highly of him. *She* thought highly of him. That should be enough for Brady.

And she could deal with her grandfather.

She'd gone to her grandmother for advice the previous day. And Grandma Joanie had told her to listen with her heart. If she was certain Brady was a good man, then one of these days, her grandfather would come around.

"You leave all that to the two of them," Joanie Hodge had instructed her as she served Madison tea and a big slice of peach pie still warm from the oven. "They'll work it out. You go after what you want. Follow where your heart leads you, Maddy. And trust it to always lead you to the right place."

That was exactly what Madison intended to do. After slipping on tiny jet earrings and spiky black heels, she straightened and appraised herself in the full-length mirror on her closet door.

Some might think she was a little overdressed for Lickety Split, but she didn't care. She liked the effect. The dress wasn't one of those long, glittery, girly pink or white confections she associated with the pageants. It wasn't *pageanty* at all. It actually looked good.

Sort of cool and sophisticated.

And unlike those days when she was competing and wearing nothing *but* fancy, frilly pastel dresses, she certainly didn't feel the least bit like she was going to barf as she looked herself over in the mirror. She wore the barest trace of rose lip gloss and a tad bit of eyeliner and mascara. Her hair fell in loose dark waves, streaming past her shoulders.

Smiling slightly, she snagged a black lacy shawl from her dresser drawer and hurriedly tossed it around her shoulders. Simply wondering what Brady's reaction would be when he saw her tonight sent an anticipatory tingle rushing over her skin.

She seized her purse, took one last peek in the mirror, then flung open the door of her apartment, only to nearly run into a tall figure in a brown leather jacket, leaning against the narrow corridor's wall.

A scream flew from her mouth, just before her brain belatedly processed who he was.

Brady.

"What are you doing here? You scared me half to death!" She leaned against the wall for support as her thumping heart slowed ever so slightly in her chest.

"Hey. Sorry. You okay?" Brady studied her, his brows knit. His thick sandy hair was neatly combed and he looked older somehow—tall, strong, and dreamily handsome. Beneath his jacket she glimpsed what was probably a brand-new pearl gray shirt, along with his boots and jeans.

She drew a breath. "I thought we were meeting at Lickety Split."

"We were, but then I got to thinking. On a *real* date the man calls for the woman at her door." Brady reached behind her to close her apartment door. "So I got here early to escort you properly."

Madison stared at him. "Are you saying this is a real date?" She waited for him to make a joke.

"As real as they come. If that's okay with you."

There was no laughter in his eyes. She knew because she searched them. She saw only warmth.

Her cheeks flooded with heat, and to keep him from noticing, in case they'd turned pink, she ducked her head as they started down the hall.

"I don't suppose it ever occurred to you to knock. Or did you just want to jump out at me like the bogeyman?"

"I didn't want to rush you. So I waited." His gaze slid appreciatively over her. "For the record, it was worth the wait. You look . . . incredible. I mean," Brady added quickly, taking her arm as they headed down the stairs, "you always look incredible but . . . tonight . . ."

She almost tripped on the bottom step, but his fingers tightened on her arm, steadying her.

"Brady, what are you talking about? You think I

366

always look incredible? Are you crazy? In my jeans, in a sweatshirt?"

"Absolutely." He flicked her a what's-wrong-with-you kind of grin. "Don't you have a clue how gorgeous, not to mention totally hot, you are? In whatever you're wearing. Especially if you're not wearing much at all."

She blushed, remembering that night in her apartment. Hot? Gorgeous? Incredible? He *was* crazy. "I'm not any of those things. I never try to be. I had enough trouble trying to be all of them when I was younger."

"I know you did—I remember. But, listen, Madison. You don't have to try. You just are." He held the door for her as they walked out onto the sidewalk. "You always have been," he added quietly.

She didn't know what to say. Brady had been her friend even before she entered a single pageant. He knew her better than anyone, except her grandparents. Her mother hadn't known her at all, or at least, had never understood that Madison had totally different wants and needs than she did. Her head was whirling as they walked down the darkened block, lit only by inter-mittent street-lights, and crossed toward Main.

"I wasn't even sure you would go through with our date . . . after what happened in my apart-ment that night," she told him softly. "I haven't heard from you, Brady. I'm sorry if you were mad when I answered the phone when my grandfather called. It's just that he gets so worried if he can't reach me—"

Brady stopped short and grabbed her arm. "I wasn't mad at you. Not because you answered the phone, not for any reason."

"Then why did you leave like that? You just jumped up and *left.* You've barely spoken to me since."

"Maddy . . ." He seemed to be searching for words as they faced each other on the quiet, darkened street, only blocks from Lickety Split. "I was furious with myself, not with you. Furious because I lost it that day, way back when I punched out Deputy Mueller after Cord died. Your grandfather's deputy, of all people! I was sure your grandfather would never get past that. He'd never trust me and he sure as *hell* wouldn't trust me with you. I didn't want him to be angry with you on my account. You've already gone through enough—"

"That's for me to decide, Brady Farraday."

She yanked her arm free and glared at him, her caramel eyes darkening.

"I'm not intimidated by my grandfather. Or by you. I make up my own mind."

"I know, Maddy, but . . . I didn't want to be the one causing any kind of hard feelings between you and him—"

"Oh, shut up, Brady. You're not going to come

between me and my grandparents. You never could. No one can. But they're not coming between you and me, either," she told him, her chin tipping up as she met his eyes.

Brady could barely keep from sweeping her up in the air and twirling her around. She was magnificent. Slender, feminine, determined. No longer the childhood friend he'd spent countless hours with when they were young, but now a woman with a will so calm and so fierce she took his breath away.

"I don't want anything to come between us, either." He pulled her close, resisting the urge to stroke his thumb along her lush bottom lip. "But I want you to be happy."

"Then I suggest you kiss me," she told him, grabbing the front of his jacket and tugging him around the corner, into the moonlit alley behind the Cuttin' Loose, away from the streetlights of Main. "Kiss me now, Brady Farraday, because I won't be happy until you do that again."

He didn't have to be asked twice. He backed her up slowly against the rear wall of the Cuttin' Loose salon and leaned down in the brisk darkness of the October night. As his mouth brushed hers, she lifted her arms and twined them around his neck. Her lips parted and her eyes shone and it seemed to Brady that every curve of her body seemed to melt like the sweetest candy against his.

He kissed her a long time, letting his lips rove along her jaw, down her throat, then return to capture her mouth. He studied her as if memorizing every single one of her features, every eyelash, freckle, and the shape of her mouth. Then he kissed her some more.

When they were both breathless, he drew back and gazed down into her flushed, upturned face, into eyes that were searching and trusting all at once.

Then she grabbed the front of his jacket again and murmured, "Ice cream can wait, Brady. I can't. Kiss me some more."

She pressed her lips to his and he grinned and did what he'd been brought up by his mother to do—always oblige a lady.

Chapter Twenty-nine

Two weeks later in Bismarck, North Dakota, Jake hurried toward his rental car. Behind him in the stands of the rodeo arena, a roar went up from the crowd. The bronc-riding competition was still under way. But he never slowed his steps or felt tempted to turn back and see what was going on.

For once the smells and sights and thrumming

energy of the rodeo hadn't grabbed him the way they always had before.

He'd originally booked his return flight for first thing in the morning, but he'd impulsively changed his plans and switched to a red-eye tonight. He could have stayed another hour or two at the rodeo, bunked at his hotel, and made it to the airport after breakfast but he found himself suddenly in a big hurry to get back.

He'd only left Lonesome Way five days before, but he missed Emma something terrible. He missed Bronco, too. He'd left the mutt in Carly's willing care, since Emma loved the animal so much. But . . . who'd have thought he'd miss that dog?

And who else do you miss? a voice inside him asked. His own voice. He couldn't seem to shut it up.

Well, yeah, he missed Carly. And that was an understatement. They'd been spending even more time together ever since her whack-job ex-boyfriend and that private detective had faced a judge. A judge who sent both of them packing.

The detective hadn't been charged with anything, but Kevin Boyd had gotten away with a suspended sentence for breaking and entering, contingent on him agreeing to leave town immediately—and to leave Carly and Emma alone.

Once the judge had listened to all the testimony, added up dates and times, and seen Emma's birth certificate as well as the results of a blood test, he'd informed Boyd that based on his own testimony as to the last date he had any contact with Carly McKinnon, along with the child's legal age and date of birth *and* the blood test results, there was no possibility that the child in question could be his.

If ever a man had left a town with his tail between his legs, it was that asshole Boyd, Jake thought. But he hadn't slunk out before Jake had warned him personally—in a soft, even, but unmistakably dangerous tone—that if he ever came within fifty miles of Carly or Emma again, he'd rearrange his face so that the devil himself wouldn't recognize him.

With Hurley already speeding home to Wyoming and Boyd gone as quick as he could book the next flight to Boston, Jake had no reason to worry about leaving Carly and Emma for a couple of days. The danger was over.

He'd called her that first night he arrived in Salt Lake City, and then each night he was in Carson City. He'd even spoken to Emma on the phone, though all she'd done was babble something about Bug and "Mumma" and "Masson," which was her way of saying "Madison." But this trip, when he'd flown out here to Bismarck for the Wilderness Falls National Rodeo, he'd had second thoughts.

He'd *wanted* to call again every morning and

every night. To hear Carly's voice. Find out about her day and Emma's day. But he'd stopped himself. He realized he couldn't continue to do that.

It wouldn't be fair.

Now that the danger was over, he had to start stepping back. Give Carly some room and take some for himself. They were getting in too deep. And Jake didn't do deep.

This is bad; you need to nip it in the bud. Now, he told himself as cheers and applause thundered from the stands behind him. He barely heard it. All he could think about was how he felt when he and Carly were together. Whether they were washing dishes or making love. Every time he was with her, every time they touched or kissed and even when he simply looked at her—he felt incredibly close to her. Closer than he'd ever felt to anyone.

It was terrifying. More terrifying than the most savage bull on the circuit. An insistent beep kept blaring in his brain, warning him of danger.

He knew they were on the brink, in danger of crossing an invisible line. Of becoming more than coparents to Emma, more than friends. More than even friends with privileges. It was uncharted territory and every instinct Jake possessed roared at him to back off.

If he called her every night he was away, she'd have every right to start thinking of them as a couple. Believing that they were more involved than they actually were. She didn't realize that there were things he could never give her or do for her—or be for her.

Which was why it was better to pull back now and not feed any more expectations.

He cared too much about Carly to ever want to see her hurt.

The amazing, beautiful mother of his daughter deserved better than what he could give her. She was strong and smart and sexy beyond words. And whenever they made love—whether Emma was over at Travis and Mia's place on a playdate with Zoey or having a sleepover at Martha's, or even tucked into her own little crib down the hall at night—he couldn't get enough of Carly. She felt so perfect in his arms. The richness of her laughter drew him like home cooking. He'd discovered somewhere along the way that those forest green eyes and her brave spirit never ceased to call to him.

But he sensed they were dancing close to a very dangerous cliff. It was time to step back from the abyss.

Frowning, he yanked open the door of his rental car and was about to slide behind the wheel when he spotted the girl.

Skinny, about eighteen. A beauty with shiny blond hair pulled up in a ponytail, and a quick, eager walk. For a moment—just one moment—something about the color of her hair and the shape of her face and the way she moved reminded him of Melanie.

He watched her run along the sidewalk and into the arms of a clean-shaven young cowboy in a tan Stetson, who scooped her up and twirled her in a circle. Her laughter rang out like tinkling crystal, and the illusion dissolved.

Melanie had never laughed like that. She'd hardly laughed at all. Ever. Aside from the color of her hair and the quick way she walked, and the brilliant blond beauty, this girl was nothing like Melanie.

Still, he stood a moment, his hands gripping the top of the car door, thinking back on the pretty and mostly silent girl he'd promised to help. The girl who'd desperately needed him.

He'd forgotten how young they'd both been back then. She was just seventeen; he was nineteen. And she was scared to death.

Her mother had died of leukemia ten years earlier. Her father was a rodeo pickup man, responsible for helping the cowboys dismount after a bucking event and for keeping the arena clear, as well as for herding and roping as needed. He was also a drunk and a bully who dragged Melanie along with him from rodeo to rodeo when she wasn't living at her aunt's house in Livingston, getting home-schooled.

Jake had first met Melanie Sutton at the Bear Claw bar in Livingston. They'd run into each other after that at a number of rodeos and became friendly. One day, he happened to spot a bruise on her arm, but she wouldn't talk about it. A month and a half later, she had a bruise on her face, a bruise so purple that no amount of CoverGirl makeup could completely disguise it.

It took a little time before Jake got her to admit that her father became violent at the slightest provocation. He beat her if she came home late after being with friends or if he caught her talking to any male under the age of forty. Or if she burned his supper, or didn't answer him fast enough when he asked her a question.

Furious, Jake was determined to confront the man and warn him what would happen if Jake ever found out he'd hit his daughter again.

But Melanie wouldn't let him. She was terrified by the very idea and begged him not to say a word to her father or to anyone else. Jake suspected others knew, too, but they all looked the other way. Her father, Duke Sutton, apparently never drank on the job and was considered one of the best pickup men in the business. No one wanted to get in Duke's way or cross him by paying too much attention to the bruises and broken bones that now and then plagued his daughter.

Melanie had always looked defeated and as skittish as a deer skidding on melting snow across a lake. Finally Jake knew why.

He made her swear to call him the next time she felt in danger. He promised he'd come and help her anytime—all she had to do was call.

He even managed to win her trust enough to get her to accompany him to a social worker's office for an initial meeting he set up. The social worker urged her to file a police report against her father and to go to a women's shelter. But Melanie panicked, too terrified of her father to even contemplate such a thing, and bolted from the meeting.

When Jake caught up with her, she was headed resolutely back to her father's RV to clean up and cook supper before Duke returned from working with his horses. She'd been crying, her eyes red and bloodshot.

Mostly it was the hopelessness that stabbed at him. Melanie didn't believe she would ever escape, so she didn't allow herself the courage to try.

He wrapped his arms around her and told her he would be there for her. That she needed to get out now, and head to a place where she'd be safe. Somewhere far away where her father wouldn't find her.

At first she refused, assuring him over and over again that she *would* run away someday, as soon as she scraped together enough money and enough courage—and a good head start. Once she finally did, she vowed, scrubbing the tears from her cheeks, her father would never find her.

Jake clasped her hands in his, right there outside the RV, and told her he'd buy her a ticket then and there. That she could go wherever she chose, someplace far away, where her father wouldn't find her. That he'd give her enough money to get started and she could pay him back down the road when she could.

Hope lit her eyes then. Real hope. Tears slipped slowly down her cheeks as he waited. And finally, she drew in an unsteady breath and nodded at him.

Jake immediately booked her on a one-way flight to Sacramento. Melanie had a childhood friend who'd moved there. They'd kept in touch over the years and her friend was now working as a nanny. She knew of another family looking for a live-in nanny and was certain Melanie would get the job if she could only get there.

The ticket he bought her was for a red-eye flight leaving that evening. Jake would drive her to the airport at nine p.m., after his event.

He escorted her back to her dad's RV to pack, then bought her a pizza and a two-liter bottle of Coke before bringing her back to his motel room to hide and eat and wait for him.

The trouble came while he was gone. Melanie must have realized she'd forgotten something in her haste to pack. A small box of postcards that had belonged to her mother. They were old black-

and-white postcards that her grandfather had sent to her mother from all over the world when he'd been in the army. Melanie had told Jake about them before, confiding that she kept the box hidden beneath the springs of her mattress so her father wouldn't destroy them during one of his rages.

She couldn't bear to leave them behind and apparently snuck home for the box when Jake was competing at the arena.

But when she reached the RV, she stumbled upon her father. For once he'd been caught drinking on the job, and had been sent home. He was in a rage, his anger no doubt fueled further because Melanie had been missing when he arrived home.

She tried to escape, to run, and even managed to punch in Jake's number on her cell phone, screaming for help. But Jake was already down in the arena, preparing for his ride, and he didn't get the call until it was too late. Until his ride was over and the thunderous applause had died down, and he'd dusted himself off and sauntered from the arena. Checking his phone, he heard her desperate pleas for help.

Help that hadn't come.

His gut clenched and in sick panic he tore out of there. He looked for her first at his motel room, then at Duke's RV.

His gut told him what he'd find before he

burst through the open door. Duke Sutton was nowhere to be seen, but there was blood everywhere.

Melanie's body was sprawled near the front. Broken. Lifeless. Nearby was an old cardboard box and a couple of dozen postcards soaked in blood.

The sheriff tracked down Duke before Jake did and found him drowning his guilt in some hole-in-the-wall bar in the next town. Jake had wanted to get his hands on the bastard first, and begged the sheriff for two minutes alone with him in a cell, but the sheriff said, "I know how you feel, son, but it ain't gonna happen. We go by the book here."

And sent him packing.

Standing outside the arena now on this chilly October day, Jake's jaw clenched, remembering all of it. How Melanie had called him. How she'd needed him, begged him for help. And he hadn't been there for her.

He'd *promised.* And now she was dead.

Because *he* hadn't kept his promise. *He* hadn't been there.

He'd been too late.

He'd known in that moment that he had no damn business making promises to anyone. He'd failed the one time he'd made a commitment to a woman, and he hadn't made one since.

Suddenly, watching the blond girl and her cowboy in the tan Stetson walk hand in hand toward a brightly lit diner, he heard a man's steady voice behind him.

"Don't let it get to you. You fall off a horse, you gotta get right back on. No ifs, ands, or buts. That's how you learned to ride in the first place, right? So I want you to go in there tomorrow and give it another try. Or else you might never know . . ."

Jake slowed and watched as a stocky man of about forty walked past him, one arm slung across the shoulders of his teenaged son. He remembered the kid from earlier. Freckles all over his face, his skin damp with nervous sweat as he climbed into the chute and onto the bronc's back. He'd tried bronc riding that day for the first time and had been tossed onto his butt in under three seconds.

Jake suddenly remembered something else. His own father's voice, saying similar words to him when he first learned to ride. Or rather, when he'd taken a tumble off Dakota for the very first time.

You fall off that horse, Jake, you get right back on. Otherwise you maybe never will. You face it, see you can do it. Don't be scared. Put your foot in the stirrup there, like I showed you. Get right back on . . .

He'd fallen off a dozen more times, but damn, he'd always swung right back into the saddle. And man, he'd learned to ride.

He halted in his tracks, stood stock-still. People in scarves and boots and light jackets dodged around him; there was chatter, horns honking; and he could smell barbecue and perfume and popcorn wafting from the rodeo stands. But in his mind, he was seeing something he'd never seen before. The one area of his life where he'd never gotten back on when he fell off.

He'd never made another promise to a woman since he was nineteen—since he'd failed Melanie. He'd never made a commitment to a woman or even let himself get close to making one.

Hell, he'd never even had a relationship with a woman that was more than a casual friendship or a one- or two- or three-night stand.

All these years—not afraid of falling. Afraid of *failing*. Failing someone close to him. Someone who needed him.

He felt a jolt down to his bones as something seemed to burst free in his soul.

Later he didn't even remember getting behind the wheel of his rental car. He pushed the speed limit on the drive to the airport and was the first in line to board the plane.

All he could think as the plane soared through the darkness was that he couldn't wait to get to Blue Bell Drive. To pull up in front of that old Victorian, to see Carly and Emma, to hold them, touch them both.

It suddenly struck him like a truckload of bricks. He didn't want to be away another minute.

He couldn't wait to get home.

Chapter Thirty

"Tell me about it. I know just how you feel," Carly murmured as Bronco gazed at her morosely.

The dog was stretched out on the rug in her sewing room as she basted the layers of the blossom quilt she needed to finish before the fund-raiser. It was two days before Halloween, Emma was asleep, and she could hear a wicked wind snarling through the darkness outside the window.

"I miss him, too, but don't ever tell him I said so. I'll have to get used to it. And maybe you will, too. He could be dumping all three of us."

She wondered if Jake would take Bronco on the road with him next time, now that he was back on the circuit. Or would he ask to leave the dog here with her and Emma?

Somehow, reluctantly, Carly had fallen in love with this big, scruffy dog. Emma adored him wildly and still called him "Bug" as a term of strongest affection, though she didn't love even Bronco nearly as much as she obviously loved Jake.

But maybe having Bronco around while Jake was gone would help keep her from missing him so much. She was talking more every day, stringing two and even three words together at a time—and lately, most of all, she'd been asking "Where Dada Shake?"

Where's Daddy Jake, in Emma-speak.

How did I let this happen? Carly wondered with a sigh. A knot suddenly tightened in the pit of her stomach. At first she'd been so careful, so resistant to letting Jake get too close. To Emma. And to her.

But these past weeks—since the break-in and the picnic at Blackbird Lake, especially—and since Kevin and his private detective had been booted out of town—she'd let her guard down. She'd let Jake in more and more—allowed him to get closer than she'd ever dreamed she would.

Jake and Emma were tighter than ever. And she and Jake—

He'd been staying here at the house every night—and not in the spare bedroom, either.

They'd made hot, intense love each night. And often fun, frisky love in the morning. Jake's love-making left her glowing and fulfilled, but always, always wanting more.

They ate breakfast together every day, working together easily as he poured cereal and made toast, and she cut up fruit and put up a pot of coffee. Emma's job, which she excelled at, was to make them grin as she chirped new words constantly from her high chair and fed Bronco bits of wheat toast and cereal from her chubby fingers.

Then Madison would show up, and Emma would shriek with excitement. While Carly headed to the quilt shop, Jake drove out every day to confer with Denny on the new guest cabins and the transition of his own cabin into a lodge. He worked the phone night and day, doing outreach, planning, and budgeting, bringing all aspects of his retreat for bullied kids together.

They'd often meet at A Bun in the Oven or the Lucky Punch for a quick lunch, then return to have dinner all together on Blue Bell Drive.

It was a wonderful routine they'd fallen into, filled with jokes and food, hugs and laughter. Just like a real honest-to-goodness family.

And then Jake had flown to Salt Lake City for the commercial shoot and to Carson City for the rodeo. He'd only been gone a few days and had called her each night. When he returned, he seemed more than glad to be back.

But this time, when he went to Bismarck, he'd stopped calling on a regular basis. He'd called only the first night, but not the next. Or the next after that.

Carly had tried to reach him yesterday and left a message. But he hadn't called her back.

She hadn't had any contact from him since that one and only call—except for a quick business-like text message:

Checking in, hope all's well, see you soon.

What the hell was up with that?

Her heart had dropped. Her throat had gone dry. Anger had risen in her and tears had formed in her eyes as she deleted the text from her phone.

She knew there was a larger message beneath the distant politeness of his text. Jake was letting her know that he was backing off. He'd contacted her only out of a sense of obligation. He didn't actually want to talk to her—or, apparently, to Emma. He was merely touching base in the most neutral, distant way possible.

Fine, Carly had told herself, pale and composed the next day, after she'd cried her heart out into her pillow the night before.

It was time for a reality check.

This was over. Whatever she'd thought was happening between her and Jake obviously *wasn't.* A leopard doesn't change his spots and a cowboy doesn't shed his wanderlust ways.

Jake was back in his cowboy-loner routine. He must be having such a good time on the road that boring family life with one woman, one kid, and a dog was just too tame for him. Perhaps he'd met another woman . . . or several women. A pack of rodeo groupies. Was there such a thing?

She felt the tears gathering in her eyes again and tried to blink them back before they overflowed. Then she heard a sound over the October wind. An engine . . . a car pulling into her driveway.

Bronco leaped up, let out a couple of excited barks. "Shhhh!" Carly hushed the dog, as she tossed aside her quilt and ran to the living room window. Before she could even process the sight of Jake's truck on her driveway, a short knock sounded at the front door.

"I thought you weren't coming back until tomorr—oh!"

Her startled words were cut off as he swept her into a tight embrace and kissed her. Standing in the doorway, the October wind whipping around them, he lifted her off her feet and caught her mouth with his in a kiss that was unlike any other they had shared. It was deep and powerful and urgent.

"Ohhhh," was all Carly could gasp at first when he finally set her down. Gazing up into his eyes, seeing the way he was looking at her, she suddenly felt the world at once spinning and settling into its rightful place.

"What . . . took you so long?" Her throat filled with emotion as she lifted a hand to his cheek.

"I had a few things to figure out."

"Such as?"

"Things like I missed you. And want you. And need you."

Seeing that she was shivering in her sea blue sweater as the wind chased up the porch and whistled right past them, he drew her into the hallway and pushed the door closed.

He absentmindedly placed a hand on Bronco's head as the dog finally stopped dancing around him like a drunken gypsy, then he led Carly into the living room.

With one swift movement he tossed his jacket onto a chair, then his arms snaked tightly around her waist so she was close against him as he kissed her tenderly on the lips.

"I couldn't get home to you fast enough."

Home?

"Jake . . ." There was a catch in her voice. She couldn't speak another word, not now. She simply gazed into his eyes, searching. He had the most beautiful eyes. Dark as a midnight blue sky. And steady. So steady. There was a tenderness in them she'd never seen before.

"I don't know why it took me so long to see it. I didn't realize until I hadn't talked to you for days and days."

"Four days," she whispered, smoothing his hair back from his brow. "You didn't call for four days. And I left you a message—I didn't even know if you got it—"

"I know, baby. I'm sorry. It will never happen again. I was an idiot. I was afraid we were getting in over our heads. That if I didn't back off, I'd hurt you. But the only one I hurt was myself—by staying away from you. I don't ever want to do that again. I *won't* ever do that again. I'm keeping you close, Carly McKinnon. You and Emma both.

Close by my side. And close to my heart. From this day forward."

He kissed her again, a deep, hungry kiss that made her knees wobble. She held on to him and kissed him back, their kisses melting into each other like butter in the summer sun.

From this day forward . . . it sounded like a sacred pledge. . . .

"What changed?" she managed to ask as they came up for air. As Bronco settled down near the fireplace, Jake drew her to the sofa and pulled her down onto his lap.

"I missed you so much I couldn't see straight. And I realized . . . I'd let something from my past bar my way to the future for too many years. I started believing all that crap about myself that everyone says, that I always used to like to hear. That I'm a born wanderer and I'll never settle down, that I'm not the marrying kind."

He stroked a hand along her delicate jaw as she snuggled on his lap. He stared for a moment at their joined hands and then looked intently into her eyes. "I let someone down once, Carly, someone important to me. And I never forgave myself for that. I never let myself get in that position again—of making a promise. I cut off my options, until I suddenly realized that when it comes to you and Emma, I want all my options on the table. There's only one hope for me to be happy now that I've tangled with you and our daughter. I need you, both of you."

His voice thickened. "I want us to be a family. I want that more than any rodeo prize or any endorsement deal or anything else. And I have plenty to do right here, getting the retreat off the ground. Running it, funding it. My traveling days are done, girl. Unless you and Emma come with me. Unless you say no . . ." His voice trailed off.

"No to what?" Cupping his face in her hands, she smiled, her heart full of love.

Jake suddenly shifted, settling her gently on the sofa beside him, then he knelt on one knee before her and seized her hands.

"Will you marry me, Carly McKinnon?" His fingers closed warm and tight around hers. "Will you make me the happiest man on the planet and give me a chance to reform my crazy cowboy ways?"

"You better believe it, Jake Tanner," she breathed, and she slid down to sit on the floor beside him, hugging him close. In a flash he had pulled her down atop him and clamped her tight, her legs straddling him, and their lips fused in a long, sweet kiss that left them grinning goofily at each other.

"You promise?" Jake said. "No welshing, Carly. You'll marry me?"

"I'll marry you tonight, tomorrow, at dawn or midnight, whenever you say."

"Damn! I don't even have a ring!" Jake groaned.

He suddenly scraped a hand through his hair. "Sorry. I figured a lot of this out right before I left for the airport and I didn't have a chance to shop before I got on the plane—"

"Jake." She pressed a kiss to his mouth. "I don't care about a ring. I care about a man. My man. That would be you." She smoothed his hair back with her fingers as he suddenly shifted, sitting up. "What are you do—"

"What does it look like I'm doing?" One strong hand took hold of the hem of her sweater and pulled it over her head. Then he unhooked her bra with a flick of his fingers and flung it aside. A moment later, those fingers slid the zipper of her jeans downward. "I'm celebrating. *We're* celebrating."

She grabbed his shirt, her fingers flying over the buttons, then turned her attention to getting him out of his jeans. In a moment they were both naked. On the floor. Laughing and touching and sealing the pact.

A half hour later, Jake slid on his jeans and Carly tied the sash of a silky blush pink robe before they tiptoed, tousled and sated and happy, into Emma's room.

"Are you sure I can't wake her up?" Jake whispered.

"Don't you dare," she whispered back.

His grin lit the shadowed room full of toys and

dolls and a big plush rocking horse. Bug was facedown in his rightful place on the miniature chair. Bronco had followed them in and was now sitting just inside the doorway, watching them with his head tilted to one side.

They stared down at Emma asleep in her crib. Her breathing was soft and even, her little fingers splayed across the Cookie Monster sheet.

"We do good work." Jake's arm encircled her waist, holding her close by his side.

Carly kissed his neck. "Yes, we do. The best."

"We should go for a few more of these. I say the more the merrier."

"Let's get married first," she suggested.

He grinned and whispered against her hair, holding her close, "Sounds like a plan."

Chapter Thirty-one

The wedding of Carly McKinnon and Jake Tanner took place on a snowy December afternoon, two weeks following the Thanksgiving dinner dance fund-raiser. Snowflakes drifted softly down upon the roof of Sage Ranch as a small group of friends and family gathered in the spacious house and filled the pretty white chairs set out in the living room.

Big Billy carried Laureen up the steps and into the ranch house so she wouldn't slip in her new silver stilettos and elegant dove gray gown.

Brady and Madison were almost late because they'd sat huddled for hours the night before in their treehouse, wrapped in coats and quilts, eating Cheez-Its and peanut butter cookies and drinking hot chocolate as they rehashed their childhood adventures and talked about the future.

Finally Brady had taken her hand after they'd climbed down the ladder and they'd gone inside his halfway renovated family home to kiss and make love and sleep before a roaring living room fire. Fortunately, Madison awakened by ten and remembered where they were supposed to be. They had time only to shower and gulp down coffee and blueberry muffins before Brady drove her back to her apartment and waited while she slipped into her slinky black cashmere dress and matching heels, applied some eyeliner, mascara, and lip gloss, then grabbed her guitar.

The ranch house smelled divine as Carly dressed upstairs in Sophie and Rafe's master bedroom, while Martha had her hands full with Emma, who kept wanting to chase Starbucks and Tidbit, their hosts' two rescued dogs. It was all Martha could do to keep her goddaughter's pale pink ruffled dress from getting dirty or torn.

"It's time," Martha finally exclaimed with relief,

standing in the doorway of the master bedroom at precisely one o'clock.

"Finally!" Carly laughed and finished slipping on her simple pale blue tourmaline earrings. They had once belonged to Annie. Now they were both her something old and her something blue, just as Martha's pearl brooch, pinned to Carly's simple one-shouldered cream dress, was her something borrowed.

As for something new—at least, relatively new —she glanced down at the princess-cut engagement ring sparkling on her finger. If that wasn't enough, she'd bought pale blue stilettos to wear down the aisle—double good luck because they were both new and blue.

She wasn't taking any chances.

Smiling at her daughter, she held out her arms.

"Guess what, Emma—it's time to go downstairs and marry your daddy."

With a laugh and a grin Emma catapulted herself into her mother's arms.

Downstairs, Madison began to play a hauntingly beautiful arrangement of the Beatles' "Here, There, and Everywhere" on her guitar. A soft appreciative gasp went up from the guests as the bride, her daughter, and her daughter's godmother swept down the stairs and into the hall.

Carly's heart felt ready to burst. When she saw Jake waiting for her in his tuxedo, she thought she might cry, but instead her face glowed with a huge smile.

Here was her love, her future. Waiting for her as snow fell beyond the window and all their friends and family looked on.

She was only dimly aware of Madison sitting off to the side, playing her guitar. Of Karla and Denny McDonald beaming at her from the second row of guests, of Sophie and Mia and Laureen all blinking back happy tears, while Jake's brothers stood at his side, grinning from ear to ear.

But it was Jake who filled her vision, just as he filled her heart. He came toward them and kissed Emma's cheek, then Martha led their daughter to a seat.

Happiness surged through her as Jake took her hands in his. His eyes gleamed into hers as they stood before Reverend Kail near the fireplace, its mantel adorned with candles and lilies and roses. She saw certainty in his eyes, and love, and tenderness, along with a cocky twinkle that was pure Jake Tanner.

By the time Reverend Kail pronounced them husband and wife, and invited Jake to kiss his bride, Carly was oh-so-ready for that kiss. She threw her arms around his neck and heard him whisper:

"This is the best day of my life."

She knew when they kissed in the glow of the

fire that they'd just sealed their marriage more than any piece of paper ever could. It wasn't until the champagne had been poured and passed and their friends and family had congratulated them, feasted, and were devouring Sophie's three-layer red velvet wedding cake, and assorted pastries were being served along with coffee and hot tea, that Jake pulled her into the side parlor where his mother had liked to sew. He closed the door and drew her into his arms.

"Emma is with Madison and Ivy," he told her before she could start to fret about their daughter. "They've corralled her—to give us a minute."

"Only a minute? I'd love an hour with you right now." Dreamily, she slid her fingers through his hair.

"We're going to have plenty of hours, wife."

Just before his mouth closed over hers, she breathed, "I'll hold you to that, husband."

It wasn't until the kiss ended that she touched his face and told him her news. And laughed at the whoop he let out, since she knew everyone in the house must have heard. And probably guessed . . .

In slightly less than eight months, they would welcome another Tanner baby into the family of sisters, brothers, aunts, uncles, cousins, and friends who all shared their joys, challenges, and lives in the town of Lonesome Way.

About the Author

Jill Gregory is a *New York Times* bestselling and award-winning author of more than thirty novels. She grew up in Chicago and received her bachelor of arts degree in English from the University of Illinois. She currently resides in Michigan with her husband. Visit her website at www.jillgregory.net or follow her on twitter @Jill_Gregory.

Center Point Large Print
600 Brooks Road / PO Box 1
Thorndike ME 04986-0001 USA

(207) 568-3717

US & Canada:
1 800 929-9108
www.centerpointlargeprint.com